Let's Not & Say We Did

Let's Not & Say We Did

THE LOVE GAME: BOOK FIVE

ELIZABETH HAYLEY

WATERHOUSE PRESS

To deadlines,
We'd never finish anything without you.

Chapter One

TAYLOR

"This feels weird," I told Ransom as we approached Brody's building.

"What does?"

When he reached up to rub my back for a second, I felt slightly better, even if the physical comfort was only temporary. It reminded me we were in this together.

"All of it," I said. "But telling everyone, especially. Right now it's just the two of us who know. But if we go upstairs and tell all our friends, we're involving them in something they might not wanna be involved in. We're not even giving them a choice. We're basically deciding to involve them in covering up a murder."

He stopped abruptly. "It's not a murder."

I looked up at Ransom, who had positioned himself in front of me. His hands on my upper arms steadied me a bit, and I felt a little guilty about it. I was practically shaking.

I knew I hadn't *welcomed* Brad into our lives. That's not why I felt guilty. I'd tried to stop him, ignored his contact like

I'd tried to do when I'd been back at school and we'd both been students at Mount Bishop University. But I should've known better than to think I could avoid someone who'd shown up hundreds of miles away from the town I'd left.

I could've done what I'd promised Ransom I'd do when Brad started making more serious threats. I could've been more forthcoming with my dad about Brad. I'd downplayed everything when I'd realized that once my dad "took care of Brad," he'd expect me to go back to school and get on with my life as if none of this had ever happened. He still hadn't *heard* me. Brad was a problem he could fix, but understanding how *affected* I'd been by the whole thing hadn't seemed to enter his mind, which made me hesitate to share my feelings with him.

So instead of opening up about Brad following me here, sending me unwanted texts and even pictures of himself around town and at the bar where I worked, I'd assured my dad that it wasn't a huge deal. I wasn't in the habit of lying, and that lie had turned out to have fatal consequences.

Though I *was* thankful the fatality had been Brad when it could've so easily been me if Ransom hadn't heard me screaming and come to my rescue.

I was so relieved when we left Brad in that alley, thinking I'd finally be able to put this nightmarish part of my life behind me. After all, who'd want to risk tangling with Ransom twice? Brad was alive and seemed fine when we left him. Or as fine as anyone could seem after a fight with Ransom. When we'd left, I'd had no doubt that parts of Brad's body would be feeling the lingering memory of Ransom's fist, but it never crossed my mind that those injuries would be enough to kill him.

"We don't have to tell them," Ransom said. "We can go back to my place or yours and figure out what to do next."

I shook my head quickly. As much as I didn't want to drag anyone else into our mess, I knew we needed these people. For what, I wasn't exactly sure. But I knew our Scooby Gang would help however they could, even if it was just to stop me from losing my mind.

"It's okay. Let's go up. They know we have something important to tell them, and you know as well as I do that they're not gonna leave us alone until they know what it is."

"'Kay" was all Ransom said. Then he pulled the door open for me, and we ascended the stairs more quickly than I would've liked.

Brody's door was cracked when we got to his apartment— probably so he didn't have to keep getting up to let people in. Even yelling "It's open" would likely have been too much for him to handle most mornings.

We entered to find most of the crew sitting around Brody's apartment in various positions and places. Carter was standing in the kitchen, leaning on the bar and eating something out of a leftover container he'd probably helped himself to in the fridge. Xander, Aniyah, and Toby were on the couch, playing on their phones. Sophia and Drew were seated at the small kitchen table drinking coffee, and Aamee and Brody were... Where the hell were Aamee and Brody?

"Wow, everyone got here before us," Ransom said. I could hear his nerves as he spoke and wondered if anyone else picked up on it.

Xander spoke first. "Yeah, well, you guys acted like it was life or death that we get here, so we came over as soon as you texted."

I tried to ignore Xander's choice of words. "Where are Brody and Aamee?" I asked, not wanting to begin until everyone was here. Or maybe I was just looking for a way to delay dropping the murder bomb on everyone.

The rest of the group looked around like they hadn't noticed their absence. A few people shrugged while others let out some grunts that didn't hold much concern for our friends' whereabouts.

"They were here a couple minutes ago," Carter announced, his mouth full.

Sophia offered a guess by way of a glance toward Brody's bedroom.

The room grew quieter until everyone was silent. Well, everyone except Aamee and Brody, whose muffled voices and occasional moans could suddenly be heard through the thin walls.

"Ew!" Sophia screamed with a shiver that seemed to run through her whole body at the thought of her brother doing... God knew what to his girlfriend in the other room. "Brody and Aamee, get out here! Taylor and Ransom are here!"

When they didn't answer and no one else spoke, Sophia begged us to start talking. Once again, the room was a bustle of noise and activity with everyone chatting and laughing. I wished we could participate in the casual conversation and the lighthearted banter like Ransom and I normally would, but despite my best efforts, I couldn't hide the seriousness of the situation.

"Really, though!" I yelled. "Can you guys please stop and come out here?"

About thirty seconds later, Brody and Aamee emerged, looking a bit disheveled and annoyed.

"What kind of donuts did you bring?" Brody asked, running a hand through his dark, messy hair.

"What? Why would we have donuts?" Ransom asked.

"Uh, because it's ten in the morning on a weekend, and you called all of us here." He shrugged. "Just seems like food would be warranted."

"We didn't bring any food," I told him.

Brody laughed before realizing we were most likely serious. "Really? You ask me to host some big event and then drag me out of bed, and you didn't even bring breakfast? Dude," he said to Ransom. "I thought we were bros."

"This is serious," Ransom said. "We have something to tell all of you, and we need you to have an open mind about it."

"Okay," Carter said slowly through a mouthful of cereal.

"I know it's gonna be difficult, but let us explain before you judge the situation." I was practically hyperventilating. "I need to sit down," I said suddenly, as I moved absent-mindedly toward the couch and squeezed in between the arm of the sofa and Aniyah, causing her to shift closer to Xander. I was sure she didn't mind, though she might have acted like she did.

"It'll be okay," she said, putting a hand on my back and rubbing gently.

"I don't think it will. All this happened so suddenly, and—"

"Taylor, whatever this is, we're here for you," Sophia said. She was my best friend and had been my best friend for two decades. Even if she meant those words, she'd most likely want to retract them once I told her Ransom and I had basically killed someone.

Breathing deeply, I tried to find the courage—and the right words—but couldn't seem to locate either.

"I'll tell them," Ransom said, obviously sensing my hesitation. "It's my fault anyway."

"Oh my God," Aamee said. "Can someone just tell us why

we're all here before I lose interest completely?"

"Sorry," Ransom said. "We haven't had much time ourselves to let the news sink in. Once you're involved, it's kind of impossible for you not to be, so I guess if you wanna leave, you should probably do that now."

"Why would we leave?" Carter asked.

Aamee groaned dramatically and headed to the kitchen. "I know my party-planning skills are unmatched, but don't expect me to be in charge of the shower. That's all you, Sophia."

Ransom looked completely confused. "What are you talking about?"

"She thinks I'm pregnant."

"You're not?" Sophia asked, sounding almost disappointed.

"No. We're not having a baby," I explained.

"Oh. Okay," Sophia said. "Then for once, I'm with Aamee. Just come out with it before I stop caring what this is about."

"We killed someone last night," Ransom blurted out.

My head snapped toward his direction, and he almost looked relieved.

"Or not really *we*. Me. *I* killed someone, and Taylor was there for it so she knows, and now you guys all know too."

"Is this like some sort of experiment for a psych class or something?" Toby asked. "Like you have to reveal something shocking and see how people close to you react? Because you probably should've chosen something more believable."

"It's true," I said.

I saw Brody roll his eyes. "I'm going back to bed."

"I'm going with him," Aamee said.

"No. Don't. You guys need to stay because we're serious and we're freaking out. It was all an accident. This guy Brad...

an ex of mine who got clingy and then stalky," I said, clearly losing my ability to find real words. "Sophia knows about him. He's the reason I decided to move here and finish my classes online during my senior year."

"Oh my God," I heard Sophia say softly, and her comment seemed to clue people into the possibility that we were being serious. "He went after you." It wasn't a question because she already knew the answer.

"Last night when I left the Yard to walk home, Brad came from out of nowhere. He'd sent me texts lately . . . pictures of himself at the Treehouse and other places nearby to let me know he was in town. But I just thought he was doing it to creep me out. I never thought he'd . . . act on any of those threats."

I had my gaze toward the ground, but I could feel everyone else's on me. Then I felt Ransom sit on the arm of the couch and put his hand on my back. His touch was gentle but firm enough to comfort me, even if only a little.

"He texted her last night, and I saw the message come up," Ransom said. "And I thought she was seeing someone else. Not that she didn't have a right to. We never talked about what was really going on between us. But I was being an asshole about it—"

"You weren't being an asshole," I said. "And none of it even matters now."

"It matters because you left by yourself, and you were upset and vulnerable. I should've been with you."

We'd already discussed all of this last night, but finding out Brad had been found dead had caused Ransom's guilt to resurface, and it would likely never go away. And I couldn't argue with the fact that if Ransom had been with me, Brad probably wouldn't have even approached me. I'd been the one to leave Brody and Drew's bar angry with Ransom, and I'd refused to let him come with me, even just to see that I got home safely. It was a mistake that would linger in my consciousness for the rest of my life.

If only I had set aside my pride, Brad wouldn't be dead and Ransom wouldn't have to worry about getting accused of a crime.

"Well," I said, taking a long breath to steady my voice, "you weren't there because I refused to let you be." I'd never make that mistake again.

I'd let Ransom in, and I never wanted him to leave. He'd been there for me physically, emotionally, mentally. And I'd been stupid to try to create distance from an amazing man because we were arguing over a shitty one.

"Okay," Aamee said. "As much as I'd like to be a part of your therapy session, can you just tell us how you killed a man now?"

"I don't know, honestly," Ransom told her. "Taylor left, and I was standing outside the Yard, deciding whether to go back in or go after her, and I heard her scream. I ran toward the sound and eventually found them in the alley next to that nail salon on Highland. He had her pinned to the wall, his hands on her neck. I definitely roughed him up and threatened him, but when we left, he was still standing." Ransom looked lost in his own thoughts, like his mind was reliving the story as he told it, whether he wanted to or not. He shook his head before saying, "No matter how much I hated the guy for what he tried to do to Taylor, I would never just *let* someone die, let alone intentionally kill them."

"Shit," Drew said. "Brad's the guy they found near Rafferty's?" His question was directed at Sophia, but it was clear they both already knew the answer.

"So you *don't* need help disposing of the body?" Aamee's blond eyebrows scrunched together in confusion, and the slump of her shoulders made her appear almost disappointed.

"No," I said. "The police found him. They reported it this morning. Sophia sent me the link to the article because it was so close to the bar, and that's when I realized. The police didn't just leave the body lying in the alley."

Aamee's gaze darted around to all of us, no doubt waiting for one of us to clarify what this had to do with *her*.

The rest of our group of friends looked absolutely stunned. I guessed most of them thought more than once about heading for the door as we explained what had happened last night. But here they all were, still sitting in Brody's apartment like soldiers waiting for instructions from their commanding officer. Too bad they had Ransom and me instead.

Brody pushed both hands through his hair and then pressed his hands to his face. "Fuck!"

Ransom glanced over at him. "Tell me about it."

RANSOM

"Okay, let's review so the timeline and locations are clear." Xander placed the notebook he'd been holding on the coffee table, and we all hovered around it like some sort of amateur organized crime group. Xander retraced the map he'd drawn according to Taylor's account of the situation and then looked to the two of us for confirmation. "Does that seem about right timewise?"

I let Taylor answer because I could only account for what

took place in the alley.

"Yeah. I think so. I'm not positive about the times, though. I'm just estimating based on last night's texts."

"Okay, so our first step is to see what cameras are in the area. Traffic light, security... Most likely the police have already secured footage of the area, but it doesn't hurt for us to know what they're looking at." He sat back and pulled his laptop out of his bag. The rest of us were silent as Xander tapped away on the keys and manipulated the screen with his fingers, though I couldn't see what he was actually looking at. "Looks like there are only five cameras in a three-block radius. That obviously doesn't account for personal devices, though chances are no one was filming much of anything at that time of night. It's not exactly Times Square, so I think we're safe where that's concerned."

He continued. "There are two traffic cameras near Rafferty's that might've caught you and Brad walking together when you say he first approached you, but it doesn't look like there are any near the area of the alley."

Taylor had said that Brad came up behind her suddenly, and that was the scream I'd heard. He'd put something against her back that she'd assumed was a gun and told her to start walking. Then he'd led her the couple of blocks to the alley where I'd eventually found them.

It all began to piece together into a clear picture the police were certain to discover. "That means they'll see Brad and Taylor together and then see me running toward them." I felt like the contents of my insides might drop out of my body and onto the floor.

"Well, that's what I was just looking at," Xander said. "I looked at the camera angles, and neither of them is clear enough to make out any faces. Taylor has a sweatshirt on with the hood up, and you could be any male with light hair. It's probably even difficult to make out your height and weight." Xander spun the computer around so the rest of us could see what he was looking at. He clicked through the camera shots that had a view of us, and it made me feel slightly better. It was dark, and the shots were from pretty far away. Then once we hit Highland, there was no video at all.

"Are you sure that's all they'd have?" I asked. "How did you even get into the footage?"

Xander looked up at me, his eyes wide and serious. "It's probably best if you don't ask questions you don't want the answer to."

"This is so much better than an unplanned pregnancy announcement," Aamee said excitedly.

"Does anyone have a muzzle?" Sophia asked.

"Would both of you stop?" Brody said. "This isn't the time for your immature jabs. Ransom and Taylor need our support. *All* of our support." He let his stare drift over each one of our friends like a parent scolding their teenagers for getting caught drinking.

The fact that Brody was the current voice of reason spoke volumes about the rest of our mental states.

Aamee rolled her eyes before saying, "I already basically offered to help hide the body. I don't know how much more supportive I can be."

"Just continue, Xander," Brody told him.

"As crazy as it is, I think Brad did you both a favor. I don't think his choice of location was an accident. He approached you in a spot where it's difficult to identify him on camera, and then he took you to a place that had no cameras at all. No doubt that was for his own benefit, but it also means it's going to be difficult for detectives to figure out who Taylor and Ransom are. It's probably even gonna be tough for them to tell that the person with Taylor is Brad. At least with any level of certainty."

"Okay, that's good," I said.

"It is," Carter agreed, "but I'm guessing over the next few days they'll start asking around at nearby businesses. And Rafferty's is one of them. Not many places are open at that hour, so I'm thinking they'll wanna know if anyone saw anything unusual or if any customers or employees resembled anyone in the video footage."

"So we'll just make sure if the cops come in, it's one of the three of us who talks to them," Drew said, referring to himself, Xander, and Brody, who all worked at the Yard, the deck bar outside Rafferty's.

"You can't be sure they won't ask other people," Taylor pointed out. "I'm sure if they come by, they'll talk to whoever's working and maybe some of the customers."

"No. We can't be sure," Brody agreed. "You guys should both stay away from that area—at least for the time being until some of this dies down. And we just have to hope if the cops do come around asking questions that no one remembers anything of value."

"Okay," I said. Though I couldn't help but think that *hope* hadn't gotten me very far in life. I wasn't sure this time would be any different.

Chapter Two

RANSOM

"If you could be any breakfast food, which would you choose?" Taylor asked me, her blond hair spilling over the puppy-shaped pillow she'd brought from her place and rehomed on my couch.

My nose crinkled. "Why?"

She lifted her head slightly so she could angle it to face me. "Why not?"

"Why would I want to be food?"

"Who *wouldn't* want to be food? Food is delicious."

"But it isn't delicious *to* food. Food doesn't get to eat itself."

Her face contorted as she clearly pondered what I said before lying back down. "You're thinking too deeply about it," she finally said.

"The fact that you're thinking about it at all is... concerning."

"Just making conversation," she muttered.

We'd been pseudo living together for two days. Two days

of both of us trying to act natural and like we weren't steeped with panic. It was more difficult to go on with my normal life after potentially murdering someone than I would've thought. Though I guess I hadn't spent a ton of time thinking about it before. Other than in that sudden, road-ragey type way where I hoped for someone to get flattened by a tractor trailer before their car burst into flames for cutting me off in traffic.

But that was normal.

What wasn't normal was running the events of an evening over and over in my head to see where I might have crossed the line and killed someone. Hypothetical murder was much easier on the conscience.

I knew Taylor was struggling with similar worries, and I didn't want to make things more difficult on her. Which was why I found myself answering her asinine question. "I'd probably be some kind of cereal. Like Kix or Frosted Flakes."

She turned her head toward me again. "Why?"

I shrugged. "Because most people can never eat them without leaving some behind in the bowl or dropping bits of it all over the place. So at least some of me wouldn't be eaten."

"First, I never leave any cereal behind. Second, what good would part of you be without the whole?"

"It's better than nothing."

The look on her face said she wasn't so sure it was. I wasn't sure how a simple question had become existential, but it was a rabbit hole I knew I didn't want to travel down. "I spy with my little eye, something . . ."

"This game is the worst," she said, though she quickly sat up so she could see the whole room.

"Lazy."

She scrunched up her face. "That's not how you play."

"Says who?"

"Says the I Spy gods."

I stood and walked over to her, bending down so I could press a kiss to her lips. "I'm the only god you need, baby."

She groaned. "That was *so* bad."

Smiling, I made my way toward the hallway that led to my bedroom. "The truth doesn't have to be good. I'm going to get ready for class. Need anything before I go?"

"Other than for my boyfriend to get better pickup lines?"

Her words stopped me in my tracks. I slowly turned in her direction. She was back on her pillow, looking at something on her phone. She looked so unconcerned with what she'd said, but I couldn't stop the thrill that shot through me.

We'd said we were dating, but neither of us had used the labels yet. I liked hearing it far more than I would've imagined.

"Say it again."

Her brow wrinkled in confusion. "Say what again?"

"Call me your boyfriend again."

A slow smile spread across her face. "Your pickup lines are shit, boyfriend."

"Noted, girlfriend."

We shared another smile before I turned and resumed my trek.

"Wait," she yelled, and my heart stopped, worry lancing through my chest that she'd changed her mind that quickly. "What's the lazy thing you saw?"

My brain took a moment to recover from the whiplash caused by talking to this woman—my girlfriend. She clearly took my hesitation for confusion because she went on. "For I Spy. You said you saw something lazy."

I snorted and, figuring it was best not to reply, hurried to my room and closed the door.

"It was me, wasn't it?" she yelled so loudly she was barely muffled through the door. "Ransom! Am I the lazy thing, you asshole?"

And leaning against the door as my girlfriend screeched at me from the living room, for the first time in two days, I laughed.

TAYLOR

After Ransom left for class with promises to swing by and pick me up for our shift at Safe Haven, I figured I should probably prove him wrong with his "lazy" comment and sign into my own classes. It had been difficult to get in the proper headspace to complete coursework when my current boyfriend had potentially murdered my ex-boyfriend while I looked on.

Though murdered wasn't the right term, was it? It was totally accidental. I mean, Ransom had punched Brad on purpose, but the *death* had been an accident. So maybe he'd . . . manslaughtered him?

As a criminal justice major, I should've been able to be a little more precise with my terms, but it was all so hard to think about, let alone break it down and get to the facts surrounding it.

Ransom had been defending me. He'd left Brad bloodied but standing. Logically I knew that there was a strong case to be made in support of what Ransom had done.

I also knew that the justice system didn't always operate in logical ways. He'd still caused someone's death with his own hands, and though a jury would most likely see Brad's death as self-defense had I been the one to cause it, Ransom was a different story. He was a former foster kid whose mother had spent time in jail for drugs. So even if I believed the law *should* operate in a specific way, I couldn't trust it to. I couldn't risk Ransom.

So the best thing to do was to wait and see what we heard about it. Our friends had promised to help, and I had to let myself trust them. Maybe if I'd trusted more of them with more of the Brad story to begin with, it wouldn't have gotten this out of hand.

I logged into my laptop to resume my course and had just begun reading over the material when my phone rang with an incoming FaceTime call from Sophia.

"Hi," I said as her olive complexion filled the screen. "What's up?"

"Um…"

Well, that wasn't a response that set me at ease. "What?"

"Don't freak out."

Rolling my eyes, I let loose a heavy sigh. "Seriously? When has saying that ever made someone *not* freak out?"

She had the good sense to look sheepish. "Since now?"

"Spill it."

"The cops were at Rafferty's." Sophia released the words quickly, as if speed would take the alarm out of them.

I pushed the laptop off my lap and stood. Pacing seemed like a crucial step in my impending panic. "Oh my God, oh my God, oh my God."

"I get why you'd be confused, but it's me. Sophia."

Stopping to glare at my friend, I said, "Why is everyone making stupid God jokes today?"

"Sorry, I was trying to lighten the mood. I'll work on my timing. And who's everyone?"

"You and Ransom."

"Oh good, you two haven't killed each other yet." At my look of disbelief, she added, "Too soon for talk of killing. Will continue working on timing. Got it."

"What did the cops want?"

"Drew said they asked if anyone had noticed an argument or someone acting strangely. They're supposedly talking to everyone within a few blocks, which we already knew they would."

My breath started coming in heavy pants. I dropped onto the couch and put my head in my hand.

"Taylor, calm down. It's all going to be okay."

"You can't know that. What if the cops find out it was Ransom who beat up Brad, and then he goes to prison and we can only have conjugal visits once a year? He'll get tired of me and decide to marry a pen pal who's affiliated with the gang he'll have to join in order to survive life on the inside."

"Wow. That's all . . . oddly well thought out."

"I've been running through potential outcomes when I can't sleep at night."

"Does he maybe not go to jail in any of these outcomes?"

"No. My mind is a seriously fucked-up place."

"Okay, well, we'll come back to that later. Anyway, my super-smart fiancé asked them if they had any cameras in the area that showed what happened."

I groaned. "Because that's not suspicious at all."

"No, no, he acted like he was asking out of concern. Like, 'Didn't any cameras capture the cold-blooded murderer who beat a man to death with his bare hands?'"

I gaped at her. "Are you for real right now?"

She waved me off. "That was, like, totally hypothetical."

"Except it's, like, totally what happened." A thought popped into my head, causing me to gasp and widen my eyes. "Do you think they could be listening to our call? Oh my God. We shouldn't be talking about this over the phone."

"Dude, you're not Manson. Chill out."

"What does that mean?"

"It means you're not important enough for them to be tapping your phone."

"Well, that's rude."

Sophia rubbed her forehead. "I'm going to need you to choose an emotion. Are you so panicked you need me to make you feel better, or are you so shallow you need to think you're the center of the universe?"

"Don't I have enough on my plate without you making me choose an identity on the fly?"

"Anyway, as I was saying before your multiple personalities started to all try to talk at once, the police didn't come out and actually say they didn't have footage, but Drew said it was heavily implied. Which blows my mind. Even your shitty apartment has a camera outside."

"It's not hooked to anything."

"Oh, well, that makes more sense."

"It also makes sense that there wouldn't be any cameras near the alley."

"Why?"

I sighed. "Brad wasn't stupid. Like Xander said, he wouldn't have grabbed me somewhere a camera would've caught him. He chose that spot intentionally."

"But he didn't even know you'd try to walk home like a

reckless lunatic. So, could he have really planned it out that well in advance?"

"I don't know. It just wouldn't surprise me if he'd scoped out the places I frequented and where he'd take me if he managed to get me alone. It wasn't like he dragged me into an alley that was on the way home. He nabbed me right at the corner of the street Rafferty's is on and then walked me in a deliberate path *to* that alley."

Sophia hesitated a second. "You didn't make it seem like Brad had a destination in mind when you first told us about it."

"It hadn't occurred to me then. But it's all I've been thinking about since, so ..." I let my words die off, not wanting to verbalize how much I was struggling, especially since I knew it was obvious.

"That's scary as hell."

I let out a hollow chuckle. "Tell me about it."

"This is still good though," Sophia said. "They obviously don't have any leads if they're wandering around talking to businesses. And no camera means no proof you guys were anywhere near there."

"Yeah, that's good."

"One more time with feeling."

I groaned. "I just hate waiting for the shoe to drop. I feel like we'll be looking over our shoulders, waiting for the cops to haul us away, for the rest of our lives."

"Then maybe you should go to the police and tell them what happened," Sophia suggested softly.

"And when they asked us why we waited *days* to come talk to them, what do we say? *Sorry, officer, we were trying to get our story straight?* That's what they're going to think. And Ransom is only in this mess because of me. I can't—"

"Taylor Emory Peterson, don't you dare finish that sentence. None of this is your fault."

"Did you just middle-name me?"

"Yes. And I'll do it again, young lady." Sophia's voice was hard and matronly as she spoke, which was a sharp contrast from the softer tone she continued with. "Tay, tell me you know this isn't on you. That asshole tried to kidnap you after stalking and harassing you for months."

I wanted to argue. Rail at her that I could've done more, been more honest, confronted Brad instead of running away. There were so many things I would've done differently. But arguing with her about blame was a waste of time. Sophia would always see me as better than I was.

"I'm just saying, it won't be me who gets into trouble. If they don't believe our version of things, it's Ransom who gets blamed for it. And I just... I can't take that risk."

Sophia was quiet for a long moment before she said, "I get it. If it were me and Drew in that situation, I'd probably do the same thing."

The self-flagellating part of me wanted to say that she and Drew would never be in a situation like this. They'd been in their fair share of hardships, but they'd always faced them together. I'd attempted to face mine alone and look where it had gotten us.

But instead of saying any of that, I simply murmured a "thanks" and counted down the seconds until I could get off the call and break down in private.

Chapter Three

RANSOM

Taylor kept saying she was fine, but she wasn't fine. Her lips were tight and flat, her eyes downcast, and her clothes baggy. Even the kids at Safe Haven seemed to have picked up on her fragile mood. They kept checking in with her, asking if she wanted to play with them and giving her pictures they'd drawn. It was like watching a dozen little Florence Nightingales hover over a wounded soldier.

I wanted to support Taylor, but I wasn't sure how. In our quest to act like everything was normal, we'd mostly avoided the topic of Brad and what had happened. But it was clear it was constantly on both of our minds, and I wasn't so sure avoiding talking about it was helping either of us.

It also worried me because I wasn't sure where the pretending stopped. How did we cement what was between us as real when we ignored some of the most important shit in our lives?

As I watched Taylor give a small smile as a little girl handed her a necklace made of dry macaroni, I vowed to do my damnedest to bring the bright, mischievous smile she normally wore back to her face. I'd gotten a glimpse of it earlier this morning, so I knew the capability was still there.

As I pondered all the ridiculous things I could do to make Taylor laugh, I felt a tug on my sleeve.

"Hey there, Cinnabon." I crouched down so I was at eye level with Cindy, a little girl I'd bonded with a few weeks ago when I'd impulsively volunteered to babysit her for a weekend.

Since that had happened, Cindy had been staying with her uncle, the director of Safe Haven, while her mom got her life sorted out. But Harry still drove her to school every morning, and she still came to Safe Haven in the afternoons so Cindy could have consistency in her routine.

Cindy pointed covertly—or as covertly as a seven-year-old could manage—at Taylor and then let a finger draw down her cheek as if tracking a tear.

"Is Taylor sad?" I said, thinking that's what Cindy was asking. Whether Cindy was just extremely shy or a selective mute, I wasn't sure, but I was grateful we'd found our own method of communicating.

She reached out and tapped my arm twice, her sign for yes.

I cast another quick glance in Taylor's direction before refocusing on Cindy. "Maybe she's just tired today. Nothing for you to worry about." I didn't want to lie to the kids. I felt like they could tell who they could depend on to be real with them. But I obviously couldn't tell Cindy that Taylor was worried we'd killed someone, so that was as close to the truth as I felt comfortable getting.

Cindy looked unsure. Then she pointed at me and repeated the motion with her hand.

I smiled. "No, Cindy, I'm not sad." *I'm scared out of my mind.* "But thank you for worrying about us. You're a pretty special kid, you know that?"

Cindy's lips turned up in a shy smile she tried to hide by ducking her head. I stood, gave her a gentle pat on the head, and walked over to Taylor. "Hey. Can I talk to you for a second?"

"Sure."

We moved over toward where we stored the snacks so we'd have a small bit of privacy.

"What's up?" she asked.

"Cindy just came over and asked me if you were sad."

Taylor's face fell, making me think I should've been more tactful with my phrasing. "Shit. Guess I'm not doing a good job of hiding I have a lot on my mind, huh?" She tried for another one of those half smiles she'd been doling out all afternoon. It almost hurt me to see it.

I crowded a bit closer to her. "Tell me how to fix it. If you want me to go to the police, I—"

She clutched my shirt in her hands. "No," she said, her tone emphatic. "Absolutely not. That is not even an option."

"Okay," I capitulated. She continued to hold on to my shirt, so I gripped her elbows. She looked like she was close to panicking. "Breathe. It's okay. We're okay."

"Just . . . you can't go to the police. Promise me."

I tried not to make promises I wasn't sure I could keep, but I figured Taylor's emotional state—as well as my desire not to make a scene in front of the kids—was enough to have me agreeing. "I won't."

She took a steadying breath and released my shirt. "I'm sorry. I just hate feeling like the police are going to walk in here any second and drag us away."

"I know. But from what you said earlier about what Sophia told you, it doesn't seem like they have any suspects." Which, in a lot of ways, made me feel even worse. Granted, there'd been no details released about the crime. For all we knew, Brad had tripped on his way out of the alley, hit his head, and died. But not setting things right didn't sit right with me. I didn't run from problems. I wasn't my mother.

I didn't want to dodge the consequences of my actions. And I wasn't trying to dodge the consequences of this one. But my priority—whether it was right or not—was Taylor. And I couldn't risk her getting swept up in everything. Once I knew she was safe, I'd come clean.

I saw Roddie, a college student who worked here with us, out of the corner of my eye. He stopped beside us, his head swinging between us for a second before saying, "Are you guys dancing?"

Taylor's eyes narrowed in what I assumed was confusion. "Why would we be dancing?"

Roddie shrugged. "Why wouldn't you be?"

Taylor stared at him for a moment before saying, "Everything with you feels harder than it should be."

Smiling widely, Roddie said, "I know, right?" and sauntered away.

Looking back at me, Taylor said, "How are we the most normal ones here?"

"That's not fair. Some of the kids are"—I looked over to where two boys were lifting up the dresses of some dolls— "kinda normal."

"Are you two dancing?"

I startled before whirling around to see Edith, Harry's cantankerous secretary, standing behind me. "Why is that everyone's first guess?"

"Would copulating be better?"

Horror swept through me at the sound of this septuagenarian saying the word "copulate." "Never again, Edith. That word leaves your mouth *never* again."

"Please. I was using that word before your dad had his first tickle in his trousers."

"Why, Edith? *Why?*" The only thing that kept my lunch down was the fact that my father was more of an abstract concept than a living reality. I would've never expected to be thankful for coming from a single-parent home, but here we were.

Edith shrugged. "I like to make you uncomfortable."

"Uncomfortable? My brain needs bleach to recover from this conversation."

Her face was smug. "Then my work here is done."

"Like forever?" I asked hopefully.

She none-to-gently slapped my cheek twice. "You wish, dear."

"Did you need something, Edith?" Taylor asked, thankfully steering the conversation in a direction that would make Edith leave more quickly.

"Harry left for a meeting, but he forgot to talk to Bill about the running toilet in the bathroom. He called to ask me to tell you to do it."

"Why can't you call and ask him?" My tone was accusing. There was no way Harry would tell me to go up and find Bill when Edith could accomplish the same task by picking up a phone.

"Because I don't run *errands*?" she said, the final word reflecting how distasteful the thought was.

"You're literally running one right now."

The glare she sent me would have flayed the skin off a weaker man. "Not that it's any of your business, but Bill and I aren't on speaking terms."

"Then send a carrier pigeon. Or, I don't know, maybe an email."

"Sarcasm is an ugly look on you," she spat.

"Well, being a lying liar who lies is a bad look on you. I'm not doing your dirty work, Edith. I refuse."

She simply stood there, arms crossed over her chest, and stared at me.

"I'm not backing down. He hates me ever since I broke the door last month."

"He hated you before that."

I gasped. "He did not."

She opened her mouth to retort with what was undoubtedly some other mistruth when Taylor spoke. "I'll go."

"That's . . . much less fun for me," Edith grumbled.

I smiled. "My hero."

"Shut up," Taylor replied before heading for the door. "If I'm not back in ten minutes . . . just wait longer."

"That line has seriously never been funny," I said, making her laugh as she left the room.

"She's a good one. You should try really hard not to screw it up."

"Thanks for the tip, Cruella."

Once Edith ran her icy gaze over everyone, she left, and I could've sworn the temperature rose without her evil presence blanketing the room.

Bill came in behind Taylor about five minutes later, giving me a disapproving look as he made his way to the bathroom.

"You know," Taylor said as she sidled up beside me, "I

always expected you to be liked by everyone. How wrong I was."

"You can't judge by Bill and Edith. They hate everyone."

"I dunno. Bill was very accommodating when I went up to see him."

"You're gorgeous. He'd be a moron to be mean to you."

A slight hint of pink rose to Taylor's cheeks as she bit her lip to keep from smiling. "You're not too tough on the eyes yourself."

"Too bad Bill and Edith have shitty eyesight."

A laugh burst from her, and I felt supremely proud of myself for prompting that sound.

"Taylor, can you help us tie the ends of our bracelets?" a little girl named Gianna asked.

"Sure," Taylor replied. The smile she bestowed on the girl was the most genuine one I'd seen since we got to work.

I watched her walk over to where a few girls were huddled at the craft table before I went to hang out with the kids who were gathered around the game console Roddie had brought in.

The rest of the night passed quickly, and before I knew it, Taylor and I were headed out to my truck. I walked around to open her door for her, getting a "such a gentleman" for the effort, but before I could swing it closed behind her, my phone started to ring.

Looking down at it, I managed to hold back a groan, which was serious progress. "It's Kari." My mom had been calling more often recently, something I'd encouraged and was trying to stay open-minded about. But the years of bad blood between us were difficult to get past, and I often found myself annoyed with her before she even started speaking.

Taylor kept her face blank as she said, "Answer it. We have time."

I leaned back against my truck next to Taylor's still-open door. "Hello."

"Ransom, hi. How are you?"

"I'm good." *Kinda.* "How are you?"

"Doing pretty good. Just running around trying to help prepare for the reunion."

"That's good that you're staying busy."

"Yeah."

Silence stretched across the line, and it felt awkward and heavy. We didn't know each other well enough to move beyond small talk often, but neither of us excelled at casual conversation. It was weird to have both so much and nothing at all to say.

"So," she began after a few moments. "About the reunion. I know you said you were going to think about it, and I was just wondering what you'd decided."

"Yeah, I did think about it, but I'm pretty busy up here. And Georgia is a little far to travel for a one-day event."

"Oh."

Her disappointment was evident, which made me feel like an asshole. No matter how much damage she'd done, she was still my mom, and hurting her made me feel like a jerk. But it was shit timing, and I also wasn't sure I was ready to hang out with a bunch of family I barely knew. Not to mention the fact that I wasn't sure where any of that family had been when I was being shuffled through the foster system.

"Okay, I understand," she continued. "Maybe I can come up to you sometime?"

I opened my mouth to respond, but Taylor grabbing my

arm stopped me. I looked over at her.

"Let's go," she said quietly. Her eyes were pleading. "Let's get away from here for a few days. Please."

I didn't think she knew what she was really asking. Leaving town to go hang out with my family felt a bit like jumping out of a frying pan and into the fire. But as Taylor looked at me hopefully, I felt myself caving.

"On second thought... is it okay if I bring my girlfriend with me to the reunion?"

Matching female squeals on both sides of the phone almost made me forget what a dumpster fire this was going to be.

Chapter Four

RANSOM

"We didn't really think this through, did we?" I grabbed the cups of coffee from where the barista had placed them on the counter and handed Taylor hers.

"I did. And in your defense, I didn't really give you a choice."

I laughed a little as I followed Taylor to a small table in front of the café. It had been unseasonably warm the last couple of days, and the cloudless sky meant we could get some fresh air while we enjoyed our drinks. Everything had been so crazy since Brad . . . happened. *I can't even allow myself to think the word.* I'd barely had a chance to process any of it, especially the part where I'd agreed to go to a family reunion to see a family I barely knew. Prison might be a better option.

"So how does all this work?" I asked. "I can probably just check with my professors." I figured I wouldn't have to miss more than two classes at the most, since I only had class a few days a week. I had pretty good grades, so I didn't see it being a problem as long as I kept up with the work. "But then there's the whole Safe Haven thing."

"I know. I feel bad about asking him for time off with such little notice—especially when it's both of us."

"Yeah," I said slowly. "He does owe us, though." Watching Harry's insane dogs and his niece had been my choice, even if the latter had been more of an accident than an actual offer. Thank God Taylor had come to our rescue and helped. So even though the favor had been a big one—and one I wasn't sure I ever wanted to repeat—I wasn't the type of guy to cash in on something like that.

I'd volunteered to help him and his husband because it was the right thing to do and he'd needed my help. Which was exactly why I knew that even if it would be an inconvenience to have Taylor and me out at the same time, he'd never say no, even if it meant filling in for one of us himself. I felt guilty about putting him in that position, but I was also glad I had the type of boss I could count on when I needed something.

"I'll talk to him. I'm sure it'll be fine. It'll only be a few days."

"I bet if you tell Harry why we're going, he'll *insist* we go," Taylor said.

I lowered my voice to a whisper even though no one was sitting at the table beside us. "You want me to tell him we're avoiding the police because we're worried about being suspects in a murder investigation?"

"Oh my God! No! I trust Harry, but I'm not sure he's the type of guy who can handle knowing something like that. He'd probably explode with that kind of information trapped inside him. I meant telling him about the family reunion. You don't have to share all the details about your past with him, but maybe if he knew you hadn't seen your mom in a while, he'd understand why you felt you needed to go."

"Okay, that's a little less jarring for him I think."

Taylor laughed, and it felt good to joke around a little, even if the jokes involved recent events. Maybe the investigation would lead nowhere, and Brad would just end up as another cold case that people would forget about.

But as much as that thought comforted me, it also made me feel like shit.

TAYLOR

I knew finding someone to cover for me at the Treehouse Bar and Grille while I was away wouldn't be an issue. People practically begged for weekend shifts. I could work Monday night if needed, though Mondays were never busy, so I doubted I'd even have to come in at all.

Our friends were supposed to be meeting at the Treehouse for dinner and drinks in about a half hour, but I'd gotten here early so I could talk to Jerry about taking off and hopefully find someone to cover me.

I made my way over to the bar to see who was working tonight, and when I saw Jesse and Harmony, I knew they'd be all over the extra hours. Harmony had just started at the Treehouse two weeks ago, so she rarely received the good shifts, and Jesse already worked Friday and Saturday from lunch until whenever someone came to relieve him. But he had a baby on the way and would happily work the full night if he got the opportunity.

I approached them excitedly with the offer, and they were just as excited to accept. That only left finding someone for my Sunday afternoon shift since both of them were already working.

"You could always ask Gail," Jesse suggested with his eyebrows raised as he grabbed some plates to take out to a table. "Sundays and Mondays are her days off."

Gail had been a host at the Treehouse since before I started working here, but she'd recently begun waiting tables too. She didn't exactly have the personality to get good tips, but I guess something was better than nothing.

I pressed my lips together to show Jesse just how enthused I was with his suggestion. Gail was nice enough, but she wasn't exactly the warm and fuzzy type. Not that I was. But Gail gave off a *don't fuck with me* vibe, which sometimes translated into a *don't speak to me at all* vibe.

"Maybe I'll just text Preston and Lila," I said. "They might want it."

"Already working," Harmony said. "Looks like Gail's your best option."

"More like my *only* option," I muttered with a glance in her direction. I put on a smile and headed over to the host station. "Hey, Gail."

Her short dark hair framed her face as she clicked around on the host station iPad. She looked up, and I could almost taste whatever oil she'd doused herself in—frankincense and some sort of floral mixture that reminded me of an old church.

"Why do you look like a four-year-old posing for a picture with Santa?" she asked.

"I don't know what that means exactly."

"Like you're trying to look happy but you wanna run away," she explained, her attention dropping back down to the iPad she'd been using.

I'd never heard a more accurate description of someone's feelings. Though she seemed about as emotionally aware as a dish towel, Gail was a shockingly good read of people.

"Because," I said, keeping up my excitement, "I have an offer for you."

"I'm not interested in being a part of your hair-care product cult."

"What?" I shook my head. "I'm not ..." I wasn't sure exactly what she was talking about, so I continued. "I wanted to offer you my shift next Sunday."

"In exchange for what?" I saw the skepticism on her face. She probably wasn't typically the recipient of people's generosity, and though there was probably a reason for that, I still felt a little bad.

"Nothing. Just tryin' to help you out, that's all."

A laugh shot out of her. "I doubt that. What is it? You need me to pee in a cup for you or something? I'm not saying no, but you should know I charge more than you're probably willing to pay for that."

I stared blankly at her while I considered retracting my offer altogether. Even though Gail wasn't typically rude to *me*, sometimes her comments felt like someone was brushing my hair with a fork.

"I don't want your pee. I just wanna know if you're interested in the hours."

Gail's stare let me know that she still didn't quite trust me, but she was considering the offer anyway. Like an animal who'd spotted food in a cage and didn't know whether to go inside.

"No catch?"

"No catch," I told her. "I'll be away, so I just need someone to cover for me."

"Okay, so it's really *me* doing *you* the favor."

This fucking girl. "Well, yeah. That's usually what happens when someone asks you to cover for them at work."

"The way you presented it made it seem like you were doing something for *me*."

"So you *don't* want the shift?"

"I never said that."

"Then you *do* want it?"

"Never said that either." She played with the ring in her nose, which I found repulsive. I could only hope she didn't do that as a server.

"Can you just tell me whether you want it or not?"

Her lips twisted in thought. "Can I get back to you?"

My instinct was to say yes and leave, but I stopped myself. "No, I need an answer now. If you don't want it, I'm sure there's someone else who will." I wasn't sure that was true, but Gail didn't know that.

She rolled her eyes like she was tired of talking to me and would say almost anything to get me to leave. "Fine, I'll take it."

We stared awkwardly at each other for a moment before I said, "Great, thanks," so I could get out of there. Standing near Gail was like swimming with a dolphin. If you stayed in the water too long, the sedative might wear off and you'd suddenly get violently pulled under.

So I headed over toward the tables by the bar and pushed a few together so there'd be enough room for all of us. It wasn't busy yet, and this section of the restaurant didn't take reservations. While I waited for the others, I put in some appetizer orders and grabbed a few pitchers of beer.

The nachos and wings arrived right as my friends began to, and once we all got settled with our food and drinks, I asked Ransom how everything went with his professors and Harry.

"Fine. Harry was happy we were going to the reunion and said it's not a big deal that we'll be gone. I think it's probably more of a hassle than he's letting on, but he seemed happy to help, so I just said thanks on behalf of both of us."

"I'll make sure I thank him too. What about your classes?"

"I emailed. They both said it wouldn't be a problem." Ransom dipped his celery into some blue cheese. "How about you? You find someone to cover for you?"

"Yeah, I should be good."

"When are you guys leaving?" Xander asked.

I shrugged because we hadn't made definite plans yet. "The reunion's on Saturday, so what were we thinking? Thursday morning maybe? Then we'll have a day to relax before we see your family. When I looked it up, it said it takes like thirteen hours to get there."

"Thursday's probably a good idea," Ransom said. "I'm sure we'll hit some traffic, but if we both switch off driving, it shouldn't be too brutal."

"You're driving?" Aamee sounded like she'd just heard someone suggest the health benefits of eating a baby's placenta.

"Yeah," I said. "We can't exactly fly."

"Why not?" Carter bit into a wing and finished it off before wiping his face.

"Because," Ransom said, dropping his voice to almost a whisper, "plane tickets will have our names attached to them. It'd be easy to figure out where we're going if the police wanna talk to us."

"If they wanted to talk to you, don't you think they already would have?" Brody asked.

"Maybe the cops are waiting until Ransom and Taylor do something suspicious, like try to flee the state, before they bring them in for questioning," Aamee suggested. She settled back in her chair with the chip she'd just grabbed and nibbled at the corner, looking pleased with herself.

"We aren't fleeing the state," I told her. "We're going to Ransom's family reunion. And that's what all of you will say if you're asked. Right?" I glared at Aamee. "Even you."

"That's insulting," she said.

"It was meant to be."

Aamee rolled her eyes, but she promised our secret was safe with her.

Xander was sitting quietly, most likely thinking about something none of us had. His brain worked like a computer when it came to analyzing . . . well, anything, really.

"What?" I asked.

It took him a moment to realize I was speaking to him, and when he did, he looked at Ransom and me. "Just wondering if it actually might look *less* suspicious to fly. Think about it . . . Anyone trying to dodge the authorities wouldn't fly. You said so yourself. So if you *do* fly, maybe it'll look like you have nothing to hide."

He wasn't wrong necessarily. "It's so much more expensive to fly, though," I said.

"Not when you factor in food and gas," Ransom explained. "And I'll pay for it. It's my reunion, and I was the one . . ."

He didn't complete the sentence, and I couldn't blame him. He didn't need to say the words for the rest of us to know what they would've been.

"You two are doomed," Xander blurted out. "You can't fly there."

Ransom and I exchanged glances before I said, "But you just—"

"I know what I just said. It was a test. And you failed worse than Brody when he's not permitted to use a calculator."

Brody appeared offended, though he most likely wasn't. "Seriously though, why do math teachers even give tests and not let you use a calculator? I mean, is there ever going to be a time when I need to do math and don't have access to my phone?"

"Probably the next time you lose it," Carter joked.

I was starting to think it was a bad idea to get everyone involved in this mess, because all of it just became messier. "Okay, can we please all focus?"

"Yes," Xander said. "Don't fly."

"Okay, you know what?" Ransom said. "I like the driving option better actually. I feel like in an airport I'd be looking over my shoulder the whole time. But this way we'll be on our own on the open road. But I do agree that driving actually might look shadier than flying."

Sophia had been quiet so far, and I wondered if it was because she couldn't believe what I'd gotten myself into or if she was upset I'd dragged her into it too. If the cops were going to question someone about me, she'd be their first stop, and I felt terrible about it.

"What do you think, Soph?" I needed to know what she thought before I made any type of decision.

She didn't say anything right away, and I watched as she shifted in her seat nervously. "I think you should get a gun."

"What?" I practically yelled. "I'm not getting a gun!" Lowering my voice, I added, "We're not running from the mob."

"Yeah, but you never know who will be involved. What if

one of Brad's friends finds out what happened and goes after you guys? I'm worried."

"We're worried too," I said. "And Jesus, thinking I might need a gun to protect myself doesn't help with that."

"Sorry," she said. "I've never had to deal with anything like this before."

"Well, neither have I. It's not like I practiced how to avoid becoming a suspect after my stalker accidentally ..." I motioned with my hand as if the movement would complete the sentence for me.

"Got killed?" Carter said, supplying the words like he thought I might have forgotten the outcome.

"Carter!" Brody snapped. "You're not helping."

"Hey, I suggested we rent some sort of private space for meetings like this a while ago so we wouldn't have to lower our voices, and Drew shot it down."

"Because it's a stupid idea," Drew said.

"You wouldn't think that if we had a Batcave."

"We have Brody's apartment. That's as close to a cave as we need."

"Hey," Brody said. "You lived in that apartment for months."

Drew stared at him before saying, "My comment stands."

"I agree. Your apartment's disgusting. Even with Aamee living there." The comment had come from Toby, who I hadn't realized was here because he was supposed to be working. He'd gotten a job as a sales consultant at a nearby gym.

"When did you get here?" I asked him over whatever insults Aamee was hurling at him.

"That doesn't matter. What matters is I told my boss I ate some bad sushi last night so I wouldn't miss this meeting of the minds. So let's figure this shit out." Toby: the voice of reason.

He had a notebook in front of him and had been taking notes, which scared me. But it was also kind of sweet that he cared so much. "I also think it's smart to drive, but you should probably come up with a reason why driving makes more sense than flying."

We all thought, silently other than the crunching of food, as we waited for someone to come up with an idea.

"Anybody?" Ransom asked.

Carter swallowed the beer in his mouth. "Anybody what?"

"For fuck's sake," Brody said. "You're worse than me."

"Sorry. I was trying to figure out which wings these were. Are they the hot honey ones or the signature?" he asked, looking at the various choices on the menu.

"Hot honey," I said.

"They're good." When he finished chewing the wing he'd just taken a bite of, he added, "So did you guys decide if you're definitely driving? Because my buddy Owen needs a ride to Virginia this weekend."

All at once, our whole group seemed to focus on him—a combination of narrowing eyes, head tilts, and eyebrows raised so high they looked like the result of a serious Botox overdose. Carter seemed oblivious to all of it, his attention still centered on his wings.

"Seriously?" Xander said on behalf of all of us.

Carter raised his gaze from his plate and finally appeared to notice the way the rest of us were looking at him. "What?"

"When were you planning to tell us that your friend needs a ride to Virginia?" Xander asked.

Now he looked as confused as the rest of us. "What do you mean? I just told you."

"That's the solution to the problem we were trying to solve," I told him. "But you said it like it was an afterthought. You had the answer the whole time."

Carter still looked lost.

"Jesus Christ," I huffed out, collapsing my face into my palms.

I felt Ransom's hand on my shoulder. "It's not worth it," he whispered.

If only Carter were capable of focusing on something for more than a few seconds, he could probably have been the next Bill Gates. Okay, maybe that was a slight exaggeration, but he would've probably been able to engage in an intelligent conversation longer than he could hold his breath.

No one said anything else to him for a while, and then Carter finally spoke again. "So I'm tellin' Owen he can get a ride with you guys, or . . ."

Chapter Five

TAYLOR

"I can't believe we agreed to this," Ransom said as he put our bags into the bed of his truck.

I was glad he had a hard cover over it so our stuff would be safe as we traveled the thirteen hours to Georgia. Though it would likely be longer since we had to drop off Owen Parrish in Virginia and would likely hit traffic at various spots during the ride. But between the two of us, we were sure we could make it in one day. Hence our seven a.m. departure.

The initial plan was to leave even earlier, but Owen said he had a meeting to go to before he could leave. And while that made little to no sense, he was giving us an excuse for the trip, so we didn't want to make a big deal out of it.

"Is that him?" I asked as a guy about our age made his way toward us with a black duffel bag thrown over his shoulder. He had shaggy blond hair and light-blue eyes. With his slender build and the carefree way he moved, he looked like the consummate surfer boy.

Ransom followed my gaze and shrugged. "I don't know

what he looks like, but probably."

When he was closer, the guy raised a hand and yelled, "Hey! You guys Random and Taylor?"

We both turned fully to face him as he approached and stopped in front of us. "It's Ransom. Nice to meet you." Ransom shook Owen's hand.

"Whoa, Ransom. That name's even more out there. Awesome." Owen seemed genuinely pleased by Ransom's name as he extended a hand to me. "Did I get your name right?"

"Yup," I said with a smile. "I like your shirt."

He smiled even wider and ran a hand down the black fabric that had a picture of Oscar the Grouch and said *Talk Dirty to Me.* "Thanks. It was a Christmas gift from my grandma."

That took me a second to recover from. "That's great."

"Yeah. She got me another one with Mr. Snuffleupagus on it that says *Every day I'm snufflin'*. It's a trip. Speaking of trips, we ready to go?"

"Yup," Ransom said as he gestured toward the bed. "You want to put your bag in there or keep it in the truck with you?"

"I'll hang on to it. I got some goodies for us in it."

"That was thoughtful," I said. "Thanks."

"It's the least I could do. I really appreciate you guys giving me a ride. My dad said if I didn't make it home for my grandpop's birthday, he was gonna draw and quarter me. And, like, I don't even know what that means, but the way he said it made it sound hella unpleasant."

"Yeah, I think it means to be cut into four pieces," I told him.

"Whoa. Hardcore." Owen sounded more impressed than horrified, which at least made me feel that we weren't delivering this cute, clearly simple young man into the hands of a sadist.

We climbed into the truck and got settled. Ransom's truck did have an extended cab, but there wasn't a ton of leg room for anyone in the back, which caused Owen to have to sprawl out across the seat.

"Sorry. It's a little tight back there," Ransom said as he looked at Owen in the rearview mirror.

"No worries, dude. I once spent eight hours in the trunk of a two-door Neon. That was a wild trip."

I wasn't quite sure how to respond to that, and it was clear Ransom didn't either because he gave a simple nod before putting the truck in gear and pulling into traffic.

"So, Owen," I said, twisting in my seat a bit to look at him. "Carter said you guys used to be in the same frat."

"Yeah, that's how we met. I only lasted a year, though. The guys wanted to dress up as women for our Halloween party, but that's, like, really stereotypical and insulting. I told them I couldn't be part of the hyperfemininity narrative they were attempting to spin and that their implicit biases were insulting to not only women but everyone who was trying to further the feminist agenda."

For the second time since we'd met, Owen had struck me momentarily mute. "That's . . . really admirable of you."

"Thanks," he said, his smile so wide he was practically glowing.

"What's your major?" I asked.

"Accounting. But then I accidentally met a doula one day, so now I'm thinking about training to be a midwife. So I took on a minor in gender studies to learn more about the female perspective."

"You . . . accidentally met a doula?"

"Yeah, I had an interview at a coffee shop, and she was

there. I thought she was there to interview me, so I sat down, which made her think I was there to interview *her*. Trippiest conversation of my life."

"I bet," I replied.

We made a little more small talk before I heard Owen ruffling through his bag. His body then poked over the seat between us.

"You guys want some brownies? I just got them this morning." He began unwrapping the Saran Wrap and then broke off a piece of the large brownie and popped it into his mouth. He then broke off another piece and handed it to me.

"Oh, um, thanks," I said as I took it.

Owen moved to hand a piece to Ransom but then pulled back as Ransom reached out to take it. "Oh, wait. You probably shouldn't eat it while you're driving."

I stopped with the brownie nearly touching my lips.

Ransom whirled around to face Owen before quickly returning his attention to the road. "Dude, are you giving us pot brownies?"

Owen looked confused by the question. "Uh, yeah."

Ransom held his hand out toward me, and I placed my brownie in it. Then he rolled down his window and threw my piece out onto the highway.

"Dude, what did you do that for? I would've eaten it."

"Get rid of yours too, Owen."

I turned and saw Owen clutch his brownie to his chest. "Why?"

"We can't have drugs in the truck."

"But...but..."

"No buts. If we get pulled over and they find that...I can't risk it."

Owen sighed. "I made a special request and everything. She put extra chocolate chips in them," he said in a tone that sounded close to how I'd imagine a chastised toddler would sound.

"Was that what your meeting was this morning?"

"Yeah. I rent a basement apartment from an older woman named Minerva who makes them. But she works the night shift at a warehouse, so I had to wait for her to get home to get some from her."

"It's gotta go," Ransom said, his tone brooking no argument.

Owen stared forlornly at his brownie. It made me a little sad to watch. He pressed the button to lower his window, gave his brownie one last look, and sneaked a large bite before throwing it out. Turning in his seat, Owen stared at where the brownie likely fell to the pavement for a second before turning around and slumping back in his seat.

"Maybe we can stop and get real brownies on the road somewhere," I offered.

Owen gave me a small smile, which was even more heartbreaking. Even after only knowing him for a little while, I could already tell he was a guy who laughed often and boisterously. Seeing an insincere smile on his face made me want to wince. "Thanks. But it won't be the same."

"Well, no, because we won't be high as kites as we hurtle down the highway," Ransom said.

I reached over and smacked him on the thigh, trying to hide the assault from Owen. When Ransom gave me a *what did I do?* look, I glared at him. *Be nice*, I mouthed.

Ransom rolled his eyes in reply, which briefly made me think he potentially wasn't the only one in the truck capable of murder. It was a shitty thing to think, but it was what it was. Everyone thought inappropriate things from time to time, right? It didn't make me a *bad* person. Though it didn't necessarily make me a very good one either.

My thoughts devolved from there, ending up at Ransom and me becoming the twenty-first-century version of Bonnie and Clyde before Owen's voice brought me back to reality.

"Can we stop at the next rest stop? I need to pee."

I looked at the clock. We'd been on the road for a little over an hour, and Owen had been quiet since the brownie incident, only humming as we drove but not speaking any actual words. Ransom and I hadn't spoken much either. It was . . . awkward between us. As if having a stranger with us made us too tense to make even casual conversation out of fear of giving away too much.

Paranoia and a guilty conscience were a duo from hell.

RANSOM

It really spoke to Owen's personality that while I hadn't meant to inflict lasting harm on Brad, I was fantasizing about strangling Owen. I knew my patience was even thinner than normal due to all the stress I was feeling, but *goddamn* this dude was irritating.

After the bullshit with the pot brownie, he proceeded to hum metal music under his breath for the next forty-five minutes. And I knew it was metal music because the sounds burst out of him at harsh, erratic intervals.

Taylor hadn't seemed bothered by it, but for me, it was like nails on a chalkboard. I'd even tried turning the radio up, but it was like once I'd heard him, my ears kept straining to see if they could *keep* hearing him.

When he'd said he had to go to the bathroom, I contemplated leaving him at the rest stop. What grown adult couldn't last longer than an hour without needing the bathroom? It didn't bode well for the rest of our trip.

"Where the hell is this guy?" I muttered.

Sitting beside me on a table made of concrete, Taylor had her head tilted toward the sun, her hands resting on the surface behind her so she could recline back a bit. "Hmm?"

"Owen. He's been in the bathroom for almost fifteen minutes."

"Maybe he has diarrhea."

I stared at her even though she couldn't see me. "Really?"

Without moving from her position, she tilted her head a bit so she could see me. "What? It's the logical explanation."

"It's also gross."

She sat up straighter and turned toward me a bit. "Why are you so tense?"

"Tense? I'm not tense. I'm just annoyed we're taking this thoughtless bum all the way to Virginia." I pushed myself off the table and stood, shoving my hands in my pockets as I started to pace.

I felt her gaze on me, but I didn't look over. I was being a total dick, and I knew it. But I wasn't sure how to stop. There was just too much going on in my head, and it was making me feel like I was losing it.

"Ransom," Taylor said.

I gave her a brief glance to show I'd heard her, but I didn't stop moving.

"Ransom," she said again, her voice sterner this time.

Stopping, I looked at her full-on.

"Come here," she said.

It made me feel like a dog or small child for her to voice a command at me like that, but I shuffled my feet closer to her before I'd even thought it through. Truth was, I *wanted* to be closer to her. Even though we'd spent a ton of time together recently, there was still a distance between us I wasn't sure how to bridge.

Owen only made that feeling worse—an actual person thrust into our bubble at a time when we had so much to figure out. I resented him for it even though it wasn't his fault. Ultimately, we'd approached *him* with the offer of transport. It wasn't fair of me to treat him like a nuisance, even though he so *was*.

When I was right in front of her, she reached up and cupped my jaw, pulling me closer and placing a soft kiss on my lips that I wanted to sink into. She began to pull back, but I surged forward, capturing her mouth again, teasing the seam of her lips with my tongue.

I felt her smile against my lips, and then she pulled back again and rested her forehead against mine. "Baby, what's wrong?"

I closed my eyes and released a deep sigh. "Everything," I whispered.

She smiled softly. "Be more specific."

Settling my hands on her hips, I enjoyed the feel of her for a second before responding. "I'm going home exactly what they all expected me to be."

She jerked her head back. "What do you mean?"

"My mom's family always expected me to turn out to be a fuckup. And now here I am, a murderer coming home to hide out from the police."

She gripped my chin tightly in her hand. "You. Are. Not. A. Murderer."

"The legal system might likely beg to differ."

Tears filled her eyes as she said, "I'm so sorry, Ransom. I didn't even think about how hard it would be to face your family under ordinary circumstances, let alone with all that's been going on. I'm such an insensitive asshole."

"Hey, hey, none of that. Only one of us can break down at a time. Wait your turn."

Her smile was wobbly, but it was there. "Sorry. Commence with your pity party."

"Thank you. Anyway, I always envisioned I'd show up to a family gathering at some point as a super-successful guy. Instead, I'm a stripper who's still in school, and oh, yeah, I may have killed a guy. I'm just . . . having a hard time reconciling how I always pictured it with how it's really going to be."

"First of all, you *are* successful. You support yourself while taking graduate classes so you can take over the world of physical therapy. You're kind and protective and funny and handsome and sweet, and—"

I put my hand over her mouth. "If you keep going, my head won't fit in the truck."

She huffed out a laugh before continuing, "I'm just saying, you're still the guy you always pictured you'd be. And as for the other thing, let's not come to any conclusions the police haven't come to yet. We don't know what happened in that alley after we left it. Let's not attribute labels until we're at least sure we have the right ones."

I knew she was saying that for my benefit. She'd also been struggling with our role in Brad's death, but I appreciated that she was trying to make me feel better. Whether I deserved it or not, I needed someone to be completely in my corner right now. And it was amazing to have that someone be her.

"I'm also showing up with the hottest woman in the world. So there's that."

She smiled. "That is a huge bright spot."

"Yup," I said as I leaned in to kiss her again.

I'm not sure how long we soaked in each other's presence before we were pulled apart by a strange shuffling noise. Whirling around, I saw Owen trying to sneak to my truck wearing a hoodie he hadn't had on when he went to the bathroom. He was also slightly bent backward and had magically gained a belly to rival Santa Claus. His hands were braced under his stomach to support the weight of it.

"Owen," I said, making the guy jerk to a stop.

His blue irises skirted in my direction, but he didn't move his head or body to face me.

"What you got there?" I asked him.

"Oh, nothing. Just got this rad new hoodie in the rest stop," he said as if I gave a shit about what he was wearing. He took another step toward my truck but had to stop again when his entire stomach seemed to wiggle before letting out a yelp. "Shit," he squealed as he moved his hands to catch whatever animal he was clearly hiding under his hoodie. Once he had himself and his shrouded accomplice situated, he braced his midsection with one hand before reaching for the door handle with the other.

"Dude, you're not getting into my truck with some wild animal," I said as I took long strides to stand in front of him, effectively pushing him back from my truck.

Owen gasped. "I would never do that! I just ... ate a lot of snacks from the vending machine."

Taylor came to stand beside me. "Owen, seriously. What's under your hoodie?"

"Cheetos and Funyuns," he replied, his voice full of bravado he obviously didn't feel. He looked like a pouty child.

"Owen," I warned. "I'm not sure why you think we're fucking idiots, but it's getting insulting. Show us what's under your hoodie before I leave your ass here."

He huffed but unzipped his sweatshirt partway. A wiry head popped out and rested on the section of his hoodie that remained zipped. The face was a reddish brown with white running from between his eyes and down his snout. His pink tongue licked his lips as his brown eyes looked at me intently.

"Did you steal someone's dog?" I asked because *what the fuck?* Where had this moron found a dog at a rest stop in the middle of a stretch of highway?

"No! I would never do that." He sounded truly affronted, which made me inclined to believe him even though I really had no way of *knowing* he wouldn't do that.

The guy could be a serial killer for all I knew. The irony of thinking that about him after what I'd done did not escape me.

"I found him," he continued. "He came right up to me when I was leaving the men's room. No collar or anything. I wandered around asking people if he was theirs, but no one claimed him. I can't just leave him here. What if he gets run over by a big rig? Or a creepy kid finds him and sets his tail on fire? That shit happens, you know. I listened to a podcast about one sadistic little asshole who used to pour gasoline on animals and then—"

"I think we get the picture," I interrupted. Oddly, I

was slightly relieved by Owen's own hatred of serial killer tendencies. Maybe he wouldn't slit our throats before we got him to Virginia.

"You can't just take him," Taylor said. "Maybe someone will come back for him."

Owen shook his head. "He's pretty dirty and skinny. Like he's been here a while."

Taylor looked at me, but all I had to offer was a shrug. I didn't have enough experience with strays—neither canine nor Owen variety—to know what to do.

"Let's go into the rest stop and see who we should call about the dog," I said. "I'm sure there's some kind of animal control or something that can come get him."

At that suggestion, Owen took a giant step backward and clutched the dog. "No way. They'll kill him."

"I'm sure they won't—" Taylor started.

"They might. And I can't risk it. Gimli deserves better."

"Gimli?" I asked.

Owen looked at me like I was stupid. "Yeah. After the dwarf from *The Lord of the Rings*." Owen reached up and scratched the dog's chin. "Looks just like him. All grumpy and scraggly."

Unable to formulate a response, I closed my eyes and shook my head in an attempt to make this nightmare go away. When I opened them, not only was the nightmare still here, but it was becoming more fully realized.

Owen unzipped his hoodie the rest of the way, allowing us to get a better look at the dog. It was probably about thirty pounds and looked to be a mutt in all senses of the word. Dirt was caked into his coarse fur that stuck out from his body like he'd been electrocuted. He was skinny, just as Owen had said, his ribs visible, but not to the point of looking like he was sick. A few weeks of good meals would probably get him back to normal. Whatever normal was for this dog.

Taylor looked up at me, her eyes pleading as she reached out with a tentative hand to stroke the dog's head. The little fucker leaned into her like he relished her attention.

"No, no, no, we gotta stay strong," I begged her.

"He is pretty cute," she said as she moved closer so she could reach more of his body to pet.

"He's probably covered in fleas."

That caused her to retract her hand pretty damn fast.

"I've been carrying him around for a while, and I haven't seen anything on him."

"You a vet now?" I asked.

Owen sniffed. "No."

"I can't risk all our stuff getting infested with whatever mites are probably all over him."

"I'll wash all your stuff and vacuum your truck out when we get to my parents' place. Besides, I've been holding him, so if he has bugs on him, I do too by now."

Owen was really underestimating my desire to leave them both here. "Well, that's comforting," I muttered, earning me an elbow in the side from Taylor.

"Please," Owen pleaded, his eyes looking suspiciously like the dog's he was clutching to his chest.

I looked heavenward. "Why? Why did you make me this way?"

Was the ability to say no completely absent from my DNA? My mom had sure said it often enough. Though I guess not when it mattered. When she should've said, *No, I will not take more drugs. No, I will not leave my kids unattended so I can hit the local bar.* Her noes had been reserved for things like *No, I will not buy you new sneakers. Just put duct tape over the holes. No, I will not come to your school concert. Those things are lame.*

Guess it could've been a family trait after all.

I sighed heavily. "Make sure you put a blanket or something on the seat so he doesn't get his hair all over it."

Owen bounced on his toes. "Oh my God, you guys are the *best*. Say thank you, Gimli."

Fuck my entire life.

Chapter Six

TAYLOR

Ransom kept checking his rearview as if the dog and Owen were plotting something duplicitous behind us. Though...I guess trying to sneak a dog into his truck was duplicitous in its own right.

"Take the next left," Owen said in between coos to his new dog. "Yes, we're going to have so much fun when we get home. Have you ever had a bath? By the smell of you, I doubt it. Yes, I do."

He sounded like he was trying to coax a baby to eat mashed vegetables. It would've been better if we'd been able to tune him out, but we'd lost cell service a little ways back and were relying on Owen to navigate us the rest of the way. The road to Owen's hometown looked like the path Dorothy took through the Haunted Forest in the *Wizard of Oz*.

"What's that noise?" Owen asked as he fed Gimli snacks and water from the stockpile he bought at the rest stop.

Ransom glanced back at him. "What noise?"

Owen waited a second before saying, "That one."

"I don't hear a noise," Ransom replied.

I actually thought I had heard something—a knocking sound—but the tense set of Ransom's shoulders kept me from voicing my observation.

"There it is again. It's getting louder. Sounds like the engine." Owen relayed all this with the calm of someone completely unable to read a room. Or truck cab, in this case.

Ransom started looking around as if he would somehow be able to see the engine if he achieved the proper angle.

"You should probably pull over," Owen advised serenely.

"There's nothing wrong with my truck," Ransom said, his tone doing little to disguise his concern.

"When was the last time you had your oil changed?"

"Owen," Ransom warned. "I take care of my truck."

"Huh. Must just be old, then."

"There's nothing—"

Ransom's sentence was interrupted by a clunking noise followed by the truck sputtering and then stalling.

"Shit," Ransom said as he glided the truck to the side of the road and turned the ignition off.

Owen sat forward so his head was between us. "Engine went."

Watching Ransom's head slowly pan toward Owen made me feel like I was living in slow motion.

Thankfully, Ransom didn't say anything to Owen but instead looked to me. "Do you have service?"

I quickly checked my phone. "Nope."

Ransom's loud sigh told me he didn't either.

Owen didn't bother to check. "There's never any service on this stretch of road."

"How far until it comes in again?" I asked.

Owen twisted his mouth. "Hard to say. It's spotty in this whole area."

"Let's get out and see if it's better outside," Ransom said.

We all climbed out of his truck. Ransom and I walked around holding up our phones as if the marginally higher altitude would help. Owen fussed over Gimli, and when I looked over, I saw why. He'd taken one of his T-shirts and put it around the dog so it served as some sort of haphazard harness. He'd then attached a belt to a hole he'd put in the back of the shirt so it functioned as a leash.

"That's . . . clever, Owen."

He beamed at me.

"How far is it to the nearest town?" Ransom asked, somehow ignoring the *MacGyver* shit Owen had fashioned around his dog.

"About six miles."

"Six miles," I whined, unable to help the plaintive sound of my voice. Trekking six miles with a high-strung boyfriend, an eccentric stranger, and a roadside mutt wasn't exactly how I wanted to spend the rest of my afternoon.

"Maybe someone will come along soon and help us," Ransom said softly, clearly trying to make me feel better.

"I doubt it," Owen the dream killer said. "I took you a back way that's a more direct route to my house. But it doesn't see a lot of traffic."

"That . . . figures," I said.

"Then we'll have to walk it," Ransom said.

"Maybe I should wait here with the truck," I offered hopefully.

"Yeah. Sure. I'll absolutely leave you in the middle of the woods with no way to call for help. Solid plan."

I glared at Ransom. "Your sarcasm is unbecoming."

"So is finding you murdered by the cast of *Deliverance*," he shot back.

"Hey. That movie was set in Georgia," Owen argued, sounding offended.

I was *not* going to think about the coincidence of that.

Ransom held up his hands. "My bad," he said in a tone that sounded less than genuine. "Lead the way to town, Owen."

Owen sniffed but began walking with Gimli trotting along beside him. "Town is kinda far," he said after a couple of minutes. "Probably faster to just take you to my house."

"What?" Ransom said dryly as he jerked to a stop.

"My house. It's only about half a mile as the crow flies. We just need to follow a path through the woods."

"Dude, why didn't you tell us your house was so close?"

"I just did." Owen sounded, and looked, truly baffled.

Ransom looked ready to throttle Owen, so I stepped between them, facing Owen. "Going to your place sounds good. Let's go."

Owen smiled at me as he turned and bounded into the woods, Gimli beside him. "You're going to love the house, Gimster. Lots of wide-open space to explore. Critters to chase. It's going to be awesome."

I couldn't help smiling as I watched them. Looking beside me, I saw Ransom frowning at me. "What?"

"This is a disaster. What are you smiling about?"

I gestured in front of us. "They're cute." Gimli's tail was wagging as Owen rambled on about anything and everything. It was difficult to dislike a guy who was clearly very well-natured, even if he was a tad oblivious.

"The guy who's leading us through the woods even though

he doesn't seem to have two brain cells to rub together and the mangy animal he found on the side of the road are cute? Really?"

I shrugged. "Really."

"I'm starting to really question your taste in people."

His response caused me to jerk my head back from him, my eyebrows climbing up my forehead. "Clearly, since I've elected to spend time with you." I hurried ahead, not wanting to be near him right now.

I heard him mutter a "Shit" behind me before rushing to catch up. "I didn't mean that how it sounded."

"Oh? How did it sound?" My tone was full-on bitchy, and I wasn't sorry in the least.

"I wasn't talking about Brad or anything. It was just a stupid joke."

"Funny."

He gently took hold of my arm, pulling me to a stop. "I'm serious. I didn't mean anything by it. I'm sorry."

I sighed. "I thought we worked through all of this at the rest stop. Our lives kind of suck right now, but we're on the same side. Can we just . . . enjoy it?"

"Enjoy . . . I'm sorry, I'm not being an asshole, but what exactly are we supposed to be enjoying right now?"

I looked around. He had a point. "The scenery?"

He huffed out a laugh. "The woods are lovely, dark, and deep."

I smiled. "That's the spirit. You should write that down."

"I would, but Robert Frost beat me to it. I had to memorize his poem in grade school. Funny what sticks with you."

"I thought it sounded familiar, but I was willing to give you the benefit of the doubt."

He put an arm around my shoulders and pulled me closer to him. "How kind of you."

"Hey, guys!" Owen called. "Why'd you stop? Are you peeing?"

Ransom looked down at me. "Still cute?"

"He has potential."

Laughing, Ransom yelled, "Coming," as we set off after Owen and into the unknown. In every sense of the word.

RANSOM

Arriving at Owen's house was a bit surreal. From the way he'd been talking, I'd been expecting something a little more rustic and simpler. But Owen's house was a large, yellow two-story home that looked like something a dollhouse would be modeled after. It had well-maintained flower beds, a trimmed yard, and fall decorations that made the place look inviting and homey.

Though that impression was dashed when I heard a shrill voice yell, "Owen Worthington Parrish, you better have brought me some of them special brownies, or you can take your ass right back where you came from."

My gaze darted around the facade of the house and settled on a second-story window where an elderly woman was poking her head out.

Owen gave me a look that let me know I was going to be suffering the wrath of the woman inside. "No, Grandma. I couldn't bring 'em."

"For Christ's sake, boy. What was even the point of coming home?"

"To celebrate his grandpa's birthday," a woman said as she came around the side of the house and looked up at Owen's grandmother. "And put the damn screen back in the window. All we need is for you to take a header out of the house. People will think we knocked you off for the insurance money."

"Joke's on them. I've got less dough than a bankrupted Pizza Hut," the woman retorted before pulling inside and pushing the screen back into place.

"Hi, Mom," Owen said as he stepped into the embrace of a middle-aged woman. She was tiny—petite—with brown hair streaked with gray that she'd pulled back into a braid. But even with the different hair color and height, she was clearly Owen's mom. He had her eyes and smile. "This is Taylor and Ransom. Guys, this is my mom, Claudette."

Claudette reached out a hand, and I grasped it quickly. She gave a firm shake that told of hands used to hard work. "Ransom. That's an interesting name."

"Yeah, I get that a lot."

"Does it have family significance?" she asked.

"Nah. My mom was probably still high on drugs from the delivery," I joked, though it was somewhat true. She was likely very high but had probably arrived at the hospital that way.

Claudette studied me for a moment before looking at Owen. "So when you said people from school were giving you a ride, I kind of expected you to show up in a car."

"It broke down on Yates Road. Figured Dad and I could go get it and tow it to the shop."

"Well, at least you were close. He's in the garage. You all hungry?"

"Starving," Owen said.

"I wasn't really talking to you," his mom said.

"We don't want to impose," Taylor started.

"You drove, what? Six hours with this one?" she asked, jerking a thumb over her shoulder. "A meal is the least I can offer. And, Owen, don't think I haven't noticed that dog you're trying to hide behind you. It doesn't come in until the vet's checked him," she said as she started up the five steps that led to the front door of the house.

"But Dr. Taggart probably won't be able to fit him in until tomorrow," Owen complained.

"Then I guess you better get him comfortable in the garage until tomorrow. Last time I let you bring a stray animal in the house, we had to fumigate the whole place."

"What if he's not a stray? Maybe I adopted him from a rescue near school."

Claudette opened the screen door and stood there, holding it open so Owen's grandmother could walk out. "Did you?"

"Well, no, of course not. I found him at a rest stop. But still, you shouldn't just assume—"

"No wild animals in the house," his mother said firmly before disappearing inside.

"You let Grandma in the house," he muttered.

"If you think my arthritis will prevent me from skinning you alive, you better think again," the old woman warned.

"You'd have to catch me first."

"Yeah, 'cause it's so hard to catch a boy who spends half of his life higher than the sun. That shit will rot your brain."

"You smoke more than I do!"

"I'm eighty-five years old and spend all day and night with your parents and grandfather. I gotta have some joy in my life." She settled into a rocking chair on the porch. "You going to introduce me to your friends?"

"I hadn't planned on it."

She snorted a laugh. "Get up here and kiss me hello, you demon child."

Owen smiled as he took the steps two at a time and bent over so he could place a kiss on her cheek.

She raised a wrinkled hand to cup his face. "How's school been?"

"Pretty good. I like my classes this semester."

"Good to hear it. If you're going to leave me all alone with these sticks-in-the-mud, at least it's for a good reason."

Owen straightened but took her hand in his. "I'm home all weekend. Just think of all the hell we can raise at Grandpa's party."

"Looking forward to it. I missed ya, kid."

Owen smiled and dropped one more kiss to her cheek. "Missed you too, old lady."

It felt as if we were intruding on a personal moment. The affection between the grandmother and grandson hadn't been clear when they'd initially been sniping at one another, but it was apparent now. I wondered what my own interactions with my family would be like.

My mom had been estranged from her own mother for my entire childhood. And while they'd clearly mended their relationship, I wasn't sure where that left me in the equation. However it would play out, I was pretty certain it wouldn't be anything like the dynamic Owen had with his family, and I envied him a bit for it.

"You sneaking that dog up to your room through the basement?" his grandmother asked.

"You know it."

The old woman stood. "I'll pretend to be doing some laundry and unlatch the storm doors for ya."

"You're the best accomplice I've ever had," Owen told her.

"Driving your parents crazy is my best feature." She turned to look at us. "I'm Jimi. There's a hall bathroom on the second floor if you wanna freshen up before my daughter-in-law stuffs ya full of food. And I made an apple cobbler yesterday you'll want to save room for."

"You made an apple cobbler?" Owen asked, drool practically forming at the corner of his lips.

"Guests get first dibs," she said, pointing a finger at him.

Owen spluttered for a second before saying, "Ransom made me throw your brownies out the window."

"Whoa, dude," I said. "You didn't say they were for your grandmother."

"I didn't *not* say it either."

"That doesn't even make sense."

"Does too."

"Does not," I gritted out.

"Guys," Taylor interrupted. "Really?"

We glared at each other before motion on the porch stole our attention. Jimi was moving toward the door, but she turned before going inside. "I'm not mad. Just disappointed." Her tone was full of recrimination, and I felt my chest constrict at her words as I continued to stare at where she'd just stood.

Owen slapped a hand against my chest. "Ignore her. She's constantly trying to reenact scenes from *Days of Our Lives*."

"You totally threw me under the bus," I accused.

"Yup," he replied, his tone telling me he regretted nothing. "I'm gonna go talk to my dad about your truck. Head on inside, and I'll meet you there in a few minutes. And my grandma was right. You're more than welcome to use the hall bathroom upstairs if you wanna splash some water on your faces. Towels are in the cabinet."

TAYLOR

When we got inside, Jimi was sitting in a rocking chair with what looked like some kind of needlepoint. I hadn't been expecting to find her partaking in such a grandmotherly hobby after what I'd seen of her on the porch. But when I got a bit closer, I saw her pattern had pot leaves all over it and felt a little more sure-footed in my assessment of her.

She was amazing.

Without looking at us, she used the hand she was holding the needle with to point up the stairs. "Bathroom's that way. Claudette has pretty much everything ready for lunch, so you don't have much time for any hanky-panky up there." She lifted her eyes to wink at Ransom. "Unless you're *really* fast."

Ransom spluttered. "I...uh...I...wow, I don't know what to say to that."

"Making people speechless is a passion of mine," Jimi said, returning her attention to her project.

"You're really good at it," he said.

"Such a smooth talker. And so handsome. How do you ever resist him?" she asked me.

Ransom, the ass, preened under her words like she hadn't just insinuated he had a hair trigger during sex. I shot him a droll look and replied dryly, "I manage somehow."

Jimi snickered as Ransom and I walked across the hardwood floors toward the stairs.

Once upstairs, we shut ourselves in the bathroom, and I leaned back against the door. "This family is like the one from *Texas Chainsaw Massacre,* except they use sarcasm instead of chainsaws."

Ransom laughed as he pulled a towel from the closet. "They're not that bad."

I sighed and moved toward the sink. "Wait until we get through lunch before you make a final assessment." I was joking, of course. The Parrishes were the type of people who put me immediately at ease, as if I could sink into their eccentricity instead of feeling like we all had to pretend to be people we weren't.

After patting some water onto my face and drying it with a towel, I moved to let Ransom have the water. As he was splashing water on himself, I watched him, wondering if I should ask what had been on the tip of my tongue since he'd introduced himself to Claudette.

"So, this is something I feel like I should know already, but . . . how *did* you get the name Ransom?"

He sat up and took the towel from me. "Well, when a woman has a baby, she has the unique privilege of naming said baby."

I slapped him on the chest. "I know *that.* But what made her pick it?"

He exhaled heavily, and the sound and the hesitant look on his face made me want to tell him he didn't have to answer. But before I could, he started talking.

"When my mom showed up at the hospital to have me, they suspected she was high. So after I was born, they had a social worker from the hospital come talk to her. Apparently my mom wasn't too friendly, and the hospital said they wouldn't release me to her if she didn't submit to a drug test. She refused, and supposedly it was quite the standoff. My mom said it was like they were holding me for ransom. Hence the name."

My heart broke for this man. This insanely wonderful and kind man who'd been dealt a shit hand from birth. Even his name was a constant reminder of how bad his life had been.

"Jesus. What ended up happening?"

"The hospital couldn't really refuse to give me to her. And while they threatened to get child welfare involved, to my knowledge they never did."

"Your mom just…told you all this?" The more I heard, the more I was worried I wouldn't be able to fake cordiality to his mother. I'd already known she'd been horrible, but for fuck's sake. Suggesting this trip had been a mistake, and I wished like hell I could take it back.

"Nah, I heard her telling it to someone she was talking to on the phone when I was a kid." He looked around for somewhere to put the towel, but I felt that it was more of an excuse to not look me in the eyes.

"Hey," I said softly as I put a hand on his arm.

When he turned toward me, I pushed myself against him, burying my face into his chest. I figured it would allow him to grapple with his feelings without me staring at him while still knowing he could lean on me.

"If you don't want to go to the reunion, I totally understand. We can tell your mom we broke down and were kidnapped by a pot-smoking granny and her dog-whispering grandson. It's not even a lie."

He chuckled, the sensation traveling from his chest and into mine. After dropping a quick kiss to my head, he pulled back a bit but kept his arms locked around me. "It's fine. I feel like I have to face them, ya know? Then I'll be able to finally start moving forward once I get over this hurdle."

"I understand. But maybe the timing isn't good. Maybe—"

He cupped my jaw in his large palm and smiled sweetly down at me. "Thank you."

My brow wrinkled in confusion. "For what?" Seriously, from the moment this man had met me, his life had only gotten harder. I was like a black cat or a broken mirror or a . . . perpetual Friday the thirteenth.

"For giving a shit. For always wanting to make things better for me."

"Even though I end up making them worse?"

"*You* never make anything worse. Ever. You've only made my life better."

I squinted my eyes in disbelief, which made him laugh again.

"I'm serious," he assured me.

I studied him for a second and saw the sincerity there. "I'm very thankful for your skewed perception of reality."

"You're ridiculous," he said, giving me a final squeeze before pulling away entirely.

"Where are you going?" I whined as his arms left me. "Come back." I wanted his hands on me all the time, but there was almost a need clutching at me. Maybe Jimi was right . . . He was impossible to resist.

"No way. I am not giving Owen's family any room to make assumptions about what we were doing in here."

"If we're loud, they won't have to assume."

That stopped him. He turned to face me, and I could see the desire written all over him. "I feel like I should be repulsed by that statement, but I'm totally turned on by it."

"Then come here and let's show Jimi how quick we can be."

Ransom stilled for a second before saying, "Yup, mentioning Owen's grandmother killed the mood for me. Thanks for that." He stepped past me and opened the bathroom door.

"Damn me and my big mouth," I mumbled as I followed him from the room, his laughter enveloping us every step of the way.

Chapter Seven

RANSOM

The moment in the bathroom had been more emotional for me than I'd expected. I'd figured Taylor would eventually ask about my name—had been surprised she hadn't already—and I'd been prepared to answer her honestly. But having to tell one of the best people I'd ever met that my mom had basically chosen my name so I'd be a big "Fuck you" to a hospital staff whose only real crime had been giving a shit about my well-being was incredibly hard.

It made me thankful to walk into a dining room full of people who appeared to be arguing about who'd been the one to name a particular chicken.

"I'm so tired of never getting the credit I deserve around here. I came up with Mother Clucker. I know it for a fact because Mom thought I said something else and threatened me with a spoon."

"She always threatened you with a spoon. Maybe if she'd ever actually hit you with it, you wouldn't be such a liar," a large man sitting across from Owen said.

From his position at the table, it was hard for me to get a full picture of him. He wasn't large in an overweight way, but rather in a hulking way that made him seem like he bench-pressed cars in his spare time.

"I can't hit him. He bruises too easily," Claudette casually commented as she dished some mac and cheese onto her plate.

"Sweet summer child," Jimi said to Owen. "We all know who the most likely person at this table is to come up with a name like that. Stop trying to steal your grandma's glory."

"Please," Owen scoffed. "You're too senile to be that clever."

"Hmm. Am I also too senile to know you sneaked that dog upstairs while your mother toiled over a hot meal for your ungrateful ass?"

"Owen Worthington Parrish, that mutt better not be in my house." This was clearly a family who liked using full names. At least where Owen was concerned.

"Mom, it's not nice to call Grandma that."

Claudette glared at her son until he grabbed his napkin from his lap and tossed it next to his plate as he stood. "You," he said, pointing a finger at Jimi, "should be locked in a home somewhere."

"I am. This one," Jimi retorted.

"If you behaved better, we could let you out more," said a man who appeared to be an older version of the man sitting across from Owen. He had the same huge frame but with graying hair.

"If you want to live to see your birthday party, you'll keep quiet," Jimi threatened.

The man simply laughed her off and continued eating.

"What are y'all doing just standing there? Come on in

and get a plate," Claudette said.

I startled a bit at her voice because I'd been watching the scene unfold before me almost as if it were a movie. Realizing I was part of the action took me aback a little.

Taylor and I moved more fully into the room, but we each came up short when we saw that the only open seats were at opposite ends of the rectangular table. It felt awkward to sit at the head of a table with a family we didn't know, and Taylor's hesitance told me she had the same thought.

"Go on, make yourselves comfortable," Claudette said as she motioned to the open chairs.

I gave Taylor a quick look before moving to one end while she walked to the other and sat down.

"Ransom, Taylor, this is my husband, Roland Jr. We call him RJ for short, and that's my father-in-law, Roland Sr."

"Nice to meet you," Taylor and I said in such perfect synchronicity, one would think we'd practiced it.

Food was passed to us around the table, and we filled our plates with ham, mac and cheese, broccoli, and biscuits.

"Owen told me about your truck. We'll take a ride out and get it with my tow truck after lunch," RJ said.

He was clean-shaven and had blond hair that looked slicked back with some kind of product. His face had wrinkles in all the places that marked a man as middle-aged, and while his size made him the kind of man I wouldn't want to get on the wrong side of, he looked kind.

"Thank you, sir."

He gave me a nod in response as he kept eating.

"You two married?" Roland Sr. asked. He looked almost identical to his son, except obviously older.

I shot Taylor a surprised look before replying. "Oh, uh, no.

We're not."

Roland Sr. looked down the other end at Taylor. "You think that's a good idea? Just traveling around with a stranger?"

Taylor's eyes widened. "He's not a stranger. We're together. Just not married."

"Hmm," the man said as he pushed his plate back so he could rest his forearms on the table. "This is a safe space, Taylor. If this man has kidnapped you for the purpose of, what do they call it now? They were talking about it on the news. Harvesting?"

I widened my eyes in alarm. Did this man think I was trying to harvest Taylor's organs?

Jimi patted her husband on the forearm. "I think you mean trafficking, dear."

He snapped his fingers. "That's it. Trafficking. You could tell us, Taylor. RJ and I can take him. And Jimi here is a wizard with ropes."

"No," Taylor said, her voice loud in the quiet room. "No, he's not... he'd never... that's not... we're fine. *I'm* fine. I'm with him... willingly?" Saying it like it was a question did not help make her sound convincing.

"Ignore him," Claudette said. "He's just messing with you."

Taylor looked at Roland Sr. as if she were begging that to be the case.

The man simply shrugged. "Gotta get my kicks somehow. So, Ransom, tell us all about yourself."

"I'm actually a little terrified to tell you anything," I teased, even though I was only partially kidding.

"Smart man," RJ said.

"Since you're sitting in my seat, I'd think you'd be a little more forthcoming," Roland Sr. said.

His words jarred me a bit. "I can move," I offered as I grabbed my plate.

Claudette sighed. "He made us leave those chairs open for you. In his words, he wanted it to feel like an interrogation. Really, ignore everything he says."

Owen bustled back into the room and reclaimed his seat. "What'd I miss?"

Roland sat back. "Did you know Ransom and Taylor like to knock over convenience stores in their spare time?"

Owen paused with his spoon halfway to his mouth before he looked up at me. "Why didn't you let me rob any with you?"

I took a deep breath and stuffed some ham into my mouth, admitting silent defeat to the Parrishes.

Chapter Eight

TAYLOR

After lunch, Ransom went with RJ, Roland Sr., and Owen to get his truck, leaving me at the mercy of Jimi and Claudette. Despite knowing that it didn't make sense for another person to cram into RJ's tow truck to take a fifteen-minute ride down the road, especially since I wouldn't be of any help beyond moral support, I also felt sort of left behind—like it was a guys-only venture.

That was until Claudette pulled a bottle of whiskey from the cupboard and Jimi sat at the kitchen table with a deck of cards.

"You play Rummy?" Jimi asked.

I slid onto a chair and looked at her. "I used to. With my grandparents. But I haven't in a long time."

"Need a refresher of the rules?"

I thought hard about whether I remembered at least the basics. "Nah, I think I got it."

Claudette sat down at an open side of the rectangular table after putting the whiskey and three shot glasses down on it.

I eyed them, both nervous and excited at what might be in store for us.

"In the afternoons, while the men run around like they're important, we play Rummy," Claudette explained.

"But we've added some rules of our own," Jimi added with a smirk.

Claudette poured the whiskey into the shot glasses and handed them out. "If you discard a numbered card, you take a sip. If you discard a face card, you take two sips. If you discard an Ace, everyone *but you* finishes what's in their glass. Got it?"

I nodded slowly, trying to figure out if there was any way drinking with these women was a good idea. But I quickly realized I didn't care, tucked my shot glass closer to me, and picked up my cards when Jimi finished dealing them.

It didn't take me long to get into the swing of the game, though I was still seriously outmatched. My grandparents had never played with the same level of competitiveness as the Parrishes.

"Claudette, I'm old. I don't have the kind of time you're taking to play a card left in my life."

"Be quiet, ya harpy. I'm thinking." Claudette played a card a moment later and looked at me. "Don't let her rush you. It's part of her strategy."

"Why would you tell her that?" Jimi snapped. "There's no family loyalty in this house."

"Clearly, judging by the way you sold Owen down the river earlier," Claudette remarked casually.

"Please. Like you're not going to cave and let him keep that dog in his room."

Claudette shrugged. "He's barely here anymore. I gotta get my kicks in when I can."

I didn't contribute much to the conversation. I was too focused on playing the right cards, which was getting increasingly difficult the longer we played—and the more we drank. I could hold my own against any college senior, but I hadn't spent much time shooting back whiskey during the previous four years.

It was also becoming increasingly clear these women could drink any co-ed under the table.

"You know what's a funny word? Queen. Queeeen. K-w-een. It does weird things to my lips. Queen," I rambled.

"Well, that didn't take long," Jimi muttered.

"What didn't?" I asked dumbly.

"Let me get you a roll," Claudette said as she stood and went to the counter to retrieve the plate of biscuits she'd served with lunch.

I chose one and bit into it. "These are so good. Do you make them yourself?"

"No, they're Pillsbury."

"That damn little dough guy makes a mean roll," I said as I shoved the rest of the biscuit into my mouth and reached for another one.

"Maybe some water," Jimi suggested.

"Nah, I'll just wash it down with the whiskey," I replied, reaching for my glass.

Claudette reached out, putting her hand over the shot glass, but my momentum caused her hand to rise with the glass so that I ended up kissing the back of her hand.

"Mmm, what kind of lotion do you use? It smells wonderful."

"Dawn dish soap," she answered.

"I'll have to check for that at Ulta." Then what I said

registered. "Oh . . . wait . . . Soap. Got it. I can just go to the grocery store."

Claudette returned with my water and set it down in front of me. Jimi started to say something, but I didn't hear her because I threw the glass of water back like it was a shot of whiskey, causing the water to slosh all over my face before dripping down onto my shirt.

"Oops," I said before breaking into a fit of giggles.

"We're gonna be in trouble," Jimi groused.

"She's in college," Claudette argued as she handed me some napkins to wipe myself off with. "How was I supposed to know she'd be such a lightweight?"

I felt indignation welling up within me. "I'll have you both know I won a prize at a frat party once for longest keg stand by a female." I reached into my jeans pocket to pull out my phone. "I think I even have a picture of it somewhere."

"That's okay, dear. We believe you," Claudette said.

"I don't," Jimi mumbled, but I pretended not to hear her because moving my fingers over my phone was hard. Had I hit my hand on something? Why were my fingers so slow and stiff?

"Have some more bread," Claudette said, pushing the basket toward me.

I eyed it warily. "I feel really full."

"Oh sweet baby Jesus, here comes the vomit," Jimi said.

"I haven't thrown up since freshman year," I defended.

"Maybe we should take a walk outside," Claudette suggested. "Maybe some fresh air will fix you up."

"Okay," I agreed because they were the hosts. If they wanted to take a random walk in the middle of the day, who was I to stop them?

I don't know how long we had walked for or where all we had gone when I heard a vehicle pull up and the sound of its doors closing.

I looked at the chickens Owen's mom kept on the property. "Do you eat them?" I asked.

"For the tenth time, *no*. We only eat their eggs." Claudette sounded tired, but I wasn't sure why.

"Uh, what's going on here?" someone asked. I turned and saw RJ, Owen, and Ransom looking down at me. The voice had been deep and a tad unfamiliar, so I assumed it was RJ who'd spoken.

Ransom's face looked concerned, but I couldn't focus much on that because the sun was backlighting him, and he looked like he was glowing.

"You look like Edward." I gasped. "Wait, didn't we talk about this once?"

"About what?" he asked.

"Team Jacob or Team Edward. After today, I am solidly Team Edward because you are fiiiine."

"What the hell happened to her?" RJ asked as I continued to gaze lovingly at Ransom. At least I assumed it was lovingly. By the look on his face, I wasn't sure I was quite pulling it off.

"We just had a couple drinks over a card game," Jimi explained.

"For the love of Pete," he mumbled.

"Who's Pete? Have we met him yet? Oh! Is he one of the chickens?"

They all looked at me like I was a bomb about to explode. That's when I realized something. "Wait. Am I on the ground?" I let my head flop to the side so I was looking at the chicken coop. A chicken was on the other side of the wire staring straight into my eyes. I looked back up at everyone. "Did I fall down and get stuck?"

"You wanted to get a closer look at the chickens and kind of ... flopped down there."

Oh. That doesn't sound like me.

I held my hand out, and Ransom grabbed it, hauling me to my feet. But once I was on my feet, I continued to sway forward, bumping up against his chest. How could someone's chest be so firm and soft at the same time?

I nuzzled in. "I like it here."

I felt his laugh more than heard it. "More than on the ground with the chicken?"

Twisting my head, I looked up at him. "I feel like you're making fun of me, but my head is starting to hurt, so I can't figure out how."

He cupped my jaw and smiled down at me. "Why don't we go up to the bathroom and clean you up a little?"

"Is that a eu ... eu ... eupheem ... euphem ... What's the word I'm trying to say?"

"Euphemism?" he supplied.

"Yeah, that. Did you mean that ... word I can't say? Because last time we were in that bathroom, we almost—"

Ransom's large hand over my mouth kept me from finishing my sentence.

I licked his palm as punishment for his rudeness.

RANSOM

After I finished picking grass out of Taylor's hair and dusted most of the dirt off her, I led her to Owen's room. Claudette had said she could rest there for a while. I was only half surprised to see Gimli lying on a heap of blankets beside the bed. His tail thumped against the floor, but he didn't otherwise move as I settled Taylor onto the bed and covered her with a quilt that was folded at the bottom.

I pressed a kiss to her forehead and whispered for her to sleep, which was unnecessary, considering soft snores were already emanating from her. I backed out of the room and gently closed the door before heading toward the voices I heard downstairs.

"I can't believe you got that young girl sauced," I heard Roland Sr. say. "I expect that kind of thing from Jimi, but you're supposed to have better sense than her."

"We'd only been playing for about a half hour," Claudette argued. "How was I supposed to know she'd get tanked so quickly?"

I walked into the kitchen and saw everyone gathered at various spots around the room. Jimi was sitting at the table, Roland was leaning against the counter, and Claudette was at the sink, cleaning what looked to be shot glasses. Owen was doing . . . something over by the pantry. His back was to the rest of us. Only RJ was missing, and I assumed that was because he was looking at my truck.

"How is she?" Roland Sr. asked when he saw me.

"Seems okay. She can sleep it off for a while before we get back on the road." I was desperately hoping my truck was an easy fix and this extended stay with the Parrishes didn't throw us too off schedule.

Claudette turned toward me, drying her hands on a dish towel. "I'm sorry. I had no idea it would go to her head so quickly."

"Honestly, she's been under a lot of stress with school and the prospect of meeting my family Saturday." *And possibly having witnessed her current boyfriend kill her old one.* "I think that played a big part in her getting a little . . ."

"Trashed?" Jimi supplied for me.

A laugh bubbled out of me. "Yes. So no one's to blame. She probably needed to blow off some steam."

Claudette nodded once and said, "Do you want some coffee?"

"That'd be great." A little caffeine jolt would do me well for the rest of the drive, especially since I doubted Taylor would be up for getting behind the wheel for a while.

Claudette busied herself pouring me a cup and brought it over with a carton of cream and a bowl of sugar, and I started doctoring my coffee how I liked it—a little cream, a lot of sugar.

"Owen," she said. "You're not fooling anyone. We all know the dog is in your room, and we all know you need to feed him. Stop stuffing snacks into your sweatshirt and just take what you need." She rolled her eyes and huffed.

Owen's head turned, and he appraised his mother for a second before looking down at the mound under his hoodie. When he returned his attention to his mom, he was glaring. "You take the fun out of everything," he groused.

"What did you even find in there that you could feed a dog?" Roland Sr. asked.

Owen came over to the table and started unloading his bounty. There was a jar of peanut butter, two cans of tuna fish, a bag of pretzels, and a package of beef jerky.

"The pretzels are for me," he explained.

His mom sighed. "Why are you even in here pilfering my food? I thought you were helping your dad."

"I was. Until I knocked his tool rack over and he told me to go away."

"You did it on purpose, didn't you?" Jimi asked, a sly smile on her face.

"Of course. I had to get in here and feed Gimli."

Claudette sighed again, louder this time. "I don't know what I'm going to do with you."

Owen smiled. "You love me."

"Against my better judgment, yes, I do."

For some reason, her comment hit me in the chest in a way I hadn't expected. I'd heard parents tell their kids they loved them without it causing an ache to bloom within me, but something about the casual way they joked about it—like their love was such a given they could tease each other about it—threw me. I couldn't ever remember hearing those words from my mom when I was growing up. The first time I did hear them, they had been from my foster mom, Melissa.

And maybe it was a case of my having forgotten. Maybe my mom had whispered it in my ear each night before she'd put me to bed. But I doubted that was the case, and she'd never done much to deserve the benefit of the doubt.

RJ came in, wiping his hands with a rag and interrupting my emotional spiral. "Well, you want the good news or the bad news?"

I ran my hand through my hair. "Bad news, I guess."

"The sound you heard is called rod knock. One of your piston rods is damaged. It's gonna take me probably a week to repair it, especially since I got other jobs at my garage in town. But the good news is, I *can* fix it. And since you were kind enough to bring Owen all the way home, I'll just charge you for parts."

"You don't have to do that. I'm happy to pay you for the labor." *Happy* was a large overstatement, but I didn't want to take advantage of anyone.

But RJ waved me off. "I'll make Owen help me. It'll be some good bonding time. Especially once he figures out he doesn't have to pretend to be a klutz just to get back to his new dog." RJ turned a knowing eye on Owen, who had the sense to look abashed.

"I'm so transparent," he muttered. Then he looked at me. "What are you guys going to do about your thingy this weekend?"

I shrugged. "Not sure. Without my truck, we don't have any way of getting there, so I'll probably just call my mom and tell her we'll have to meet up with her another time."

"We're a ways away from the nearest airport, but we do have a bus station in town," Jimi said. "I'm not sure what your financial situation is like, but if you could afford it, you could look into when the next bus leaves."

The thought of spending hours on a bus wasn't particularly appealing, but neither was canceling the trip. As disastrous as it had been so far, there was an air of adventure associated with it that I was beginning to feel exhilarated by. And since we'd have to face reality when we got home, I wasn't willing to give up on our trip just yet.

"And I could drive your truck up to school when it's done so you don't have to come back through here afterward," Owen offered. "I'm not coming back to school until next weekend."

And while my initial reaction was to balk at Owen driving my truck, no one in his family looked alarmed by the offer, which put me at ease. If I'd learned nothing from my short time with the Parrishes, it was that they were brutally honest.

If Owen were a danger behind the wheel, they'd say so.

"That would be great. All of it . . . would be great. Thank you all, very much. For being so helpful and welcoming. I truly appreciate it."

They all waved off my thanks, but I'd meant every word. I'd learned more about the kind of family I might want to have in the future—if kids were ever a possibility I warmed up to—during one afternoon with them than I had in my previous twenty-six years. And I'd be eternally grateful for it.

Chapter Nine

RANSOM

We arrived at the bus station a little after five in the evening. Owen wished us good luck, promised us he and his dad would take good care of my truck, and said that he'd see us when we got back. I grabbed our bags out of the trunk and set them on the sidewalk by a bench outside the bus station as we watched Owen and his dad drive away.

"Do you wanna wait here with our bags while I go get our tickets? Then maybe we can see if there's something we can grab to eat. We won't get to Georgia until morning at the earliest."

"Eleven forty-two to be exact," Taylor said, looking pleased with herself. "I already got our tickets." It was good to see her looking like her old self again. When she'd first woken up from her stupor, she'd still been a little tipsy. But Jimi had mixed up some kind of concoction, told Taylor to drink it without asking any questions, and then gave her some crackers. Fifteen minutes later, Taylor was more alert and said she'd felt remarkably well.

"Seriously? Thanks! How much were they?"

"Don't worry about it. You already have to pay for your truck to get fixed. Besides, I have a credit card I barely ever use. When I went to look at the departure times, I decided just to get them. My dad doesn't even check the statements."

I sat down next to her on the bench and leaned forward with my forearms on my thighs. Even though we'd be sitting for hours, I couldn't help wanting to be next to her.

"Thank you." I leaned over to give her a small kiss, which she seemed to enjoy, because when I pulled back, her eyes were closed.

"Why'd you stop?" she asked, her eyelids lifting but still appearing heavy.

"Because we're sitting on a bench in front of a Greyhound station, and I just put my hand in something unidentifiable."

"That's . . . so gross."

I brought my hand away from the bench and eyed the sticky brown substance. "I think it's Coke, so I guess it could be worse."

"Did you smell it?"

"No! Why would I smell it? I'm not trying to contract a disease before the bus leaves." Craning my neck, I searched through the window for a restroom sign. "I'm gonna go wash my hands. I'll be right back." I didn't want to point out that there was a man about twenty yards away licking the back of his hands like a cat cleaning himself, so I just hurried off to scrub what I hoped was soda from my own hand.

When I returned, Taylor was on the map app of her phone. "There isn't much of a selection in terms of food that's close enough to walk to."

"I'm not really surprised by that. What time does the bus leave again?"

"Not for another hour and a half. I can keep looking. We could always call for an Uber to take us somewhere."

I glanced around the area—there were a few stores in the distance that probably made the bulk of their profits selling cigarettes and lottery tickets. I knew towns like this one well, and though I didn't want to stick around for longer than I had to, I was heading to the town where my mother lived, so I was aware I'd be trading one nowhere town for another. I felt a little guilty for having that thought, but I'd tried so hard to make something of myself—to leave a life I'd been given for one that I chose. Being back in a place like the one that reminded me so much of my childhood caused my nerves to react in a way that I hadn't expected them to.

"I'm not sure how many Ubers come out here," I said. "We might be waiting a while."

"Excuse me," a gruff voice cut in, and I startled at his words but did my best to appear unaffected. I didn't think I truly had any reason to be nervous at the moment, but I'd allowed myself to let my guard down. I turned to face the man who couldn't have been any taller than Taylor. He had a gray beard and the skin of a man who'd spent most of his life working in the sun. "I heard you talkin' about findin' a place to eat?"

"That's right," I said.

"Ain't much around here, but there's a small farm up the road. They run a little restaurant there. Nothin' fancy, but the food's good. It's kinda a town favorite around here."

"Thanks," I said. "Maybe we'll check it out."

"We appreciate the recommendation," Taylor said. "Where exactly is this place?"

He pointed away from the direction we'd come from. "Maybe 'bout a quarter mile or so down the road. Just past the traffic light up 'ere. Just knock on the door. They don't do much advertisin' since it's mostly locals who go."

We both thanked him again, and once he was a safe distance off, I looked toward Taylor. "Thoughts?" It did seem kind of strange, but I knew from experience that towns like this one had their own way of doing things.

Taylor shrugged. "It's either that or starve until lunchtime tomorrow."

TAYLOR

We walked the quarter mile toward the farm like the man said, passing a convenience store and then a gas station that I didn't think sold anything else besides gas. And sure enough, just past the traffic light, there was a farmhouse. It was a cute white home with a front porch that spanned the width of the house. In need of a paint job, it wasn't in perfect condition by any means, but I didn't expect it to be. And the fact that it was a bit weathered made it slightly more charming somehow.

I could see some horses toward the back of the house and a few goats a bit farther away.

"Should we just go knock?" Ransom asked, stopping at the end of the driveway.

"That's what he said to do."

"It doesn't look like they have a restaurant here."

"I didn't think it would. They probably don't want tourists bothering them all the time," I told him.

Ransom raised an eyebrow. "I'd doubt many people are in a hurry to tour this town."

"Let's just go knock. What's the worst that could happen?"

"I'm thinking the Virginia equivalent of the Manson family."

I rolled my eyes at him, already starting to walk up the driveway because I knew he wouldn't let me go up there alone. When I got to the porch, I rang the bell, and when I didn't hear anything, I knocked.

We could hear voices inside, and it sounded like a teenage girl was yelling for someone else to open the door, and then we heard someone else yell for her to open it. A few moments later, the wood door pulled open and a tall, lean girl who looked to be about eighteen or nineteen stood behind the screen door.

"Can I help you?" she asked, but her tone didn't match her words, because she looked like the last thing she wanted to do was help us.

Despite the cooler weather, she wore cutoff shorts and a tank top that revealed most of her stomach.

"Hi," Ransom said, and I could tell he was trying to sound pleasant, even though I knew he was a bit skeptical about eating here. "We were hoping to get something to eat."

The girl narrowed her already thin eyes at us. "Who do you work for?"

"What? No one," Ransom told her. "We're catching a bus in a little while, and a guy at the station told us you guys serve food."

Without a word, the girl turned away and yelled, "Mom, two strangers are here asking for food." Then she disappeared out of sight.

"See," I whispered. "They think we're tourists."

"They have guns hanging on the wall," Ransom pointed out as he peered into their house.

"If they're on the wall, I doubt they're loaded. They're

probably just for show. And people around here are probably used to that sort of thing." I was beginning to think Sophia's suggestion of bringing a gun along wasn't the worst idea, but I didn't bring it up to Ransom.

"If you say so." He laughed, but it sounded empty.

When someone came to the door again, it was a woman I assumed was the girl's mother, though she appeared older than what I would've imagined she'd look like. Her gray hair was neatly tucked into a bun on the top of her head, and she wore an apron that said *Be nice or I'll poison your food.*

It was a strange choice of sayings for a restaurant, but I wasn't about to point that out. "We just wanted to get something to eat before our bus comes in a little while," I told her. "Do you have any tables available? Is this even the right door? Someone told us there was a restaurant here, but we didn't see a separate entrance or anything."

The woman turned back toward the inside of her house, mumbling for us to give her a minute. Ransom and I had a nonverbal conversation with each other that consisted of widened eyes, sideways glances, and shrugs.

We didn't even notice when the woman returned.

"Restaurant's in the barn out back, but we're fixin' it up, so it's not open right now. All we can offer ya is a seat at our kitchen table, but we're happy to do that if it suits you all right. Unfortunately that'll mean you won't get to order off a menu, but I promise ya everything I cook is good."

I looked at Ransom and tried to gauge his reaction. Both of us seemed a little hesitant but figured we didn't have any better options.

"That'd be fine," he said. "Are you sure you don't mind havin' us?"

"Not at all."

We started to enter the home, but she positioned herself in the entranceway. "It'll be twenty each for the meal. Just a flat fee since you aren't choosin' yer food."

Ransom pulled out his wallet and handed the woman three twenties. "Consider it an advance tip."

She gave us a stern nod. "Now that that's settled, let me introduce ya to everyone."

She brought us into the living room, told us that her name was Mae and we could call her what everyone else called her, which was Mama. "Some of the little ones call me Mama Mae, but it strikes me as a little formal."

I wondered if she was the mother of all the children that were running around the house, but after about ten minutes, several of them had gotten picked up, and I realized that Mama Mae ran a home daycare. I wondered what kind of regulations allowed childcare facilities to display guns on the walls of the play areas, but I doubted Mama Mae had gotten her center approved by any state agencies.

Mae instructed us to sit at the large oval table that took up most of her kitchen, and soon the rest of the family joined us. It felt a bit odd to be seated at the table with strangers, but they probably felt the same way about having us here.

I could tell her oldest son, Todd, who looked to be about twelve, thought his mother shouldn't have invited us in because he ate with his head down and his eyes directed right at us from across the table. He didn't say anything, but his stare said everything he was thinking: he didn't trust us one bit.

The two younger boys, who Mama introduced as seven-year-old twins Trenton and Tripp, were the complete opposite. They hadn't stopped talking since they'd sat down. Their sister,

Samantha, who we'd first seen when she answered the door, was clearly getting annoyed by their chatter, but I thought the dark-haired boys were cute. They talked about their teacher, Ms. Miles, and fed parts of their dinner to the two dogs who'd planted themselves on either side of the boys.

Mae and her husband, Clint, were either oblivious to the dogs helping the boys finish their dinner or they just didn't care. Though I wasn't sure if Clint even realized Ransom and I were at the table, so I doubted he'd noticed his sons feeding their vegetables to the dogs. He was too focused on his meatloaf and trying to see the score of the game on the TV in the other room.

"This is really good, Mama Mae," I said. "It's been years since I've had a home-cooked meal as good as this one."

"Mama Mae?" Samantha said, her voice radiating the type of disgust only a teenage girl could produce. "Is that what she told you to call her?"

"Yeah," Ransom answered, obviously as confused as I was.

"That's my name," Mama Mae snapped at her daughter.

"It's not her name," Clint cut in. "No one calls her that."

I looked around at the other kids and then back at Mama Mae . . . or whatever her name was. "I'm confused."

"Her name's Mae," Todd explained. "But no one calls her Mama. We just call her Mom."

"She's been trying to get that Mama thing to stick since I was born," Samantha said. "She needs to give it up."

"And you need to be quiet, little girl, or I'll rip that piercing right out of your tongue so you can't use it anymore."

Samantha ripped off a piece of a roll she'd been holding and stuck out her tongue at her mother. Sure enough, there was a silver bar through it.

"Can I get my tongue pierced too?" one of the twins asked.

"No, Tripp," Mae said. "Samantha's in high school, and she doesn't listen to rules."

"There was never a rule that I couldn't get my tongue pierced."

"There was," Clint said. "You just never knew about it because you didn't ask before you put a hole through your body."

"Everyone has holes in their body. What's one more?"

"Pleeease," Tripp begged. "I can stick my tongue out at show-and-tell, and Ms. Miles can't yell at me."

"Can I be excused?" Todd asked.

"Go 'head," Clint told him. "Just put your plate in the sink before you go."

Todd got up without another word and headed upstairs.

"So when are the renovations expected to be finished?" Ransom asked.

"What renovations?" Clint looked up from where he'd been buttering his corn.

"In the restaurant."

"Oh, yeah. It'll probably be a while before that's up and runnin' again," Clint said.

Samantha laughed. "Yeah. Like never."

I would've assumed Clint was taking care of the renovations himself and his daughter's comment had been a shot at him, but he'd seemed confused when Ransom had brought it up. Maybe he'd been slacking so much he'd forgotten about them completely.

A few minutes later, the boys finished eating and cleared their plates. When Samantha disappeared too, I got up to help Mae with the dishes.

"Don't be ridiculous," she said. "You're our guests."

"I hope we didn't intrude," Ransom said.

"Of course not. Besides, you're paying customers. You wanna take some pumpkin pie for the road?"

Ransom gave her a wide grin. "Wouldn't feel right turning down pie," he said. "So if it's not too much trouble..."

Mae smiled just as wide as Ransom had. "I'll box it right up for you in one of Mama Mae's doggie bags."

Mae moved around the kitchen, pulling a pie out of the refrigerator and sliding out two slices. Once everything was wrapped up, she handed the bag to Ransom.

"Gives me somethin' to look forward to on our sixteen-hour bus ride."

"Where y'all headed, anyway?"

"Georgia." I didn't like to lie, but the second the truth left my mouth, I regretted it. I didn't exactly think Mae and her family had any interest in getting involved with a police investigation, and I doubted the authorities would even know we'd been here. Ransom didn't seem to mind that I'd shared our destination, but I couldn't help but wonder if I should start being less free with the information.

"That's nice," Mae said. "I have some family down there. It's such a pretty state."

"It is," Ransom agreed. "I grew up down there, so we're going to visit some family."

"Meeting the parents, huh?" Mae said to me, her raised eyebrows saying more than her words had.

I laughed nervously. "Yeah. Wish me luck."

"Well, good luck, sweetheart. I'm sure they'll love you."

Ransom looked at the time on his phone. "We should probably get going. Thanks again for the meal."

Mama Mae said goodbye, and her husband grunted

something from his recliner that I assumed was directed at us as well, though I had no idea what it could've been.

Once we were outside and a little ways from the house, Ransom said, "Well, that was . . . weird."

"Weird," I agreed, "but good. At least we got a home-cooked meal out of it."

"Definitely. They didn't have to serve us dinner with the restaurant closed."

I'd been taking in the scenery—or what I could see of it in the dark—when something in the distance caught my eye. I waited until I got close enough to be sure I was seeing correctly before I pointed it out to Ransom.

"Look at that," I said, already beginning to laugh.

It took Ransom a moment to realize I'd been talking about something other than the goat sleeping on top of a car. At the end of a driveway, next to a large red mailbox, was a large white wooden sign with black script.

"Jezebel's Restaurant," Ransom said. There was an arrow on the sign that pointed to the back of the house. In the dark we could clearly see a large room attached to the farmhouse. Through the large glass windows, we could see people sitting at tables eating. "Oh my God."

"I know," I said, both of us frozen in the dark as we watched a server walk over to a table with a bottle of wine. "Did we just pay a random family to eat dinner with them?"

"I think we did."

"Let's never mention this again," he said.

And as we began walking toward the bus station again, I muttered, "Already forgotten."

Chapter Ten

RANSOM

God, my neck hurt. And my back. And pretty much every muscle in my body. Being stuck on a bus was no way to spend a night, especially when you're over six feet. I closed my eyes tightly, rubbing them for a minute before I got up the courage to open them and face the sunlight I could see through my eyelids.

It took me a few seconds for my eyes to adjust, and once they did, I looked beside me. A sleeping Taylor rested her head on me, and I wondered if she'd been like that all night. Despite the uncomfortable position, I didn't remember really waking up. Looking at my phone, I saw it was ten thirty in the morning. We must've been getting close.

Not wanting to wake Taylor, I tried to remain as still as possible. It had been a long night, and I didn't know how much sleep she'd gotten. I leaned my head on hers as she slept and stared out the window at the scenery as it passed, looking for something I might recognize.

I'd been all over Georgia as a kid, and though I likely

wouldn't remember specific details, I hoped something would remind me of the place I'd been raised, though I had no idea why, considering I had tried so hard to forget it.

Nothing looked familiar, necessarily, but I also hadn't been anywhere near Decatur County, Georgia, in . . . well, I couldn't remember the last time I'd been here. The town where I lived with my mom and my sister, Hudson, was as short on money as it was on people. Since there weren't many job opportunities, and most of the few thousand residents hadn't had much more than a high school education, the majority had struggled to pay the few bills they had.

Most of my time in foster homes had been in this county, in one small town or another, and I had eventually landed in an after-school program, which was where I'd ended up meeting Melissa. It'd been free, and my foster mom at that time put me in there because she didn't trust me home on my own.

At first, I hated going. It was just one more place I had to meet new people and make new friends. But Melissa made it easy for me to feel part of the group. And eventually, when the home I'd been living in didn't work out, she and Matt took me in, and their family of three became four.

I felt Taylor move around a little until eventually she woke up completely.

"Good morning," she said with a stretch.

"Is it?"

"Is it what?"

"A *good* morning? Do we know that yet?"

She smiled but said, "You're such a downer." Looking out the window, she said, "Georgia's pretty."

"Oh, we aren't in Georgia quite yet," said a woman across the aisle from us.

"Really?" I asked. "How is that possible? We should be like a half hour away or less."

"We are. Shouldn't be more than fifteen minutes or so."

Now I was completely confused. If we were only fifteen minutes away, I couldn't fathom how we wouldn't be in Georgia by now when we were headed to the southern border of it. Much like this entire trip so far, none of it made sense.

I heard Taylor mutter an "Oh God" and then saw her dig through her purse frantically. It made me just as anxious as she looked, but when I asked what was wrong, she didn't answer.

"Taylor, what's wrong?" I asked again. "What is it?"

She was looking at her phone now and mumbling something about how this couldn't be right.

"What?" I asked again, this time more sternly. "You're really freaking me out. Can you please answer me?"

My mind played a sort of slideshow of horrible possibilities. Had she seen someone or something that made her worry the authorities wanted to question us? Had she seen a text come through on her watch from someone back home that worried her? Anything was possible, and if she didn't tell me what was happening right the fuck now—

"Don't kill me."

"First of all, that is a horrible choice of words right now. And second, what the hell are you talking about? Why would I wanna kill you?"

I hoped she was overreacting, but the horrified look on her face as she stared at her phone told me she wasn't.

"Okay, I'm not sure how this happened, but we're in Vermont."

"Vermont," I repeated. "I don't... How are we in Vermont?"

Without looking up from her phone, she squeaked out an answer. "Because I evidently bought us tickets there."

TAYLOR

The bus pulled out of the long, angled space, cracking the thin sheet of ice that had begun to form over a small puddle and splashing black water onto the sidewalk of the bus terminal.

"It's cold," Ransom said, as if I hadn't noticed.

Expecting to be heading south and to a slightly warmer climate, neither of us had brought anything heavier than a thin jacket. It was supposed to be close to sixty-five degrees all weekend. In the *state* of Georgia, at least. The town of Georgia, in Vermont, was a different story.

"I'm sorry," I said again. I'd immediately apologized once I'd realized my mistake, which, admittedly was a pretty big one. But it'd been an accident—one I'd thought anyone could make. Though Ransom insisted otherwise.

I chanced a glance to my right to look at him. His posture revealed how deflated he felt, and I couldn't blame him.

"If it sets your mind at ease at all, I'm sure the cops won't think to look for us here," I told him.

"That's not even funny."

I'd been serious when I'd said it. "Sorry," I said again.

Ransom dropped the bags he'd been holding and adjusted his baseball cap before resting his hands on his head and letting out a heavy sigh. He looked around at our unfamiliar surroundings, no doubt deciding what to do next. Finally, he picked up the bags again and walked over to a bench in front of the building.

I followed but was too nervous to sit, so I stood instead. "Maybe there's another bus we can take. If we leave soon, we can probably get there sometime in the middle of the night. We'd still have time to make the reunion."

Ransom looked up at me slowly. It was the kind of movement you might see someone do in a horror movie when a demon possessed them. "I'm not sitting on a bus for another half a day."

"Ooh, what about a train? That'd be faster. Or we could rent a car. Then we can stop wherever we want to take a break."

His silence told me neither of those two ideas thrilled him.

"Okay, so not a car, bus, or train," I said. "What about a plane?"

Ransom stood suddenly, startling me even though I was sure he didn't mean to scare me. "Jesus, Taylor. You sound like a Dr. Seuss book. You can't just name modes of transportation like it'll fix this."

I knew it was out of frustration, but his voice had gotten louder, and it made me uncomfortable, mainly because we were still in public. "Don't yell at me."

"I'm not yelling," he said even more loudly. "I just ... How do you expect me to react?" He gestured around him. "Look where we are!"

"I think it's a cute town."

"I'm not talking about whether or not the town is *cute.*" He said the word like it offended him. "I'm talking about the fact that you bought us tickets to a place that's farther from our destination than where we started!"

"I said I'm sorry. It was an accident. You didn't realize either. I'm sure the sign on the bus said where it was headed."

He shook his head, and the expression on his face told me I'd hit a nerve that didn't want to get touched. I couldn't say I felt bad about it either. If Ransom thought he could talk to me like this, and in public, it'd do him well to learn he'd get the same in return.

"No way," he said. "You don't get to blame this on me. *You're* the one who bought the tickets. Who doesn't know the difference between a town and a state? You thought a bus just went to the state of Georgia? Like there was only one station in the whole state?"

"I'm not well-versed in public transportation."

"Clearly." He scoffed. "Maybe you're right. I should've known someone who grew up flying first class with her dad's miles wouldn't have any idea how to buy a bus ticket."

I stared at him blankly because I couldn't decide if I was offended by his assumption or impressed that his assumption was true.

He blew out a deep breath and massaged his temples. "I'm sorry. I know you were just trying to help. It's been a long couple of days, and being mad doesn't make things any better," he said quietly when I hadn't spoken after a few seconds. "And I shouldn't have said that. If anyone should know you can't control what happens to you in your childhood, it's me. If kids aren't responsible for the bad things that happen to them, they shouldn't be responsible for the good ones either."

I chose not to comment on anything he'd just said, figuring it was better just to move forward. "We'll figure it out."

"Maybe it's a sign."

"What do you mean, a sign?"

"I don't know. Like . . . the universe is telling us . . . or *me* that it's a bad idea to try to reconnect with my family."

Hoping to convey my skepticism, I raised my eyebrows at him. "So the universe had me buy a bus ticket to the wrong state?"

I was glad when he laughed at that so I could too.

"Seriously," I said. "You can't believe that. We're in Georgia, Vermont, because this is the kind of shit we get ourselves into, not because the universe wanted to tell you how to deal with a family reunion."

"You're right. I shouldn't blame the universe. We're in Vermont because you can't read."

Ransom tried to keep a straight face, but he failed miserably, and before we knew it, both of us were trying to catch our breaths from laughter.

When we finally managed to calm down, I pulled out my phone. "I was serious about the plane suggestion, though. I know it's not the best idea to buy a plane ticket with our names on them, but if we want to make it to the reunion, it's probably our only real shot to get there in time."

He sighed like he didn't want to accept that was our only option but knew he'd probably have to. "Full disclosure? Flying scares me a little. I was glad when we realized it wouldn't be a smart plan."

I took the opportunity to wrap my arms around him, and then he did the same. It always amazed me how small I felt against him.

"I'll protect you," I told him, looking up with a smile.

"It's a nice gesture, but unless you brought your Iron Man suit with you, I doubt you can stop a 747 from crashing to the ground."

My eyes grew hooded, and I did my best to sound as seductive as I could standing outside the bus station of an unfamiliar town in the cold. "Oh, you have no idea what kinds of outfits I brought with me on this little trip, and if we don't get to a hotel soon, you may never get to find out."

"I feel like you're trying to be sexy, but now I'm imagining a Captain America mask in there or something," Ransom teased.

"Um...Captain America *is* sexy."

Ransom shook his head at me. "What am I gonna do with you?"

"Let me get us two plane tickets to Wherever You're From, Georgia?"

"Ha!" he laughed. "Like I'd ever let *you* book our flight. I'm not even trusting you to make dinner plans from now on."

I groaned. "Are you ever gonna let this go?"

"If I had to guess, I'd say probably not."

RANSOM

By some miracle, we were able to get a flight from Burlington, Vermont, to the Southwest Georgia Regional Airport, which was the closest one to the location of the reunion. Even more of a miracle was that the flight went fairly smoothly other than having a connecting flight in Atlanta. And even though the second plane was delayed by a little over an hour, we still arrived in Albany, Georgia, before midnight.

I was just happy we'd gotten here safely and I hadn't felt sick on the plane. The realization that traveling would've been a large part of my life had I become a professional football player almost made me thankful my career had changed course. Almost.

We just had to pick up our rental car and head to the hotel we'd booked, which was about an hour from the airport. And since the reunion didn't begin until eleven the next morning and the hotel was only a few minutes away from it, we'd have plenty of time to sleep in and eat before getting ready.

"You sure we're not in New York?" Taylor joked, pointing to a sign that said Albany.

"Oh. Maybe," I said dryly as we walked through the terminal looking for directions to car rentals.

I was glad we hadn't packed so much that we'd had to check our bags. At least that would save a little time. I was exhausted. I hadn't slept on the plane since I'd been anxious. I hoped I could sleep once we got to the hotel because I knew my anxiety wouldn't go away anytime soon with the reunion tomorrow. But at least being in a bed with Taylor would relax me a little.

Though on second thought, access to a bed might mean we *wouldn't* be sleeping much.

My phone had dinged with a text, and when I had a second to look at it, I removed it from my pocket. It was from Xander.

Glad you guys landed safely.

I wondered who'd told Xander we'd flown, and I couldn't figure out what the connection would've been because no one else knew about it.

Yeah, thanks. How'd you know we flew?

His text came back almost immediately.

Same way the authorities will.

You're not helping the situation.

Neither are you.

Fucker. When I saw a sign for baggage claim, I pointed it out, and we followed the directions until we arrived at the baggage carousels.

"The car rentals should be around here somewhere." I put our bags down near a wall and asked Taylor, "Do you wanna wait here while I find it and check in?"

"It's fine. I'll come. I think it's down there," she said, pointing behind me.

When I turned around, I saw a counter with the name of the car rental company hanging over it. No wonder we hadn't spotted it right away; it was completely dark.

"Are they closed?" I heard the defeat in my voice but also the uncertainty. I'd reserved a car online and even put down a time that we'd arrive. Though that time had passed an hour and a half ago thanks to the late departure of our connecting flight.

"I was wondering the exact same thing."

We both began walking toward the desk in silence, and once we arrived, there was no doubt we wouldn't be renting a car tonight. They'd closed at ten, and it was past eleven.

"Before you say anything, this is *not* my fault, and we're not even."

Taylor smiled as much as her exhaustion would probably let her. "I didn't say anything." She looked around. "You wanna just go outside and get a cab? I'm sure we can call in the morning and get the rental place to drop the car off to our hotel."

E L I Z A B E T H   H A Y L E Y

"That'd be a good plan if it weren't for the fact that the hotel is like an hour away. It'll probably cost a fortune, and I'm not sure I feel like spending that long in a cab after the last twenty-four hours."

"You sure? It would pretty much complete our reenactment of *Planes, Trains, and Automobiles*," she joked. Even Taylor's raised eyebrow, which she knew I thought was cute, couldn't convince me. "I'm honestly fine with whatever gets us to a bed and a shower. Except walking. I have to draw the line somewhere."

I was glad that was where she drew the line, because when she heard my next suggestion, she'd have to agree to it, even though I wasn't a hundred percent on board with it myself.

Chapter Eleven

RANSOM

Taylor shifted her weight from side to side nervously as we waited on the sidewalk outside the baggage claim area. I was nervous too, and I rubbed at a stain on the sidewalk with the toe of my boot. Rain pelted the areas of ground that weren't covered, leaving puddles that reflected the overhead lights in the water.

I felt bad I'd called Matt and Melissa, but I also knew they wouldn't want me taking a cab to a hotel an hour away when their house was only twenty minutes from the airport. It was late, but Matt and Melissa had always been night owls, even before Emily's death. And the loss of their only child had meant that on most nights, sleep was difficult to come by at all.

"I wish I'd had time to prepare to meet your family."

Looking up at Taylor, I took in her features—the long blond hair pulled back into a messy bun, a face absent of any makeup—not that she'd needed it—and eyelids that seemed heavy with the weariness of the past couple of days. Despite all that, she still looked beautiful, though I was sure she would've argued with me. But I understood why she wouldn't feel she was in the best condition to meet the two people who'd helped me develop into the man I was today.

"Sorry," I told her. "Nothing about this trip has been ideal, so in that regard, it's kind of on par."

"Yeah, I guess." She was quiet for a moment before she asked, "Do I need to know anything?"

"Like what?"

She shrugged. "I don't know. Just … anything."

"Not that I can think of. I mean, they aren't running a Satanic cult out of their basement or anything."

"Dammit, what will I have in common with them, then?"

I laughed, marveling at Taylor's ability to keep her sense of humor about her during the most stressful of times. Even though she worried about meeting them, she still helped me find some levity in the situation.

We waited a few more minutes before I spotted a burgundy SUV in the distance. "That's Melissa," I said, thinking that Matt probably hadn't driven because he'd been drinking tonight. As the truck got closer, I could see him in the passenger's seat, though, and I was happy they'd both come.

Melissa put the hazards on and practically jumped out of the driver's seat and ran around the front of the car to wrap me in a hug. I'd forgotten how tiny she was, how fragile. Her barely five-foot frame felt almost childlike in my arms, but somehow her embrace was still as comforting as it had always been.

"I'm so glad you called," she said.

All I found myself able to say was "Me too."

When Melissa and I finally let go and I looked to my side, Matt was standing beside the door he'd just gotten out of. We stared at each other for a few seconds before moving toward the other. Matt wrapped his arms around me and patted my back hard. He smelled like Acqua Di Gio and cheap bourbon—a scent I hadn't known I'd missed until I smelled it again.

"This must be Taylor," Melissa said. She walked over to her and took hold of both her hands, holding them in between her own, and looked at her. It wasn't an intimidating stare like a mother might give her son's new girlfriend. The opposite, actually. She looked happy, thankful. Like I'd surprised her with a gift she hadn't known she wanted.

"Sorry, yes," I said. "This is Taylor. Taylor, this is Melissa and Matt."

"We met already," Matt said. "I couldn't leave this poor girl waiting awkwardly on the curb without introducing myself."

"It's so nice to meet you," Melissa said.

"It's nice to finally meet you too," Taylor told her. "I've heard so much about you. Ransom speaks highly of you both."

"Really?" Matt raised his eyebrows in clear disbelief. "I'm shocked he speaks about us at all."

He'd presented the comment almost as a joke, but there was some truth to it, and we all knew it. I'd pulled away, and in response to that, they'd pulled away too until we all existed at a comfortable distance.

"Well, get in already," Melissa told us. "It's freezing out here."

Wind stung our faces, but it was nothing compared to the Georgia of the North we'd experienced earlier.

Matt opened the door so Taylor could climb in, and once I put the bags in the trunk, I followed her, buckling myself in. I knew Melissa wouldn't start driving until we were all safely strapped in, even Matt.

Brad Paisley's voice came through the speakers, and I

figured the choice in station had been Matt's since Melissa couldn't stand country. I wondered if she'd driven all the way to the airport with it on or if he'd just switched the station when she'd gotten out of the car just to annoy her. I figured the latter was more likely.

Shifting the Chevy Tahoe into drive, Melissa took one last look in the rearview mirror, no doubt to make sure we had our belts buckled, and then pulled out onto the main road. And a few minutes later, we were on the highway heading to the only house that had ever felt like home to me.

TAYLOR

I'd thought that meeting Matt and Melissa would feel strange somehow, and the more I thought about it, the more I realized the idea of spending time with them caused me more anxiety than meeting his biological family would have. This was the family he'd loved, the family that had loved him. They were something to him. Important.

There was no way I could fuck up meeting his blood relatives, because that soup was already so salty no one wanted to taste it anyway. But this was different. The picture frames in this house held photos of Ransom as a boy: a few baby pictures and then one when he looked to be about four, lying on the ground in front of an old TV that was probably in his mother's house. But there were also more recent ones—playing baseball, sitting cross-legged in front of a Christmas tree holding up a new Xbox.

He had a bedroom here, which was still completely intact from what I could tell. Trophies and awards lined the wooden shelves on the walls, and a small desk sat in the corner where I imagined a younger Ransom used to do his homework in high school.

After we'd fallen asleep in his bed, which was nowhere big enough for the both of us, I'd gotten up earlier than I'd expected to considering our late arrival. Then I'd taken a shower and wandered downstairs.

The house was quiet except for the fourteen-year-old chocolate lab, Buddy. His arthritis prevented him from walking upstairs at night, so he slept on the kitchen floor because he liked the feel of the cold tile. Ransom had said that even when Buddy slept upstairs, he'd chosen to make the bathroom floor his bed for the same reason.

Buddy woke right up when I got downstairs and stood to greet me, his long nails clicking and sliding on the hard floor as he fought to maintain his footing on the slick tile. His fur was rough with age, and his face now had more white than brown. But as I greeted him, kneeling to let him lick me, his tail didn't seem to be affected by his years. It moved back and forth as quickly as I imagined it did when he'd been a puppy.

"Sorry I woke you, Buddy," I whispered. "You wanna go out?"

He clearly knew what that meant because he immediately headed over to the door that led to the fenced yard. It wasn't overly large and had little landscaping, but it definitely had enough grass for Buddy to run around.

While Buddy was outside, I quietly searched for coffee and filters so I could get a pot going before Ransom and his parents awoke. Once I found them, I scooped out the coffee, measured the correct amount of water, and switched the coffeemaker on. I took a seat at the oval table that sat in the kitchen as I waited for the coffee to brew. There really was nothing more comforting than the sound and smell of coffee brewing on a weekend morning.

I could see why Ransom had so easily felt like the Holt house was home to him even though he'd become a part of the family as a teen. The downstairs only had three rooms—a kitchen that served as the dining room as well; a living room that had two charcoal-colored couches, a few small tables, and a TV; and a room connecting the two, which had probably been meant as a dining room but seemed to serve as more of an office than anything else right now.

Though the home was considerably smaller than the one I'd grown up in, I could tell Matt and Melissa took pride in it. Everything had a place and a purpose, and even though the home was older, nothing about it seemed neglected. The paint was still pristine—even on the molding around the windows and doors, which in older homes often got neglected—and the wooden cabinets seemed like they'd recently gotten new hinges. I wondered if household projects were how Matt kept busy at home.

Once the coffee finished brewing, I poured myself a cup in a mug that had the logo of a local café on it. In the fridge, I found some creamer, and since there weren't any dirty dishes in the sink, I washed and dried the spoon I'd used and returned it to its place in the drawer.

Buddy came to the door a few minutes later and, once inside, found a place on the couch that I could only assume was his spot since the pilling on the cushions was more pronounced there.

I sat down next to him, petting him with one hand and sipping my coffee with the other. Buddy fell back to sleep quickly, his white eyebrows twitching with dreams. Once I was done with my coffee and I didn't think Buddy would notice if I got up, I washed my mug and headed back upstairs to snuggle up to Ransom.

When I entered the room, I was surprised to see he was already awake. His hair stuck up in different directions—messier than usual because of our two days of travel. His eyes were intense and pensive as he stared at his phone, and I didn't think he noticed me when I entered.

He spoke without looking away from his phone. "Hudson wants to go to breakfast this morning. She said Kari's helping set up for the reunion, but she'd like to get together beforehand so things aren't so weird later."

"You should go," I told him, plopping down next to him on the bed.

"She asked if we'd both go."

Well, that was…unexpected. Hudson's reasoning did have its merits. It might be easier for both of us if we at least met with her before introducing—or in Ransom's case, *re*introducing—ourselves to the rest of his family. But it still felt like some sort of an intrusion for me to tag along. He didn't talk to his sister much, and he hadn't seen her in years. It made more sense, at least to me, for just the two of them to go.

"I mean … I'll go. If you want me to. But if you wanna go by yourself, I totally get it. It might be easier to talk without an outsider there."

"You're not an outsider," Ransom assured me, his head snapping toward me apologetically, even though he didn't have anything to be sorry for.

"I know. I just meant—"

"Hudson should be the one who feels weird, not you."

I understood what he was saying even though he hadn't explicitly vocalized it, and it shouldn't have made me feel as good as it did. That was his sister—his blood. But the connection Ransom and I had was stronger than the one he had with his own sibling. And while that made me feel sad for Ransom and Hudson because circumstances beyond their control had driven them apart, the realization that our bond was stronger than theirs didn't feel all bad. I could be a pretty shitty person sometimes.

When I didn't answer, he spoke again. "I don't know what to tell her. I haven't answered yet and I feel like I should go, but I don't wanna go without you."

"Okay, I'll go," I said, trying my best not to be nervous for the both of us.

"But I don't want you to feel *forced* to go either."

"I don't feel forced."

"Or not forced, necessarily. I know you don't think I'm making you do something. More like you feel that—"

"Ransom, I get it. You don't have to explain. I'd feel the same way if I were in your position." Or I thought so, at least. There was no way I could know for sure.

He sighed heavily as he typed out a reply, and I couldn't help but wonder if I'd taken the weight that had been on his shoulders and placed it on my own.

Chapter Twelve

TAYLOR

Ransom was nearly vibrating with...something when we arrived at the diner where we were meeting his sister. I wasn't sure if it was excitement, anxiety, or a combination of the two, but the grunts I'd received in response to my first attempts at conversation kept me from asking further. He seemed to want to be alone with his thoughts, and I was happy to let him work through whatever he needed to.

He clutched my hand in his as he scanned the fifties-themed diner for Hudson. "There she is," he said breathily before giving me a soft tug and leading me to a booth along a wall of windows.

The nineteen-year-old girl brightened when she saw him, standing as we approached.

She looked as all-American girl as I'd expected, being related to Ransom. Her hair was a light brown, but she had the same gleaming blue eyes as her brother. She was willowy and pretty, with a light dusting of freckles across the bridge of her nose.

As soon as Ransom was within reach, she jumped up and threw her arms around his neck. He returned the embrace, lifting her off the ground. They stayed like that for a long moment, and I tried to not seem too awkward as I stood there watching them.

When Ransom put her down, she dashed a hand over her eyes and sniffled before turning to me. "Hi," she said with a wide smile. "You must be Taylor."

I smiled back at her as I stepped forward and held out my hand, which she eagerly grasped. She was a bit shorter than me but had the same confident presence that Ransom did, as if her charisma was a tangible thing.

We shuffled around and slid into the booth, Hudson on one side, Ransom and me on the other. She beamed at him the way one would imagine an adoring younger sister would. It threw me a little because I knew the two seldom spoke. Not out of some kind of dislike, but more born out of the fact that they'd grown up as virtual strangers. Despite that distance, anyone with eyes could see the way Hudson marveled at her brother.

Not that I could blame her. I was pretty sure I often looked at him the same way.

"Jeez, Blink, I can't even believe how grown up you look," Ransom said.

Hudson rolled her eyes. "Oh my God, stop calling me that."

Ransom shrugged, his lips tilted up in a smirk. "It's your name."

"No one calls me that anymore!"

Wait...anymore? "Your name is actually Blink?" The words escaped my mouth before I could process their level of tackiness.

"No," she replied, looking alarmed that I would think she had such a comical name.

"It's one-eighty-two," Ransom supplied.

"One-eighty... what? I need to hear this story."

Hudson covered her face with her hands, which made me even more curious.

"Our mom had a little ... trouble with the birth certificate paperwork," Hudson explained, looking embarrassed. "She accidentally wrote our address on the line where my name was supposed to go."

"Hence, One-eighty-two Hudson Lane Moxon. When I heard it, all I could think of was the band Blink-182, so that's what I called her," Ransom explained as if this was some cute family memory and not the tragic tale of a mother who couldn't even name her kids without fucking it up. "At least Mom noticed her mistake and managed to put our last name in the right spot."

"If she noticed, why didn't she fix it?"

Hudson sighed. "I've asked her. Supposedly a nurse was looking over her shoulder and pointed out the error, but she said she was too embarrassed to admit she messed up, so she just left it."

"That's ... wow."

"I know. I keep meaning to get it changed now that I'm over eighteen, but I just ... haven't. I at least need to get the 182 off there."

"She secretly likes it," Ransom said.

"No. I do not."

"Why wouldn't your mom change it before?" I tried to imagine a mother who hadn't bothered to change her child's name so it didn't match her address. That seemed even more sad than being named that in the first place. It was one thing to make a mistake, but to never try to correct it in nineteen years seemed especially harsh.

Hudson bit her lip. "I lived with my aunt Renee growing up, and she offered to help, but my mom always had legal custody, so we would've had to get her involved and that was difficult on a good day, so we just . . . left it."

I'd never been more thankful for my overbearing father and flaky mother than now. "Elementary school must've been brutal," I remarked.

"Eh, it wasn't too bad. I just owned it, ya know. And I think people felt sort of sorry for me and told their kids not to hassle me about it."

Her response was almost flippant, which made it all the more depressing.

She began to toy with the plastic menu that was on the table. "Enough about me. Tell me about you guys. How was your trip?"

Ransom and I shared a look before he turned to her. "Interesting."

"Cataclysmic," I added.

"But we made it, so . . ." His words trailed off as a teenage boy approached our table.

"Hi, sorry for the wait. I'm Dylan. What do you want to drink?"

"Dylan!" an older woman scolded from where she'd been hovering at the table behind him. "Say 'Can I start you off with something to drink?'"

"That's what I said," Dylan argued.

The woman glared at him, and he huffed before turning his attention back to us. "Can I start you off with something

LET'S NOT & SAY WE DID

to drink? Cyanide? Arsenic?"

"That's it, back into the kitchen with you," the woman said as she grabbed the kid by the collar and tugged.

Dylan laughed. "I'm kidding. They know I was kidding, right?"

"I'm very sorry about him. We're short-staffed, and I thought my son could handle the responsibility." The woman said the words as if each one was a dart aimed at his vital organs.

"I'm so handling it," Dylan said.

"It's fine," Ransom said. "I'll have orange juice and water."

"I'll have the same," Hudson added.

"Me too."

Dylan walked away with his mother whispering harshly in his ear.

"What are you guys getting?" I asked because the table had fallen into an awkward silence after Dylan's departure.

"I'm not sure," Hudson said. "But we should probably get something light. There's going to be enough food at this thing to feed a small army."

"How much family are you expecting?" I asked.

"Tons. I don't even know where they're all coming from. Growing up, it was just Mom, Aunt Renee, and our grandmother. But now all of the sudden there are aunts, uncles, cousins. It's going to be intense."

Ransom stiffened next to me, and I instinctively put a hand on his leg.

"I didn't think there'd be that many people there," he said.

"Me neither. But evidently Grandma is one of *eleven*. I knew she came from a big family, but eleven is ... intense. Like, seriously, did her parents do anything other than each other?"

"That ... didn't need to be said," Ransom replied, looking disgusted.

Hudson smiled. "Sorry."

Dylan came back and handed out our drinks.

We watched the tray teeter precariously on his hand as he unloaded it.

"Whew. That's harder than it looks," he said as he tucked the tray under his arm and pulled a pad of paper from his apron. "You know what you want?"

"Dylan," his mother growled. She was a bit farther away this time but clearly still within earshot.

"I'm so sorry, sir, m'ladies." He added a bow for good measure before continuing. "What fine cuisine can I procure for you on this fine morning?"

We smothered laughs as we ordered. When Dylan had retreated to the kitchen, we exchanged glances and smiled awkwardly, all of us clearly unsure how to pick the conversation up again.

"So," Hudson said after taking a sip of her juice, "how are you feeling about seeing Mom?"

Ransom began mindlessly tearing his napkin into pieces on the table. "Honestly, I'm not sure. I think I feel so many things, it's impossible to sort them out."

"I was kind of surprised you agreed to come. Seeing Mom is one thing, but the rest of the family too? It's a brave move."

Ransom shrugged. "As much as ripping off a Band-Aid can be brave, I guess. It just seemed easier to get it all over with at once. And there will probably be lots of distractions to keep things from getting too awkward."

"That's true," Hudson mused.

I sat silently beside Ransom, my mind full of the things he wasn't saying. That he wouldn't have agreed to come if it hadn't been for me. I knew he and I had already covered all of this, but the guilt continued to gnaw at me. Truth was, Ransom probably wasn't ready to confront his mom, let alone all his extended family. But he was doing it anyway because I'd insisted it would be a good idea.

While part of me wanted to be warmed at the lengths he would go to to make me happy, I couldn't help but feel truly selfish that I'd put him in that position. What did this man even see in me?

"So, Taylor, Ransom told me you're going to be a lawyer?" Hudson asked.

I was a little surprised Ransom had told her anything about me, though I wasn't sure why. Maybe because things between us had been such a whirlwind, and I hadn't known how much he confided in his estranged sister.

"Yeah. I'm just waiting for my LSAT scores, and then I'll start applying to schools."

Saying it out loud made me realize I hadn't checked the email I used for educational and professional purposes. I had it on my phone, but I'd never been able to figure out how to get it to send me alerts for new emails, so I had to remember to check it regularly. Ever since the Brad...*incident*...I hadn't thought to open it.

But now that the thought was in my head, I wasn't able to resist toying with my phone, my fingers itching to open it to check my email.

"That's awesome. Any idea where you want to go?"

I did, but that wasn't a rabbit hole I wanted to go down. It had always been my dream to move to the West Coast after graduation, so it made sense to go to law school out there. But I'd been so focused on the dumpster fire that was my life these past few months that not only had I not given it much more thought, I also hadn't broached the topic with Ransom. Doing so in a diner while we met with the sister he hadn't seen in years didn't feel like the right time to drop that bomb.

"I plan to apply to a bunch of places and see who accepts me. I'll make a decision from there." Which at least wasn't a total lie. I'd always intended to apply locally too, even though that was more of a safety net than anything else.

Hudson's phone dinged with a text, and she picked it up to read it. "Aunt Renee is being weird this week."

"How so?" Ransom asked.

While Hudson explained that their aunt Renee had been snippy the past few days and had been constantly checking in with Hudson, I took the opportunity to surreptitiously open my phone.

I scrolled through my email, and there, like a bright, shining beacon, sat my LSAT results. They'd come through a couple of days ago. What kind of moron planned their entire life around achieving one goal and then went completely brain-dead when they were in the home stretch of achieving that goal?

It had been bad enough that I hadn't put the time I should've into studying for them—even though I had been preparing for them for the past year—but to not have been obsessively checking for my results showed just how crazy my life had become.

I needed to figure out a way to get myself back in order, and I logically knew that involved confronting everything surrounding what had happened with Brad. I just wasn't sure how I was going to do that yet.

"Anyway, enough about her," Hudson said. She turned her attention back to me before I could open the email and actually see my scores. "It must feel so good to know what you want your future to look like. I have no idea what I want to do," Hudson said, her voice sounding a little sad.

"You're still young. You have plenty of time to figure it out," Ransom said.

"I guess," she said, sounding unconvinced.

"Are you in school or working while you figure it out?" I asked, putting my phone away. It was frustrating to not be able to check them, but it was probably best to wait anyway. I'd need to give the results my undivided attention, and I couldn't do that yet. Not to mention I was pretty sure I hadn't done well and would rather be alone when I sobbed into a pillow for hours.

"I wanted to take classes, but . . ." She shrugged instead of finishing her sentence.

"But what?" Ransom prompted.

She toyed with the tip of her straw instead of making eye contact with Ransom. "Aunt Renee thought it was a waste of time. Mom agreed."

I felt Ransom tense beside me. "Why would it be a waste of time?"

Hudson smiled, but it didn't reach her eyes. "I wasn't exactly an honor roll student in high school. They didn't think it was worth throwing money away for classes I probably wouldn't pass."

"That's bullshit," Ransom said, his voice practically a snarl. "If you were taking classes you were interested in, you'd probably do really well."

"I dunno. Aunt Renee always said it was good I was pretty. Otherwise I'd be up a creek without a paddle." Hudson said the words as if they were a joke, but it was obvious they hurt her.

It wasn't the first time I'd felt the desire to beat the shit out of their aunt. When I'd heard how she'd taken Hudson while leaving Ransom to fend for himself in the foster care system, I'd instantly wanted to inflict bodily harm on the woman. But hearing how she'd basically told her niece that her only aspirations should be to become a trophy wife made me want to murder her.

And unfortunately for her, that wasn't completely out of my wheelhouse anymore.

"Hudson, listen to me, okay?" Ransom said seriously as he slid his forearms onto the table so he could lean toward his sister. "People told me shit like that my entire life. Between my ADHD and dyslexia, most people didn't think I'd amount to much. It's why I focused so much on football. All it took was the Holts believing I could, and I want to be that for you. You can accomplish anything you want. And I'll be there to help you any way I can."

She smiled a small, shy grin that demonstrated how much his words meant to her. "Thank you. I'll keep that in mind."

"Please do," he said, his words pleading, as if he was begging her to believe in herself.

I'd already felt grateful to Melissa's family for, in many ways, saving Ransom and allowing him to grow into the wonderful man he was meant to be. But the full force of how differently his life might have been without them made my eyes prick with tears. He deserved the world, and he'd come so close to never realizing that.

Our breakfast came soon after, dangling precariously from Dylan's spindly limbs. But he managed to set everything down without dropping anything, and we settled into lighter conversation as we ate. Ransom settled the tab when we were done, and we walked outside, telling Hudson we'd follow her to the reunion, which was set to start in about fifteen minutes.

After turning on Matt's SUV, Ransom turned to me. "Ready for this shitshow?"

"Born ready," I joked. "Are you ready?" I asked more seriously.

He gave me a small smile. "As I'll ever be."

And as he pulled out in traffic behind Hudson, I guessed that would have to be enough.

Chapter Thirteen

RANSOM

We pulled into the parking lot next to Hudson's small blue Civic. I took in the large park sprawled in front of us and saw people bustling about, putting the finishing touches on various things for the reunion. The lot had a number of cars already in it, and others were pulling in around us.

Suddenly, things felt very, very real.

My breath quickened as I wondered what these people would think of me, what I'd talk to them about, what painful memories might resurface.

A hand on my arm, giving it a gentle but firm squeeze, pulled my mind from the what-ifs. I turned to find Taylor looking at me, concern evident on her face.

"You okay?" she asked.

"Yeah," I croaked. *Jesus.* I cleared my throat before continuing. "Yeah, I'm fine."

She studied me for a second before sitting back in her seat. "What's the worst-case scenario?"

I huffed out a humorless laugh. "I'm not sure I even want

to think about the *worst*-case scenario."

"Humor me."

I rubbed my hand through my hair as I thought. "I guess it's that they all think I'm not worth knowing. Or someone says something nasty and I start a brawl."

Her jaw worked as she sat silently for a moment before shifting her body to face me. "These people... I get they're your family, but they're strangers too. And they didn't have to be. A lot of them *chose* to be. It's not you who should worry about *their* judgments. *They* should worry about *yours*. You're here, giving them a chance that most of them probably don't even deserve. And if they don't see that for the gift it is, then *fuck* them. All of them."

She reached out and gently caressed my cheek with her fingertips. "They don't determine your worth, Ransom. You know who you are. You know what you're worth. And everyone who knows you—truly knows you—is fully aware of what an honor it is to have you in our lives. You're the best person I know. And nothing that happens today will change that. Even if you start a brawl." She said the last part with a smile, and I was thankful she could still joke with me about something like this after all that happened with Brad.

Maybe I was reading too much into it, but it made me feel as if she knew I'd never intentionally hurt someone—at least not in a permanent way. While I'd always do what I could to protect her, I wasn't a danger to her or other people. I wasn't even aware I'd been worried she'd be scared of me until she set me at ease about it.

"Thank you," I said.

She gave me a wry look. "You don't really have anything to thank me for. You wouldn't even be facing this situation if it weren't for me."

I looked out the window at where the family I didn't know was gathering and finally felt myself unclench. "I think I needed to face it." Looking at her, I continued. "And I think I needed to face it with you. Knowing you have my back… I can face this because I have you on my side."

She moved so fast she was almost a blur. She pressed her lips to mine in a fierce, though short, kiss and then pulled back just far enough to look me in the eyes. "I will *always* have your back."

"And I'll have yours."

"Good," she said before smacking another kiss to my lips. "Then let's go make this reunion our bitch."

I laughed loudly, the action loosening the remaining heaviness in my chest. "Let's."

We climbed out of the car and made our way to where Hudson was waiting for us. I appreciated that she'd waited, as if she'd sensed I'd need some extra support. I let Hudson lead as we made our way toward a giant table situated at the far end of the grassy park where food was being set up.

"Mom," Hudson said when we got close.

And then there she was. She'd been bent over as she sorted the food, and I hadn't recognized her until she looked up with bright-blue eyes I'd always been told were identical to my own. Her hair was a lighter shade of blond than it had been when I'd been growing up, but it suited her.

She was a bit plumper than she'd been last time I'd seen her, a little more weathered, but I'd still have known her anywhere.

Her eyes widened when she saw me, as if she were surprised, despite knowing I was coming. It took her a moment to react, and we both just stood there and stared at each other as if we were each taking measure of the other. And even though this woman didn't necessarily deserve the consideration, I couldn't help but wonder if I lived up to her expectation.

"Ransom," she whispered, and the word seemed to push her into motion. She came around the table quickly, closing in on me and wrapping me in a tight hug.

It took me a moment to react. I wasn't used to maternal affection from this woman. Even during the better times, she hadn't been very demonstrative. Add that to the fact that I hadn't seen her in close to a decade, and my body had to catch up to my brain and accept that this wasn't a stranger hugging me.

I returned the hug, my hold on her loose and tentative. But my reticence didn't seem to have affected her, because when she pulled back, tears were shining in her eyes and her smile was wide.

She reached up and cupped my cheek. "Look at you. So handsome. It's so good to see you."

I cleared my throat before replying. "It's good to see you too."

She gazed at me for a moment longer before she noticed Taylor standing beside me. Stepping back, she dashed at her eyes before running a hand down her flowy floral shirt. "How rude of me. You must be Taylor. I'm Kari."

Taylor shook the hand my mom had stretched toward her and smiled. "Nice to meet you."

"You too. I'm so glad you both could come." My mom looked around as if the environment would somehow inspire conversation. "Are you hungry? We have tons of food."

"We actually just had breakfast with Hudson," I said.

"Oh, that's right. I knew that. Um, well, do you want me to introduce you around, or...?" She left the sentence hanging there, making it apparent there weren't likely many alternatives to her doing just that.

I wondered who the meet-and-greet portion of the day would be more awkward for—me, my mom, or the rest of the family? For all intents and purposes, I'd been the son who'd been thrown away. But despite how awful it was to feel like trash, it was perhaps even worse for them to be confronted with said trash, knowing they'd been the ones who had discarded it.

Not that my extended family had owed me anything. Most of them had had enough of Kari's shit before I'd even been born and likely had no idea I'd even *been* born, let alone what had become of me. But I still felt like one of their skeletons slipping out of the closet. Would they give me a chance, or would they try to stuff me under the nearest mattress until I was simply a lump that made them marginally uncomfortable when they lay a certain way?

There wasn't much else to do other than find out. But I didn't necessarily want to be pranced around like some kind of show pony my mom tried to sell to potential buyers.

"That's okay," I said. "We'll just... mingle."

My mom looked both apprehensive and relieved. My guess was that she'd known the right thing to do was introduce me, but it also wasn't something she particularly *wanted* to do. Not that I could blame her. I wasn't sure where she stood with the rest of the family, and honestly, it couldn't have been easy to have the child social services had taken away from you show up to an event like this. I gave her credit for wanting me here, even though it highlighted her greatest failure: her inability to take care of her children.

"Okay, well, I'll catch up with you in a bit," Kari said, and I nodded.

I took Taylor's hand in mine and turned to look out over the rest of the park and the people milling around in it.

Hudson stood on my other side. "So, you want to meet the crazy ones, the crazier ones, or the craziest ones?"

I shared a look with Taylor, and she smiled. Turning back to Hudson, I said, "May as well go all in."

Hudson smirked. "Uncle Lester it is."

She started off, and though the evil glint in her eyes made me wary, I followed. Whether it was to my benefit or destruction . . . I guessed I'd find out.

TAYLOR

Uncle Lester could've been anywhere between forty and eighty. His back was slightly rounded, giving him that hunched-over look often associated with old age, but he also used words like *lit* and *salty* and asked if we were coming to "spill the tea" when we walked over.

I only knew he wasn't a teenager because his hands were weathered and the skin on his arms was loose and saggy.

Usually one's face gave the strongest evidence of age, but since Uncle Lester was wearing some sort of Steampunk bird mask, I wasn't getting any help in that department.

"So you became a Yankee, eh?" he asked Ransom, his voice muffled by the mask.

The question made me lean harder toward him being eighty. Or two hundred and eighty.

"Uh, I guess," Ransom answered, his words coming out like a question.

"Shame. Strong fella like you coulda helped the cause."

"Cause?" Ransom asked, and I almost wished he hadn't.

If Uncle Lester started on some sort of Civil War-era, racially charged rant, I was going to explode.

"Yeah. People down here are trying to overturn laws that have ruled our great state since its inception."

I felt Ransom stiffen beside me, but Hudson placed a hand on his arm and whispered, "Wait for it."

"Take my hometown of Gainesville, for example. There, it's illegal to eat a chicken with a fork, a perfectly reasonable law. And people want to overturn it! Everyone knows, chicken is meant to be eaten and enjoyed with your hands. We need all the help fighting off these psychopaths we can get. You look good and intimidatin'. We need more of that down here."

Whew. So Uncle Lester was just insane. What a relief.

Ransom looked flustered, and I'd have felt for him if this weren't one of the most entertaining conversations I'd ever been a part of.

"I don't, uh, I'm pretty settled up there," he said. "Sorry."

The bird head shook back and forth slowly. "Such a pity. Well, let me know if you change your mind. Got a comfortable couch you can stay on until you find your own place. Course, that's where Mable sleeps, but I'm sure she'd share."

"Who's Mable?" I asked, expecting him to say anything from his daughter to a dog.

"My chicken."

Damn, hadn't seen that one coming.

"Don't worry," he continued. "I won't eat her with my hands. And certainly not with a blasted fork!"

"Uncle Lester," Hudson said, leaning toward him, conspiring. "Is that Aunt Fiona over there? I wonder if she ever bought that rake."

"I bet she didn't. She's been a heathen since the womb."
He started to move past us. "Fiona! Fiona, I got a rake to pick
with you."

"Rake?" I asked Hudson as we watched Lester point a
finger at an older woman who looked about ready to physically
remove his head from his body.

"She lives in Acworth, where every citizen *must* own a
rake. She refuses to buy one to drive Lester crazy."

"Seems like an easy task," I muttered.

"Yeah, he's really eccentric but harmless overall. He once
gave me fifty dollars because he said my shoes looked worn."

"That's nice," Ransom said.

"It was. I mean, I'm pretty sure he did it to get under Aunt
Renee's skin, but still. New shoes are new shoes."

Ransom let out a heavy sigh and rolled his shoulders.
"Okay. Who's next?"

"Well, that depends. There's our cousin Ronald, who
always wears fedoras and speaks with a British accent, great-
aunt Hazel, who thinks she can predict your future if she rubs
your feet—sidebar, I'm destined to go on a crime spree that's
somehow caused by a misunderstanding—or Hector. I'm
not sure how we're related to him, but he claims he grew the
world's largest peanut, but due to jealousy and a vicious streak
a mile wide, his wife ate the peanut before them 'boys from
Guinness,' as he called them, could get out there to measure.
He tried gluing the shell back together, but the damage had
been done."

"Wow. Are they still married?" I asked, curious if one
could overcome a betrayal of that magnitude.

"No, they divorced soon after. He still lives in her

basement, though. He had to move down there when she remarried."

I looked over at Ransom. "Holy shit. I think you may be the most normal one here."

"Hey," Hudson protested as Ransom grabbed me in a loose headlock, causing me to burst out laughing.

"You're messing up my hair, you Neanderthal."

"According to Uncle Lester, Georgia needs more Neanderthals."

He let go, and I beamed up at him. "Too bad they can't have you."

"Oh no?" he asked, his eyes sparkling in the sun.

"Nope. You're all mine."

Ransom smiled and was leaning down to kiss me when Hudson said, "That reminds me, I'll have to introduce you to Baxter. He once stole a mannequin from a department store and went running down the street with her, yelling about how she asked to go live with him. Spent some time in the asylum after that stunt." She shook her head sadly. "Never been the same since."

I was just about to beg to never meet this Baxter person, when someone spoke from behind us.

"Ransom?"

We turned to see an older woman with white hair puffed up to make her look about three inches taller than she was. But even with her short stature, there was an intimidating air about her. She was solidly built, but not overweight, and looked like she was more than capable of knocking grown men on their asses.

Mostly, though, it was probably the serious set of her face that made her seem unapproachable. She didn't smile, her brows were held in a rigid line, and her eyes looked almost… disinterested. Like she was deigning to speak to us without any real desire to do so.

"I'm your grandma. Been a long time since I've seen you." She gave Ransom a quick look over. "Looks like you grew up all right."

I wanted to say something spiteful like it was no thanks to her that was the case, but I held it back. I don't think she missed the sharp intake of breath I'd taken, making it clear I'd wanted to interject but hadn't.

"Who's this?" she asked, sounding like she expected him to say I was some grifter he'd picked up on the way down here.

Ransom wrapped his arm tighter around me. "This is my girlfriend, Taylor. Taylor, this is my grandma Irene."

"Taylor," she repeated. "Never really understood people who used last names for first names."

"Hmm, Hudson must've been a hard sell for you, then," I snapped back before I could censor myself.

She raised one of her eyebrows slightly, and if I had to guess, I would've said she looked almost impressed by my retort. If she was, she was in for a treat. I had snark for days ready for this lady.

We all stood there looking at each other. It was clear none of us knew what to say, and since everything that entered my mind contained an expletive, I decided to sit this one out.

Hudson moved toward Ransom and embraced his arm. "Isn't he handsome, Grandma? And smart. He's getting his master's degree."

Ransom shuffled a little, looking uncomfortable by the praise, probably because it sounded like Hudson was trying to sell her grandmother on him—something that shouldn't have been necessary. But I gave her credit for trying. The poor girl was in a difficult position, and she was doing her best to navigate it with a sunny smile and a positive attitude.

"That's nice," the older woman said, sounding as someone might when accepting a preschool art project covered in glue and popsicle sticks. "What in?"

"Sports medicine," Ransom replied.

She nodded. "That makes sense. You always were good at sports. Shame what happened at Ohio."

Ransom was visibly taken aback, likely shocked she knew anything about his interests, let alone the career-ending knee injury he'd suffered in college.

"Yeah," he said, his voice thick. "Figured becoming an athletic trainer or physical therapist would let me still have something to do with the game. Especially since football was the only thing I was ever really good at."

"Well, it's good to play to your strengths," his grandmother said.

I wasn't sure if Ransom had said what he did thinking that being self-deprecating would endear him to her or if he really thought he wasn't good at anything else, but I couldn't let this woman or Ransom, for that matter, think he was short on talents.

"That's not the only thing he's good at," I said. "He's great with kids. He's by far the most popular counselor at the after-school program where we work. He's also who our boss there trusts the most because he's dependable and responsible. He's on track to graduate from his program with high honors, he's funny, he's kind, he's a great friend and an even better boyfriend. There's nothing he can't do if he sets his mind to it."

I was nearly out of breath when I finished my diatribe, but

I didn't regret a word of it. Maybe I was guilty of the same thing Hudson had done—tried to make Ransom sound good to his grandmother. But fuck it. Nothing I said had been a lie, and if she'd made any attempt to know him, I wouldn't have had to tell her anything. She would've already found it out for herself.

She was quiet for a moment, lips pursed. "That's quite a list. Did y'all practice that on the way down?" She smirked as if her words were funny.

Ransom cleared his throat. "Why would we do that? It would imply a desire to impress you. Something I can assure you I feel no need to do."

His grandmother appraised him before giving him a full smile, without any hint of malice or judgment. "I'm glad to hear it. No one here is worth trying to impress." She stepped forward and reached out, patting Ransom on the forearm. "I'm glad you came, Ransom. And I'm glad you managed to turn out so well. God knows we weren't much help to you in that regard."

She cast a brief look in my direction before turning her attention back to him, her lips clearly fighting a smile. "Maybe your guard dog will let us visit a little more later." And with that, she began to walk off.

"Did she just call me a dog?" I asked loudly, causing the infuriating woman to cackle as she headed toward another group of people.

Hudson looked perplexed. "I don't think I've ever heard her laugh like that."

"I tend to bring the best out in people," I replied.

Ransom snorted at that, the jerk.

Chapter Fourteen

RANSOM

I'd spoken to so many people within the first hour of arriving at the reunion that my throat had started to ache. At some point, Hudson had wandered off, leaving us to tackle the masses on our own. Most people had been genial and welcoming, even if there seemed to be an alarming number of eccentric personalities in my family.

But then there were people like the ones we'd found ourselves stuck talking to for the past few minutes, like Cal. He'd introduced himself as my mother's distant cousin but also as my great-uncle. When Taylor had looked at him quizzically, he'd shrugged and said he'd "married twins."

I had no idea how that would impact his place in my family tree, but I was also fairly certain I didn't want to find out.

When my gaze drifted to the woman beside him, who I assumed was his wife, he said, "Oh, Billy Jo's not one of them. We met after I divorced the first twin for the second time."

Wow. For a somewhat portly and homely man, "Uncle" Cal seemed to get a lot of action.

"This is my oldest son, Cal Jr. Junior, meet your cousin . . . I'm sorry, I'm not sure I ever knew your name."

I felt Taylor take a step forward, and I imagined it was so she could rip Cal's head from his body, but I reached out to grab her hand, shooting her what I hoped was a calming look. It didn't seem to work. She looked furious, and oddly, that made me less so.

This clown was no one to me. The people who knew and loved me were in my corner, and that's what mattered. The fact that Taylor felt each slight against me so viscerally made me feel whole in a way I wasn't sure I ever had.

I extended my hand. "Ransom."

Cal Jr. clasped it, pumping it once as his father slapped his rotund belly like some sort of down-on-his-luck Santa Claus.

"I *did* know that," he said through guffaws. "We had a good laugh about that one when you were born. Ransom. For the love of Pete, what was Kari thinking?" He sobered, but the mirth didn't leave his eyes—though it did morph into something decidedly crueler. "Though I guess you and I both know she wasn't exactly thinking straight, was she, *Ransom*?"

That sent him into peals of laughter again, and despite my earlier feelings of calm, rage was quickly bubbling up.

"It is funny, isn't it?" Taylor said beside me.

I snapped my attention to her, the hurt crushing my chest as if an anvil had been dropped on it. Though when I looked at her, I noticed she wasn't laughing.

"It's almost as funny as some hillbilly with a twin fetish mocking his own family at what should be a celebration of his relationship with them."

Cal's laughter slowed as he swept his glinty stare over Taylor. "You talkin' about me?" He chewed the inside of his cheek as he forced a neutral expression to his face.

I assumed the psychopathic nonchalance he was trying to exude was something he thought made him more intimidating. Instead, it made him look like a constipated actor who was working too hard to sell his lines.

"Hmm, clever too," Taylor replied. "That's a surprise."

A flush crept up Cal's neck as his anger seemed to be literally bubbling to the surface. He took a step toward her, his finger outstretched. "Now you listen—"

That's as far as he got. Instinctively, I'd moved to fill the space between them, causing Cal's finger to graze my chest before he quickly retracted it. I had at least four inches on the man, causing him to have to tilt his head back to look me in the face. And from the way his eyes widened, I'd hazard a guess he didn't enjoy the position he found himself in.

"You say one word out of line to her," I growled, "and you'll be leaving here in an ambulance. Got it?"

A slither of fear slid through his gaze at my threat, but as he registered the small crowd that had gathered around us, he puffed up like the proud little rooster he clearly was and attempted to shrug my warning off as he stepped back.

"Threatening your family, huh?" His attention shifted briefly to Taylor. "Wish I could say *I* was surprised. Being a criminal is pretty much in your blood."

His words were exactly what I'd feared before we'd come, and despite them coming from a man who was clearly a total lowlife, it still stung. I tried to maintain a blank facade, but from the way his lips turned into a smirk, he knew his words had left a mark.

I felt Taylor move behind me, but whatever she was going to say was cut off by a voice that was so icy, it likely could've been used to combat global warming.

"Must be," Grandma Irene said, her eyes holding so much malice, Pennywise the Clown would think twice before fucking with her. "Especially since *you* also share that blood. Between that *lady friend* you got caught with in your car a while back and that restitution you had to pay your boss after parts from his shop were magically found in your garage, it seems being a criminal is something you have a bit of expertise in."

"I was set up. Damn cops in town have it out for me," Cal blustered, spittle flying from his mouth in his frenzy to defend himself.

"Hmm, yes, you with your pants around your knees as a woman somehow fell, openmouthed, onto your...member definitely screams setup. What was her name? Cherry? Candy? I forget. Didn't forget the rumor she may have been a minor, though. Care to clear that one up for us?"

"I ... I ... I can't believe ... you ..." Cal scrambled to form his thoughts as he gestured to me, apparently caught off guard by my grandmother's attack of him in defense of me.

She moved in on him, sliding her small body between him and me, her eyes never leaving his. "You can't believe what? That I'd put all your business in the street? Or park, as it were. Guess it's been too long since you've seen me, Calvin. You've clearly forgotten how long my memory is and that all gossip trains run through my station first and foremost. Oh, and that I don't give a flying fuck about you and yours. So you better get away from my grandson before I start talking about what really landed you in Georgia State Prison a few years back."

Cal had grown progressively paler as my grandmother spoke, and he stood there, gaping like a fish, as she continued to stare him down. Finally, he cleared his throat and took a quick look around before uttering a brusque "let's go" to his family, who filed behind him like stupid little ducklings.

Once he was far enough away, my grandmother turned and said to the crowd that had gathered, "What do y'all look so surprised about? It's not a Moxon reunion if there's not a row smack in the middle of it."

That broke the tension, causing everyone to chuckle as they dispersed.

My grandmother stayed in front of me, waiting until everyone was out of earshot before asking, "You okay?"

"Yeah. Yeah, I'm fine. Thanks." *Thanks.* The word was so insufficient to express what I felt. Having her defend me felt . . . fulfilling. As if a hole I hadn't even known I'd been carrying around inside was a little less empty.

She reached up and patted me on the cheek twice, a small smile playing on her lips. "Don't mention it. I love getting the chance to unleash my inner bitch once in a while." She peered around me to where Taylor stood. "How about you, honey?"

At some point, Taylor had fisted the back of my shirt, and I felt her pull it even tighter when my grandmother addressed her.

"I'm . . . I don't know what I am," Taylor answered.

"He's a vicious bastard. Don't let him get to ya."

"Oh, no, I'm not . . . He's not worth my energy. But . . ." Taylor trailed off, and I turned so I could wrap an arm around her shoulders and pull her beside me.

My grandmother stood and waited for Taylor to finish.

Once she'd nestled into me, Taylor released a breath. "I was trying really hard to not like you, but damn, that was impressive."

My eyes widened. I couldn't believe Taylor had actually

just said that out loud.

But my grandma simply laughed loudly. "I have my moments."

"That was a seriously epic moment. I'm sad I didn't film it so I could study your ways."

"Oh honey, I have no doubt that by the time you're my age, you'll have far surpassed my bitchiness."

That had sounded like an insult to me, but Taylor beamed, so I guessed this was a woman thing I was never gonna understand.

The smile fell from my grandmother's lips, but there was still laughter in her eyes. "I'd like to take the two of you to dinner after this circus is over. I think it would be nice for us to . . . reconnect in a setting where there aren't a bunch of busybodies wandering about."

I looked over at Taylor, who shrugged as if to say it was okay with her, before replying. "Sure. We'd like that."

"Good. I'll invite your mom and Hudson along." With that decided, she turned to where the food was being unwrapped in preparation for everyone eating. "Good Lord, Lucille, why don't you just send out an engraved invitation to every bug within a mile? Sweet Jesus." And with that, she stalked off toward whoever Lucille was.

Taylor and I stood beside each other in silence for a second before she broke it. "You know, I need to thank you."

I jerked my head to look at her. "For what?"

"My mom, who's basically a transient with expensive taste, has never seemed as normal as she does after spending an afternoon with your family."

I shot her a droll look. "So happy I could improve your assessment of your mom."

She wrapped her arms around my bicep and rested her head against me. "Despite the insanity that must be some kind of hereditary trait, I have to say, a lot of these people are pretty great. Uncle Cal notwithstanding."

I dropped a kiss to the top of her head and said, "You're so twisted."

And while she laughed at my words, I noticed she didn't argue. We really were a match made in heaven.

Chapter Fifteen

TAYLOR

As I watched Ransom play football with a group of kids, I couldn't help but smile. Even though I got to watch him with kids on a regular basis, there was something about seeing him interact with them while playing a sport he clearly loved.

Maybe it was because Safe Haven was a job and we had to be somewhat responsible there, whereas here, Ransom seemed to not think twice about knocking eight-year-olds to the grass if they got in his way. But he also seemed...freer here. He celebrated with the kids, lifting them up on his shoulders when one of them scored, and he also trash-talked them, laughing loudly when one of them gave as good as he got.

I inwardly groaned. As if Ransom needed to get *more* appealing. God.

Deciding I needed to stop perving on him while he played with children, I took out my phone and opened my email. My LSAT scores were still there waiting for me.

Part of me was desperate to see how I did, while the other part was worried that if I'd done poorly, I'd be in a mood for the rest of the day. I'd never intentionally ruin Ransom's time with his family, but I was worried I wouldn't be able to pretend well enough for him not to notice something was up with me.

That said, I wasn't sure I could wait. Having waited this long already made me feel like I had restraint rivaled only by Wonder Woman. I was just about to click open the results when someone sat beside me.

I turned to see Kari, who was watching Ransom with a soft look on her face.

"He's something else, isn't he?" she said, her voice full of awe and pride and maybe a bit of relief as well.

I smiled, setting my phone down and joining her in watching the man I was sure we both loved, because really, who wouldn't? To not love Ransom would've exposed Kari as the monster it was easy to label her as, but I didn't think it was that simple. In reality, as I watched her watch her son, I felt that Kari was probably incredibly complicated.

"He was always...good. I don't mean behavior-wise, because that boy could test the patience of a saint with how high-energy he was, but he was always kind in a way others weren't." She hesitated, letting her head drop for a moment before lifting it again. "He wasn't shown a lot of kindness growing up." She turned to face me, looking alarmed. "Not that I ever let anyone hurt him. Physically at least."

I didn't react other than to offer her a small smile. I didn't have words to give her. She should've done better by Ransom, and there was no reason to act like we didn't both know it. But it could've been worse—*she* could've been worse. And it seemed like a disservice to not acknowledge that her intentions hadn't been bad, even if her follow-through was shit.

"But people weren't *nice* either," she continued. "They

put him down, and I let them. Not just people I brought around when I was high, but people who should've known better. Been better." She gave me a humorless smile. "Including me."

"I'm not sure I'm the one you should be saying this to," I said, not because I didn't want to hear it, but because I shouldn't be the one to hear it *first*.

She brought up her legs so she could hug her knees. "I know," she said quietly. "It's just . . . hard. I don't know why it's harder to tell him than it is to tell a stranger."

"Maybe because my opinion doesn't matter," I offered.

She looked at me for a moment before nodding. "Yeah. Yeah, that's probably it. Not that I don't care about what you think. You're clearly important to Ransom, and I value you because of that, but . . . yeah."

We sat there quietly for a bit, watching Ransom drag four kids over the goal line as they tried to prevent him from scoring.

Kari laughed beside me. "I know I don't deserve it, but I hope he'll give me another chance to know him."

I bit my lip, wondering what to say. I didn't want to speak for Ransom or betray him in any way. But I also thought Ransom wanted to have a relationship with his mom, and whatever he wanted, I wanted to do my best to get for him.

"I think letting him know you *want* another chance would go a long way to convincing him to give you one. And then maybe patience with a good dose of perseverance mixed in will help him see you're in it for the long haul but won't push, either."

She pursed her lips, seeming to run over what I'd said. Then she gave a single, emphatic nod. "I can do that."

For Ransom's sake, I truly hoped she could.

After a few more minutes, Kari spoke again. "I'm going to go check in and make sure no one needs help with anything. My mom told me about dinner. I'm looking forward to getting to know you better." She cast a look at the field. "Both of you."

"Me too," I said with a smile.

She started to walk away, and I turned back to the game, but her voice startled me a few seconds later. "Thank you."

I looked up at her in confusion. "What for?"

"For looking at him the way you do." Then she walked away, and I watched her go before refocusing on my man. I wasn't sure how I looked at him, but if it was with half the love I felt for him, I was sure it was an intense thing to witness, and I was glad it was so apparent to others. Ransom deserved that.

I watched the rest of the game, my fingers twirling my phone, but I didn't open it. The conversation with Kari highlighted how today wasn't about me. There'd be time for LSAT results later.

A little while later, Ransom ambled over to me, slightly out of breath and sweaty—which was how I liked him best. He dropped to the ground, stole a large gulp of the water bottle I had resting beside me, and then flopped back onto the grass.

The tree behind us offered a decent amount of shade from the Georgia sun. While it wasn't as warm as I'd expected—due to my limited knowledge of geography, I'd assumed most southern states never dipped below seventy degrees—I could see how he'd have gotten hot running around.

"Tired?" I asked.

"Exhausted."

"Hmm, who'd have thought the big, strong college football player would be wiped out by a bunch of kids?"

He moved the arm he had resting over his eyes so he could

glare at me. "Really?"

"What?" I said innocently. "Just an observation."

"They were like a wild pack of dogs. Lawless and untrained."

"Mm-hmm."

"It's amazing I made it out of there alive."

"Definitely," I said, clearly patronizing him.

"I have the stamina of a stallion."

A snort burst out of me, and by the way his lips were thinned as if he were fighting a smile, I knew he was equally amused. It felt good to banter with him. Over the past week, we'd been stuck in an us-against-the-world mentality, but it was fun to get back to how we started: teasing each other mercilessly.

"Is it an aged stallion that you're referring to, or...?"

His eyes danced, and I was struck by what a good look happiness was on him. "Behave, or I'll show you just how young and virile I am."

I scrunched up my face. "Is that supposed to be a threat? If so, you're really bad at them."

"Behave," he said through a grin.

"Me? You're the one who came over here all"—I waved my hand in his general direction—"like that and started making suggestive comments."

"Are you saying you want me to do more than make suggestions?"

"When are you going to stop asking questions with obvious answers?"

He waggled his eyebrows in response, causing me to scoff in mock disgust.

"Whatever."

He rolled over to his stomach, which put him closer to me, his side brushing up against me. "When we're not in the middle of a field surrounded by my family, I'll try to be more ... vague with my questioning."

"Hmm, how are you going to do that?" I asked. My voice sounded breathy and needy, and Jesus Christ, this was inappropriate on so many levels.

He thought for a minute, his eyes blazing into mine, before he spoke. "I might ask how wet you are. After your shower, of course."

I huffed out a small laugh, even though the low, husky note in his voice was also a major turn-on. "Is that all?"

"It'll be Christmas in a little over a month. I've been wondering how big of a ... package you might want. Maybe we can discuss that later."

"Sounds like a worthy discussion."

"Maybe I'll get you a drum set. You know, so we can do a lot of ... banging on it."

Laughter won over sexual tension, and I collapsed beside him, my body shaking from his ridiculousness. By the time I calmed down, we were lying face-to-face, and he had an arm wrapped around me. I lifted my hand so I could trail my fingertips down his cheek. "No one makes me laugh like you."

He hugged me tighter. "They better not."

"No one makes me happier, either."

Looking deep into my eyes, he said, "Ditto." Then he pressed a kiss to my lips that was much too short, though probably adequate considering where we were.

We basked in each other's presence for a minute before I sat up again, not wanting his family to think we were getting it on in the grass.

"Your mom came to talk to me."

He groaned and pushed himself up so he was sitting as well. "You have the shittiest segues."

"Sorry not sorry."

"I saw her over here. What was she saying?"

I shrugged. "Just how happy she was that you found such an amazing girlfriend and that you should probably spoil me to make sure I never leave you."

"Sounds about right."

"She's probably going to pull you aside at some point. She's . . . proud of you. And happy at how great you turned out. As she damn well should be."

"Easy, tiger," he said as he leaned over and lightly nipped my shoulder.

"Savage," I said as I flicked him away.

He was quiet for a second and then said with so much nonchalance that it seemed forced, "My aunt Renee hasn't come over to talk to me."

"Is she here?"

"I've caught a few glimpses of her, but she's kept her distance. I wonder if it's intentional or if I'm just reading too much into it."

I could tell that the idea of it potentially being intentional bothered him, so I did the only thing I could think of: deflect. "Maybe she's intimidated by what a strong, attractive physical specimen you've brought with you today."

"Hudson isn't that strong."

I scoffed and backhanded him lightly. Then I scooted closer and let my head rest on his shoulder. "I'm sure it's just a coincidence." I hadn't meant the words as an empty platitude. What could the reason be for her to stay away? If Ransom's mom and grandmother had embraced his being there, why would his aunt have an issue?

Ransom sighed. "I guess we'll see."

We would. And I hoped for Renee's safety, it was all a misunderstanding. Because I wouldn't hesitate to cut a bitch.

RANSOM

Once the reunion had wound down, Hudson found me and said our grandma had suggested dinner at a small restaurant about ten minutes up the street. She rode with us so we wouldn't get lost, and my mom and grandma followed.

I hadn't expected Aunt Renee to show up, but she walked in behind the other two women as if she were being led to her execution while sucking on lemons. That was one question answered: she had been avoiding me on purpose at the reunion.

She made no move to greet me in any way and seemed determined to look anywhere but in my direction. I wasn't even sure why she'd come if she didn't want to be here, but the sharp glare my grandma shot her gave me some clue.

Despite it being Saturday, we didn't have to wait long for a table, which I was thankful for since the dark cloud that was my aunt Renee had made it tense as we all stood there awkwardly. Taylor and Hudson had done their best to lighten the atmosphere, but even they were strained for topics as they remarked on how retro the wood paneling on the walls was and whether "that guy over there looks like Chris Hemsworth or Chris Evans."

When the hostess showed us to our table, there was some odd version of musical chairs played before we all settled. My grandmother wanted me to sit more toward the middle of the table, which made Renee roll her eyes and plop down at one end of the rectangular table.

Once the hostess left us with our menus, my mom opened hers with a flourish and said, "What does everyone feel like?"

"A drink," Renee muttered as she looked around, likely for our server.

I saw my mom tense, but she didn't comment. Hudson also cast nervous glances around the table, even though she pretended to be focusing on her menu.

Grandma Irene had no such hesitation. "What else is new?" she said. She'd tossed the question out casually, but it landed like a grenade, causing all of us to turn to Renee so we could watch her reaction, which was positively glacial.

"I think you mistook me for your *other* daughter," Renee shot back, casting a vicious look at Kari.

My mom seemed to draw in on herself, dropping her head and putting her hands in her lap. I wondered about their relationship and why my mom didn't stand up for herself, but I was completely out of my depth with these people. Their dynamic was nuts, and I hated that I'd been dragged into what was clearly old and deep family drama.

My grandmother still never looked up from her menu as she hummed. "Did I? I don't think so." Then she set her menu down and looked at my mother. "Kari, when was the last time you had a drink?"

My mom looked like she wished the floor would open and swallow her into any of the circles of hell—which was fair since I was certain hell was less hostile than this environment at the moment.

"Uh, it's been, um …" She cleared her throat. "It's been

sixteen months and a few days."

"Each day is an accomplishment," Grandma prodded. "Take credit for them all. How many days?"

"Seventeen."

Grandma didn't smile at my mom, but the look on her face was clearly pleased. Proud, even. Then she glared down the table at Renee. "See? I got it right after all."

Renee scoffed. "Because she's known for being so honest."

My grandmother set her arms on the table so she could lean forward and have a more direct line of sight to her daughter. "When you said you were joining us, I told you I expected you to be civil. If that's something you're incapable of, you know where the door is."

Wait? Renee chose to come?

"I was. You're the one giving me a hard time," Renee argued.

Grandma Irene rolled her eyes, but the arrival of our server kept her from replying.

Once we'd ordered drinks and been read the specials, we were left alone again.

Irene, probably in an attempt to move to safer topics, turned her attention to Taylor. "So tell me, Taylor, what do you do?"

Taylor looked a little startled at having been addressed, but she recovered quickly. "Oh, um, I'm finishing my last semester of school."

"What's your major?"

"Criminal justice."

Renee scoffed again. "What does someone do with a degree in that?"

Taylor stared at Renee, her gaze unwavering. "Go to law school."

That shut Renee up pretty quickly.

"What law school are you going to?" Kari asked, her voice carrying genuine interest.

Taylor smiled at her. "I'm not sure yet. I have applications ready to go to a few schools, but I need to wait to get my LSAT scores before sending them out. Since I don't plan on starting until next fall, I still have a bit of time."

That caught my attention, and I felt like the worst boyfriend ever for not asking about it sooner. "Shouldn't you be getting your results soon?"

She hesitated, not enough so that anyone else would've noticed, but I definitely did. "Yeah. Any day now."

I narrowed my eyes slightly to show my confusion, but Taylor averted hers and picked up the water glass the server had filled. Figuring this wasn't the time to get into it, I let it go. For the moment.

"That's exciting," Hudson said, her smile genuine.

"If I pass it will be," Taylor replied with a self-deprecating laugh.

I reached over and gave her thigh a squeeze. "You will." And I believed it. While I knew she'd had a lot on her plate these past few months, I also knew she was wickedly smart. And if she didn't pass this time, she could always take them again. Though having a potential murder investigation hanging over us probably wouldn't help her concentration.

But it would be okay. I'd deal with all of that once we were back home. And while I could never push what had happened from my mind, I tried to push it to the back. It gnawed at me, knowing that I was finally getting to know my biological family, despite the fact that the impression they were getting of me would be shot to shit once I went to the police and confessed everything.

I'd be exactly what Cal and probably Renee thought I was. Even worse, maybe. They'd probably feel vindicated in their dislike of me once the news broke, but I hoped I at least made enough of an impression on Irene, Kari, and Hudson that they wouldn't think I was a monster.

And maybe I shouldn't even care about what they thought. Maybe their opinions didn't deserve to matter to me at all. But on some level, they did, and there was nothing I could do to alter that fact.

Taylor gave me a grateful smile before our attention was once again stolen by the server delivering our drinks. Then he took our orders before retreating again.

We all sat in silence for a second before Hudson broke it. "How much longer do you have before you finish school, Ransom?"

I sat back and tried to clear my brain of my maudlin thoughts and focus on the present. "One more semester." Despite my best attempts, I couldn't stop the errant thought that that semester might never get completed if I went to prison.

"That's amazing," Kari gushed. "I'm ... I'm not sure I have a right to feel this way, but ... I'm proud of you and all you've accomplished. It had to have been incredibly hard, but you never gave up."

She might have been right. Maybe she *didn't* have a right to be proud, considering the lack of any role she'd played in my success. But all the same, her words hit somewhere deep inside me and soothed a hurt that had probably been aching for most of my life.

"Thank you," I said, my voice rough with emotion I tried like hell to conceal.

LET'S NOT & SAY WE DID

Taylor's hand found mine under the table and twined them together.

"Please," Renee said. "We all know he isn't capable of getting through college, let alone a master's program, on his own. Probably paid someone to do his work."

I felt blindsided by the words from a woman who didn't know the first thing about me. Sure, the kid she'd known hadn't had an easy time of it. Between my ADHD and dyslexia, school was a disaster. But I was nine years old the last time she saw me. She had no idea how hard I'd worked to overcome all my troubles to make sure I had a shot at a better future.

"You don't know anything about what I'm capable of."

She rolled her eyes in dismissal as she took a gulp of the vodka on the rocks she'd ordered.

"What exactly is your problem?" Taylor said, her voice loud enough to attract the attention of those at nearby tables.

Renee set her glass down and bored her eyes into Taylor. "Be careful who you're speaking to like that, little girl."

"Or you'll do . . . what?" Taylor asked.

"Aunt Renee, please," Hudson pleaded quietly as I whispered in Taylor's ear that it was okay.

"The hell it is," she replied.

"See! This! *This* is my problem," Renee practically yelled, interrupting my attempts to calm Taylor. "Everyone is all of the sudden Team Ransom. He went off and found himself a new family, and we're supposed to just welcome him back into this one like some kind of prodigal son. He was nothing but trouble when he was a kid and probably isn't any better now, but we're all supposed to just forget that he was a thorn in all our sides, causing social services to be all up in our business for *years*. Now you all want to act like he's some messiah."

She stood, causing her chair to topple backward. "I've had to listen to Kari and Hudson drone on about the wonderful Ransom for the past few months, like he's something special. Well, it must've been nice for you"—she pointed at me—"to be getting a fancy college degree and living your life while everyone back here acts like you walk on water. Meanwhile, I've been taking care of everybody, raising kids that aren't mine, and spending money I don't have. But *you're* the hero of this situation? It's bullshit. You were a good-for-nothing kid, and you're probably a good-for-nothing man."

I let each of her words collect within me until I too rose from my chair, though it felt more as if I'd levitated, my anger rising like a wave beneath me. The words that were on the tip of my tongue would be enough to drown us all if I let them.

My mom finally spoke up, saying, "That's enough, Renee. You have no right to—"

I lifted a hand to silence her. While it was appreciated, I hadn't needed her to fight my battles in a long time.

"So that's what it is, Renee?" I said. "You think *you're* the hero? Why? Because you swooped in to save your niece while sending your nephew to foster care? Because you justified that decision by whispering poison in everyone's ears, much like the shit you're saying now?"

Some of her bravado faded, but that didn't slow me down. She wasn't the only one with things to get off her chest, and I was damn well going to be heard.

"Enlighten us," I continued. "Is it because I proved you wrong? Is it because you feel guilty that I was clearly capable of more than you ever gave me credit for? Or is it the glaring evidence that all it takes to be successful in life is to get the hell away from you?"

Taylor stood beside me and hugged my arm. Whether it was in support or to keep me from flying over the table at Renee, I wasn't sure, but I appreciated it all the same.

"You can sit there with your self-righteous opinions of who I am and what I'm capable of. You can try to justify how you treated me with these myths you've fabricated about the kind of man I am. But the reality is, you don't have the slightest clue about me or my life because you *chose* not to know. And that's what kills you. No offense to anyone, but I'm the most successful and functional person at this table, and you had no part in it. And that's what bothers you the most, isn't it? You have to live with all the guilt and without any of the credit."

She scoffed. "I don't feel any guilt. You weren't my son. I didn't owe you anything."

I used my legs to scoot my chair back and stepped away from the table, Taylor close beside me. "You're right. You didn't. You don't. But you feel it anyway, don't you? You have to. Otherwise you wouldn't have come here to tell me how much I don't belong. You need me gone because I'm a reminder of all sorts of bad feelings and worse actions."

Looking down at Taylor, I unwrapped her hands from my bicep so I could tangle my fingers with hers. "You didn't need to cause a scene just to make it clear I'm not a part of this family. I've *always* known I didn't belong. You made that clear to me from the time I was old enough to understand words."

I made brief eye contact with the other people at the table. People who were family but also...weren't. "I'm not sorry I came here and saw all of you. It helped me put some things to rest. But that's all this was. An ending...not a beginning. And while I'm not saying I won't answer your calls if they come, this"—I gestured to all of them—"except for Hudson, isn't my family. And I won't be dragged down by your bullshit drama and petty opinions anymore. You don't deserve to have that kind of impact on my life."

Almost everyone at the table was quiet as they looked anywhere but at me. The only one who met my eyes was Hudson, and I sent her a small smile. "I'll call you soon." I didn't want her to think any of that had been directed at her. A relationship with my sister was one of the only good things I'd gotten out of this clusterfuck, other than closure.

She smiled. "I can't wait."

I returned the smile before leading Taylor away from the table and the dysfunction I was born into. And as we wove our way through the room full of gawkers who weren't even pretending to mind their own business, I couldn't even find it in myself to be embarrassed. I was too busy being able to finally take a deep breath as the final constraints of a past I hadn't chosen fell away.

TAYLOR

We were quiet as we buckled our seat belts and pulled onto the road. Ransom had set the GPS for Melissa and Matt's, and we were both content for a little while to sit back and listen to the robotic voice navigate us through Georgia.

But I was only able stay quiet for so long. "Wouldn't it be awesome if the GPS voice was someone like Samuel L. Jackson? 'Turn here, motherfucker!'"

I smiled when I heard his chuckle beside me. Part of me wanted to keep cracking jokes, but I also didn't want to avoid the bitchy elephant in the room.

"So, your aunt is an interesting character."

Ransom snorted. "That's one way of saying it."

"You were totally badass though. Like a linguistic Superman. Take those truth bombs, Ratchet Renee."

He glanced over at me. "Did you just say 'ratchet'?"

"If the adjective fits," I replied with a shrug.

He ran a hand through his hair before setting it on my thigh. "I'm sorry if we made you uncomfortable."

"As if. I love a good scene. I'm just sorry I didn't have a more starring role in it."

He laughed again, and I was thankful he was in a place where he could get some humor out of it.

The things his aunt had said had been...gutting. Her intention had been to hurt him, and while I wasn't sure what a person would get out of inflicting pain on someone she barely knew, I hoped we'd foiled any pleasure she'd tried to elicit from the encounter.

"The next public airing of grievances can be all yours," he said.

I beamed at him. "You're so good to me." I caressed his hand for a moment before continuing. "Are you really okay, though?"

He sighed and seemed to really think about my words before responding. "Yeah. I am. Don't get me wrong, that was...brutal. But as I stood there looking at them, it dawned on me that, with the exception of Blink, I truly didn't give a shit what they thought of me. It was...freeing."

"I'm glad. You have so many people who love you. Screw everyone else."

His lips curled up slightly. "People love me, huh? Interested in giving me names of some of these people?"

Ugh, of course he went there.

Not that I hadn't included myself in the statement. I'd probably been at least partway in love with Ransom since he came running when I'd had that panic attack over Brad. Maybe even before then. But this wasn't the way I'd envisioned saying the words. Especially since I'd pictured *him* saying them first. I gently slapped his arm.

"Don't fish. It's unattractive."

"I'm not looking for compliments, just clarification."

I sat back and crossed my arms over my chest as I fake pouted. "I'm not having this discussion while you're driving." At the very least, I was going to have his sole focus when we had this conversation.

"Want me to pull over?"

I couldn't help but crack up at that. "Oh my God, stop torturing me."

His smile said he wasn't upset about me dodging the conversation. We'd have it. Just...later.

"Though if you want to pull over to go through a drive-thru, I'd be down with that," I said, thinking that it might be a good idea to grab something for dinner since we'd left before it had a chance to begin.

"Your wish is my command."

And the crazy thing was, I knew he meant it. In all things. And wasn't that a frightening power to wield?

Chapter Sixteen

RANSOM

Melissa and Matt had insisted that Taylor and I stay with them a second night instead of heading to the hotel. Then we could spend the day with them Sunday and take a flight back early Monday morning. At first I'd been a little hesitant, though I wasn't sure why. This had been my home, even if it had only been for a few years.

But since we'd arrived here late last night, we hadn't spent much time in it. We'd gone to sleep almost as soon as we'd gotten in, and this morning we'd gone to breakfast with Hudson.

I couldn't help but feel guilty about how accommodating they were being, letting us sleep here and loaning us Matt's SUV, but they seemed more than happy to help.

It was a little after eight when Taylor and I returned to Matt and Melissa's, exhausted from having to socialize all day.

Melissa nearly jumped off the couch to meet us at the back door as we kicked off our shoes. "How did it go? Tell me everything. Or nothing. Whatever you'd prefer." She waved her hands in the air like she was trying to dismiss her own comment.

"It's fine. Things went all right. They're . . . an interesting bunch."

Matt walked in a few moments later under the guise of looking for a snack in the fridge, even though he closed it without removing anything. "How'd Kari seem?"

It surprised me that Matt had been the one to ask about her first. Melissa was usually the one to ask about her.

"The best I've ever seen her, actually." I slid into a chair at the kitchen table, exhausted from the emotions of the day but not quite ready to retreat to my room like an introverted teenager.

Taylor sat in a chair beside me and gave me a warm smile. She'd been so supportive today—and really every day since we'd started dating. Other than Matt, Melissa, and Emily, Taylor was the only person in my life I felt had my back completely and unconditionally. I mean, who else would volunteer to go to an awkward-as-fuck family reunion as a way of escaping a murder investigation? She really was one of a kind.

"That's a relief," Matt said, and I wondered who it was a relief for.

I assumed he meant it was a relief for me, but I was sure he was also glad that the reunion and Kari's condition hadn't made things more difficult for me.

"You never know with Kari," he added.

"Matt," Melissa scolded with only a word.

"Just sayin'."

I could tell by Melissa's stare that she didn't think his comment needed to be shared. Mainly because it went without saying. Kari was unpredictable. She always had been, and that would probably always be the case.

Even if she'd changed for the better permanently, she'd spent most of her time as a mother bouncing from being completely unreliable to suffocatingly invested at her best. I had few memories from my early childhood of Kari being clean, and those memories were jam-packed with fort-building using cushions from our old couch and impromptu dance parties while Kari sang along to whatever came on the radio.

And while any kid would be happy to get that kind of attention and spend those moments with their mom, as an adult I recognized it for what it was: Kari's attempt at cramming pleasant maternal interactions into a small amount of time because she knew she'd inevitably fuck up again. And when she did, those memories were all the three of us would be left with.

And those moments made the cliff we'd all eventually fall from steeper—made the impact at the bottom that much more painful each time. Because while I had known we could only dangle at the edge for so long before we tumbled off, that knowledge didn't stop it from hurting.

Kari always had the potential to do better than she did. And Hudson and I were frequently reminded of that. It made me wonder if we would've been better off with a mother who'd simply given up completely instead of popping in and out of our lives.

Even now, I still couldn't be sure who she kept trying for: us or herself.

Melissa sat down at the table with us, and Matt brought over some bowls, spoons, and a half-gallon of chocolate marshmallow ice cream, which had always been one of my favorites.

"They're probably stuffed from the reunion," Melissa told him.

Matt raised an eyebrow at her like she was crazy. "There's always room for ice cream."

"I can't disagree," I said, grabbing a bowl and helping myself to a few scoops.

"I think I might have to pass," Taylor said. "Though if I have to look at it much longer, I may not be able to resist."

Matt put some in a bowl and slid it her way. "This way it'll be ready for you once you're ready for *it*."

"Thanks," Taylor said with a laugh.

As I ate a few small spoonfuls, I looked around at the kitchen. Melissa still had the gray hand towels with drawings of dogs that resembled Buddy, and the teapot that only got used when we had company sat on the stove on a trivet Matt had made by sticking rubber feet to a piece of leftover ceramic tile he had from when he replaced the bathroom floor.

Not much had changed since I'd lived here seven years ago or so, but somehow nothing had stayed the same either. It was an odd paradox I struggled to make sense of.

"You know what we need?" Matt said. He stood up and headed for the living room. None of us tried to guess what he'd come back with, but when I saw the old Parcheesi box tucked under his arm, I should've known.

"Really?" Melissa asked.

"You say it like you don't wanna play," Matt told her.

The game had been a staple of the Holt game nights Matt and Melissa had insisted we implement once a week as a way to keep Emily and me in the house more. I'm not sure if their intention was to spend more time with us or keep us out of trouble because we were both in high school, but looking back on it, I was glad they'd required us to stay at home one weekend night.

"I'll play," I said.

"What game is it?" Taylor asked.

"Parcheesi," I told her. "It's fun."

"It's actually *Pa*cheesi," Matt said. "Ransom and Melissa like to put the *r* in there, even though it doesn't exist."

"The real game is called Parcheesi," Melissa said in our defense. "Matt got a knock-off he saw somewhere."

"Whatever. Tissues still wipe your nose even if they aren't Kleenex," Matt said, brushing her off as he set up the game in the middle of the table. Melissa got up to put the ice cream away, clearly accepting that she was going to play whether she wanted to or not. She always gave Matt a hard time, saying the game annoyed her when we all knew it didn't.

Matt gave me the blue pieces, and I put them in my circle. "You have a color preference, Taylor?"

"Red's good, I guess," she told him, and I assumed it was because she was seated in front of that circle. "Is this hard to learn?"

"Not really. We'll help you as we go." Matt reached to his right to give her the red and then placed the green in his own circle and the yellow in Melissa's. Seated at the kitchen table as I stared at the old gameboard caused a kind of nostalgia I wasn't sure I wanted to experience. I hadn't played Parcheesi— or *Pa*cheesi—in years, and the last time we'd played, it had been Emily seated beside me.

We must've played this game a hundred times while I lived with the Holts, and I could count on one hand the number of times Emily had won. She'd get nervous when any of us started to get some of our pieces in the home space and then try to join forces with whoever was doing the worst. Unfortunately for her, her alliance barely ever worked, and even when it did, it usually wasn't her who benefited most from it.

"Did your family play board games when you were young, Taylor?" Melissa asked.

Taylor looked momentarily stunned, as if she were unsure of how to answer. "Not . . . often," she finally said. "My parents split up when I was pretty young, and they both ended up remarrying. We kind of just did our own thing most of the time."

"Oh, I'm sorry to hear that," Melissa said. "About your parents."

"Thank you, but it's really fine. It was probably for the best. I can't imagine the two of them living together all these years later. They're totally different people."

"Marriage definitely isn't easy," she said. "Especially when you're married to this one." I saw her raise her eyebrows at Matt, and it made me happy to see they could still tease each other like they'd done . . . before.

I remember a couple of months after I'd moved in, Matt had come up from working in the basement while Melissa was cooking dinner. He took the Scotch tape he had in his hand and grabbed a hold of her. Then he wrapped her up so tightly in the tape, she couldn't move anything but her legs. Or at least she acted like she couldn't. Emily and I laughed hysterically, along with Matt, while Melissa threatened that we wouldn't have a dinner to eat unless one of us untaped her so she could finish cooking it.

Finally, Matt gave in and unwrapped her, pulling her into a hug once she was released. She threatened that he'd better sleep with one eye open that night, but she still kissed him back when he put his lips on hers. I'd pretend I was just as grossed out as Emily was whenever they'd display any sort of public affection, but deep inside it made me happy to be in a home with people as loving as the Holts, and I'd often let my mind wander to one day in the not-so-distant future when maybe I'd have a wife who would kiss me like that and a home that felt like mine.

Now I just hoped my home wouldn't be an eight-by-ten cell.

TAYLOR

It'd taken me a few turns to get the point of the game, but once I did, I was fully invested. I wanted to get one of my pieces into the home space before Ransom got any of his in there. I doubted I'd actually win on my first time playing, but there was always a chance I'd get a little beginner's luck.

"Okay, so since Ransom just rolled a double," Melissa explained, "and he has all his pieces out of the nest, he's allowed to move his pieces a total of fourteen spaces. But since he rolled twos, he needs to break up his moves in increments of twos and fives."

I had no idea how I could feel so dumb playing a game they told me Emily had learned when she was five. "Wait, what? Why fives?"

Ransom flipped over the dice and showed me the fives on the other side. "The opposite sides always equal seven, so if I'd rolled fours, for example, there'd be threes on the other side."

That made sense, but I'd probably screw it up if I had to do it later. I just hoped I wouldn't get any doubles so I didn't have to worry about it. "Oh, okay. I think I get it."

Ransom studied the board before deciding on his move. He counted his first five out loud and hit the yellow piece with his own when he landed on a space occupied by one of Melissa's pieces.

"Get out of here," he teased.

"Come on," Melissa said. "I only have one other piece out."

The way he stared at her made me wonder how intense he must have been on the football field if he took a board game this seriously.

"I take no mercy," he said. "And I'll take my twenty now."

"Twenty! Why do you get an extra twenty?" I asked.

"Because he captured another piece," Matt explained. "You get twenty extra moves, but they have to be taken all at once and with the piece that did the capturing."

"No one told me that."

Ransom moved on to his other pieces, deciding to move one of them the remaining nine, which brought him close to the path to home. He rolled again, getting doubles again, but this time it was two ones. "Oh, is *that* why you've been playing so conservatively this whole time?" he joked as he studied the board again.

"I've been lulling you into a false sense of security," I deadpanned.

Ransom moved his piece that was farthest from home up the pathway.

Melissa and Matt laughed, and then they both exchanged glances before they started chanting, "Dou-bles, dou-bles, dou-bles."

"Your witchcraft isn't gonna work on me," Ransom said to

them. "May as well save your breath for complaining after you lose." He held the dice in his hand and blew into his fist.

"What happens if you get doubles again?" I asked.

"I have to move my farthest piece back to the nest."

This wasn't a difficult game to understand, necessarily, but it was a lot to remember. They hadn't told me most of the rules until something happened that necessitated explaining them, probably because it would've been completely overwhelming to hear them all at once. Like reading an entire economics textbook when you had a quiz on only one chapter.

Matt and Melissa were still chanting, and I looked over at them with a devious smile before joining in. "Dou-bles, dou-bles."

"You picked the wrong side," Ransom joked.

"Just roll," Matt told him. "We don't have all night."

"Actually you *do* have all night," Ransom told him. Then he tossed the dice onto the table, and all of us watched them jump around.

They landed, and all of us moved whatever way we had to in order to see them.

"Yes!" Ransom yelled.

The roll came up a six and a four, so Ransom advanced a few of his pieces safely.

"My turn." I grabbed the dice off the table, shook them in my hand, and rolled a three and a five.

I used the three to capture one of Matt's pieces and was able to take another of my pieces from the nest with the five I rolled. Then I moved my twenty extra spaces I got because I'd captured Matt, and it landed me right onto a space Ransom currently occupied.

"Back to your nest, little bird," I said. I picked up his blue piece and put it back for him, basking in my capture. Ransom's eyes were alight with competition, like he enjoyed the back-and-forth almost as much as he liked being in the lead. I moved my other twenty spaces and then sat back in my chair happily. "I love this game."

Melissa picked up the dice and rolled. "You'd love it more if you remembered to go up your home row." Then she moved her pieces and slid the dice to Matt.

"Oooh, that's cold," Matt said. "That's no way to treat our guest."

It took me a moment to realize what she was talking about, and once I did, I felt like a complete moron. In my excitement, I'd completely forgotten to turn toward the home space, which was in the center of the board, and now I'd be forced to go around again.

"Can I get a mulligan or something since it's my first time?"

The Holts all looked at each other, their eyes darting back and forth like they were deciding how to proceed in a language only they could understand.

"That's gonna be a no," Ransom said. "No mercy, remember?"

And that's how the rest of the night continued. None of us taking pity on anyone else. If someone had a chance to capture someone, they did it, and everyone carefully plotted their strategy with every roll. It took three hours before the game finally ended with Melissa as the winner. When she rolled a two, advancing her last piece into the home space, she practically jumped out of her chair.

"I love Parcheesi!" she said. "Losers put the game away."

Matt and Ransom shook their heads and rolled their eyes

at her, but I could tell their annoyance was all for sport.

"I thought it was *Pa*cheesi," Matt said.

"Whatever it's called, I love it!" she said again.

And even though I hadn't come close to having any chance of winning, I realized I loved it too.

RANSOM

Taylor and I made our way upstairs not long after the game ended, both of us flopping inelegantly onto the bed and groaning out our exhaustion from the day.

"I don't ever want to move from this spot," Taylor said, her voice muffled against the pillow.

"Well, you're going to have to because you're on top of the covers."

"So?"

"So I need them."

"For what?"

"To sleep under." *Why the hell else would I need them?*

"It's warm in here. We don't need them."

"I *do* need them."

She twisted her head in my direction without moving the rest of her body, making her look like some kind of snake. "Why?"

I sighed, exasperated. "This is the dumbest conversation ever. I like to sleep under the covers, which is their purpose."

"You *like* to sleep under them, or you *need* to sleep under them?"

"What?" Had she dropped some LSD when I hadn't been looking?

"I had this friend in grade school who thought her covers protected her from monsters. I was always like, 'They're fabric, Erin, not armor.' But she didn't care. She wouldn't even let a foot sneak out the sides." She moved closer until her face was inches from mine. "Are you scared of monsters, Erin? I mean Ransom."

I shot her a withering look. "As much as I love being compared to a little girl, no, I don't think a blanket protects me. I just . . . like them."

"Like a security blankie?"

I took the pillow out from under my head and hit her in the face with it, causing her to burst out laughing. I then gathered her close, and she rested her head on my chest.

We lazed in contented silence for a few minutes before I remembered something. "Wait, what's going on with your LSATs?"

She tensed. "What do you mean?"

"You looked weird earlier when the subject came up."

"Just what every girl wants to hear from her boyfriend— that she looks weird."

"Shut up," I said before placing a kiss on her head to offset the words. "Did you get them?"

"Maybe."

"Hmm, this is a fun game. Much preferable to you just coming out and telling me about them."

She chuckled. "I got them this morning, but I haven't opened the results yet."

I jerked up, causing her to fall to the mattress with a squeak. "What are you waiting for?"

She sighed and sat up next to me. "I dunno. I guess I didn't want to make today about me."

"Because having it be about me went so well?" I teased.

After rolling her eyes, she brought her knees up so she could rest her chin on them. She darted her gaze over to peek at me before staring straight ahead. "What if my score sucks?"

"Then you take it again."

"Maybe it would be a sign that I should do something else."

I cocked my head a bit at her words. "Do you *want* to do something else?" She'd never given me any indication she did, but so much had changed in the past couple of months. I wouldn't blame her for reevaluating things.

"No," she said almost immediately.

"Then that settles it. If you failed, which is a totally hypothetical concern since you haven't even opened the damn results yet, then you'll take them again. And you'll keep taking them until you pass."

"You make it sound really simple."

"Isn't it?"

She shrugged in reply.

I scooched closer and wrapped an arm around her. "We have a lot of shit going on that makes life harder. But this doesn't have to be one of those things. I get that the test is tough, but so are you. You just gotta keep trying."

She let out a sharp exhale before resting her head on my shoulder. "Thanks for the pep talk, coach."

"You got it, slugger."

"Can you hand me my phone?" she asked.

I retrieved it from where she'd set it on the nightstand before collapsing onto the bed. She pulled up her email and selected the one with the link to her results.

"Here goes nothing," she muttered before clicking.

I tried to look over her shoulder after she logged in, but I didn't have much clue what I was seeing.

Suddenly, her body sagged as if a pressure valve had been released.

"What? What is it?" Was it a good sag or a bad sag? Why wasn't she talking? She was almost always talking!

"My score is good," she said with a sniffle. "Really good." She let out a small laugh that sounded watery.

"Holy shit! That's amazing!" I tackled her to the bed and began peppering her face with kisses. When I pulled back, her smile was blinding. "Congratulations," I said softly.

"Thank you," she replied.

As I looked down on this amazing woman who had accomplished this incredible thing while dealing with a shitstorm, who'd supported me against a family I hadn't seen in over fifteen years, who I knew I could always count on, in whatever way I needed her, I was filled with such incredible emotions, I couldn't suppress them.

"I love you."

And maybe the timing was shit with all we were dealing with and what might happen to us in the future, but she deserved to know. Even if this trip turned out to be the last time we had together, at least she'd know I'd loved her. That I'd do it all again with her, even if we had only a little while.

Her eyes shined as tears sprang in them. She blinked, and they spilled over, leaving tracks down her cheeks. If it weren't for the fact that she was still smiling, I would've been worried.

She tightened her arms around my neck and pulled me down so my lips were nearly grazing hers. "I love you too," she said. "So much."

And with that, we were kissing, our tongues tangling in

a dance that spoke in ways words couldn't. She'd twisted me up from the first time I'd seen her, and I'd only become more wrapped up in her as time had worn on.

I might not always be able to touch her like this. But I'd sure as hell always remember it.

We undressed each other slowly until we were naked and writhing against each other in ecstasy.

A small voice in the back of my head said maybe this was a tacky thing to do in Matt and Melissa's house, but I told that voice to fuck right the hell off. This moment was too big to stop.

Her hands caressed my body as I slid inside her, her gasp filling the air before being followed by a low moan. We tried to stay quiet, but our soft sounds of pleasure became a soundtrack that couldn't be stifled.

And as her body quaked beneath me, I followed her off that cliff.

Just like I'd follow her anywhere else.

Chapter Seventeen

TAYLOR

Despite the exhaustion of the day, my mind kept me from getting much actual rest. I'd drifted in and out of sleep for much of the night, spending most of my time trapped in that space that exists between dreams and conscious thoughts, making it difficult to tell the difference between the two.

And though my brain had seemed aware of each passing thought at the time I'd had them, when I woke up for good a little after seven in the morning, I couldn't make much sense of details. They existed only as images flashing through my memory like pictures on a phone after a long night of drinking. Matt and Melissa. Ransom. Hudson and Kari. I'd also thought—or dreamed—of Emily, though I couldn't remember the specifics.

In the dream, I hadn't been able to recognize her face, and I couldn't remember it now. I wasn't sure the picture my mind had drawn of her even resembled the real person.

Of course, the Holts had pictures of their daughter throughout their home, but I hadn't had a good opportunity to look closely at any of them yet. I'd wanted to, though. I'd seen them on the wall, and I'd wanted to walk over and stand in front of the frames and really *see* the person who'd been loved by so many people, even if I'd never gotten a chance to know her.

Carefully, I pulled the covers off and crept across the room to where I'd plugged in my phone to charge last night. I grabbed a sweatshirt from the top of my suitcase and shrugged it on when I got into the hallway. As I descended the stairs, I texted Sophia to see if she was awake.

I am now.

Sorry :)

No you're not.

You're right. I'm not. I've barely talked to you, and I gotta catch you up on the reunion yesterday.

I wandered into the kitchen and got a glass of water. When I was done, Sophia's text was waiting for me.

I didn't wanna ask, but . . . did everyone survive?

A few seconds later another text came through.

Sorry. Really poor choice of words.

We need to talk about that too.

I'd been avoiding thinking about the investigation into Brad's death, which was easier because I was states away. But I knew my level of comfort would begin to vanish as soon as the miles did. Sooner or later, I'd have to face what we'd done and accept whatever came of it.

I considered calling her, but she beat me to it. We'd all agreed not to put anything that could be incriminating in writing, and so far we'd been careful.

"Hey," I said, pulling my hood up before heading out onto the back porch. It was enclosed, but it also had no heat, so it was colder than I liked this early in the morning.

"Hey," Sophia said back. "Figured it was easier just to call. Even to talk about all the reunion stuff."

I didn't really feel like getting into the details right now, but I knew she'd been thinking about all of it almost as much as I had. Sophia had always given a shit about my life even when I didn't have anything interesting happening, so I knew she must be practically vibrating with curiosity considering the current state of my life.

"Yeah, that's fine. I'm on the porch. I think everyone's still asleep. It's cold out here, so I'll have to give you the details later, but it was pretty much what we both expected. Lots of family drama that's been years in the making. But I think Ransom's glad he went. I met his sister, and she was totally cool. His mom seems good. He's definitely got an eclectic mix of relatives, so we were both a little overwhelmed."

That last part was seriously understated, but I'd have to fill Sophia in on Uncle Lester and the rest in person so I could do their eccentricities justice.

"That's understandable. I'm just glad you guys made it through unscathed, especially with everything else you have going on."

"Thanks. Yeah," I said, "we're glad it's over too. But now we have to deal with the rest of this shit." I glanced out to the backyard like I thought I might see an FBI agent peeking out from the bushes or something. Guess I hadn't put my paranoia on the back burner after all. "Have there been any... developments?"

"Not that we've heard. I'm sure they're working on it, but the police obviously aren't sharing the details of their investigation with us, and it's not like we can ask."

"Right," I said with a sigh. "I guess no news is good news in this situation."

"Have you heard from any of your college friends about it? Did any of them know why he'd come here?"

"Actually, no."

For some reason, I hadn't even thought of that, though it made perfect sense. If the police wanted to know who killed Brad, they'd most likely want to know what he was doing in a city where he didn't live, and the only connection to that city was me. If it hadn't already, it wouldn't be long before the investigation extended to my school and the small group of friends I'd left there. And then there were Brad's friends I had to worry about too. I'm sure Brad hadn't said many pleasant things about me since we'd broken up.

"Oh, okay. Drew heard Brad's family is holding a vigil for him in a few days, the night before the funeral. I thought maybe your friends would've told you about it."

"No. They didn't tell me anything." I pressed on my eyes with my free hand, suddenly feeling my body heat up despite the low temperature on the porch. "But they know I'd never go. I never told them how crazy Brad had gotten, but they knew I wanted nothing to do with him. That much I made clear. If they're planning to go, I'm sure they wouldn't tell me."

"Sorry. I shouldn't have mentioned it. I'm sure the last thing you need to think about right now is this guy's family standing around a beach with a bunch of candles and pictures of him."

"It's on a beach?" I'd said the words softly, more to myself than to Sophia.

"Yeah," she answered curiously. "Why? Does that matter?"

"No," I said quickly. "Not really." I knew Brad had grown up near the beach. He'd loved water and had once told me he and his older brother Jonathan had sneaked out of the house after their parents went to sleep so they could hang out on the beach. It was the summer before Jonathan went away to college, and Brad wanted to spend every second possible with the brother he'd idolized since birth.

He'd described even the drive there as a thrill because it was illegal to be on the beach that late at night, but Jon was four years older than Brad and had just gotten his license. He'd promised Brad the worst that could happen was that they'd get fined and told to go home.

It probably would've been true, but Jon had brought a six-pack with him. He'd given thirteen-year-old Brad two of the beers. After deciding it would be fun to go for a dip in a stranger's beachfront hot tub, Jon and Brad's night of freedom ended in the back of a police car. Since Jon had been drinking and hadn't been permitted to drive home, their parents' car was left on the side street near the beach where Jon had parked it.

His mom had been furious, more so than their dad, because she'd insisted something could've happened to them. What if they'd decided to swim in the ocean instead of the hot tub, she'd said, and one or both of them drowned in the nighttime sea? What if the cops hadn't come and Jonathan had gotten into a car accident on the way home?

When Brad told the story, he'd shared his mom's fears with an eye roll and a laugh. Like most teenagers, especially boys, the fatal possibilities his mom had described had seemed ridiculous to them, even as a college-aged kid.

As far as he was concerned, he was invincible. Until he wasn't.

All good parents worried about their kids. Even my own mom, who'd spent the better part of the year with her husband doing who knows what in Australia, still called to check in on me routinely.

And even though her actions didn't always show it, Kari also cared about her children.

I wondered if out of all the morbid fears that must've run through Brad's mother's mind—both rational and completely unlikely—she never once considered that her son's life might end alone in the alley of an unfamiliar city.

"Taylor. Tay-lor."

Like I was being woken from a dream, Sophia's voice began to materialize like water vapors rising to form a cloud. By the time I became consciously aware that she'd been trying to get my attention, she was practically yelling at me. "Are you there?"

"Yeah. Sorry. I . . . I must've lost the call for a second. The reception here is so unreliable."

"Oh."

"I should go," I told her with no explanation as to why.

Thankfully, she didn't ask, and once I hung up, I headed back inside.

ELIZABETH HAYLEY

I tried to push all thoughts of Brad below the surface, but it was next to impossible, especially when Ransom wasn't awake yet to distract me. I didn't want to risk waking Melissa and Matt by taking a shower or making any sort of noise upstairs, so I opted to make some coffee.

I poured enough water in the coffeemaker to make a full pot so everyone else could have some when they got up, and I scooped about five heaping spoonfuls of grounds into the filter.

As I waited for it to brew, I walked around the downstairs, finally getting a chance to look at the pictures I'd seen only briefly since I'd been here.

Ransom's college graduation picture and Emily's from high school hung next to each other over the love seat in the living room. I'd obviously known about Emily's battle with cancer and how close she and Ransom had been. It was sad, of course, to hear about, but standing here in the home where she lived, looking at pictures of her . . . it suddenly felt more real.

My chest ached for the Holts because even though there wasn't an empty spot on the wall where Emily's college graduation photo should've gone, I had no doubt there was a hole in their hearts that should've held memories like those. I tried to remember if anyone had even mentioned Emily last night while we'd played Parcheesi, but it was difficult to remember because yesterday had been filled with so many new people and stories.

"I'm assuming Ransom told you?"

Melissa's voice startled me, and I turned around to see her at the bottom of the stairs. I hadn't even heard her come down until she'd spoken.

"About Emily, I mean."

I held my coffee mug tighter, wanting its warmth to

comfort me, even though I wasn't the one who needed comforting.

"He did," I said. "I'm so sorry." The words sounded empty. They were anything but. I couldn't imagine losing someone close to me, let alone a child, but my condolences sounded generic because I hadn't been prepared to deliver them. "She was beautiful," I added.

"Inside and out." Melissa forced a tight grin. "This one's my favorite of the two of them." She pointed to one of the photos that hung on the stairway wall.

I'd noticed the collage of frames on my way upstairs last night, but it hadn't been an appropriate time to stop and look at them. As I moved closer, I saw how, regardless of size, shape, or color, each of the frames seemed to fit like a puzzle piece in its given place—part of a larger whole that would feel incomplete without it.

And in those frames were snapshots of a life I'm sure, to Melissa and Matt, felt like a different one entirely. There were shots of Christmases and birthdays, softball games, and cheesy family photos. Beautiful moments frozen in time so that each single instance captured told a story all its own.

The one Melissa had pointed to was of Ransom and Emily lying on their backs in the snow. The shot was taken from above, and between them was a younger Buddy, lying on his back as well. All of them, even Buddy somehow, were smiling. Their arms and legs were outstretched, and I could see where the snow had been pressed down while they'd made snow angels. I could see why Melissa loved it so much.

"It was the first snow day the kids had after Ransom moved in with us. Emily and Buddy had always been inseparable, and when Ransom came, the kids got along so well, Buddy thought he was about to be replaced."

Melissa laughed, but I could hear the faint sniffle beneath it. I wondered how often she stopped to notice these pictures. Did she just pass by them because the memories were too painful? Or did she look at them daily because a reminder of what she'd lost made it easier to celebrate what had once been?

"Was Buddy replaced?" I asked, my smile small as I turned toward Melissa.

"Almost. Emily and Rans were meant to be siblings. Or best friends. Or both, I guess. I'm not exactly sure who the third wheel was—Buddy or Ransom. But somehow all three became so attached, we wouldn't see one without the other two close behind."

"That's so sweet." *And so sad.*

"Yeah," she said softly. "Buddy hasn't been the same since we lost Emily. And I guess you could say we lost Ransom soon after."

I looked into Melissa's eyes, and through my own tears I could see hers. Neither of us allowed any to fall, but they were there nonetheless, and I was sure we both knew it.

I opened my mouth to speak, but thankfully Melissa said something before I had to.

"It's okay," she said, placing her hand on my arm for a moment, like she sensed I might apologize on his behalf. "We all have our own way of dealing with it. And Ransom's had a lot of loss in his life. He just couldn't take another."

Even though I knew about everything Ransom had gone through, I hadn't thought of it like that. How he'd lost one of the only good people in his life after losing so many bad ones.

"He doesn't owe anything to anyone but himself at this point in his life." She sighed heavily, but it sounded like it was more out of sadness than frustration. "I'm just glad he's happy and he's moving on with his life. Moving *forward*. If there's one thing parents want for their children, it's for them to be happy. And Ransom's happy. I know that boy, and even though he was exhausted and probably felt bad about calling us to pick you guys up, he looked happy."

"You think so?" I wondered what the old Ransom was like, the one Melissa and Matt had known. The one *Emily* had known. But then I decided it was probably for the best that I only knew this one.

Despite the heaviness of the conversation, Melissa's lips slipped into a smile, and she seemed more at ease than she had a few moments ago. "I know so."

I didn't want to think about the implication that his happiness had anything to do with me, because as much as I didn't want the credit for making him happy, I also didn't want the burden of keeping him that way.

In the back of my mind, I worried about what would happen if things didn't work out between us. I always did. It was part of my self-diagnosed neuroses that didn't allow me to follow through with anything without overthinking it. And with a secret between us as devastating as the one we were carrying, I couldn't decide if we'd grow closer or further apart as a result of it.

I smiled back but was unable to find any words to express what I was feeling. My parents' marriage hadn't worked out for several reasons—some of them still unknown to me. But right now, I was in the house of a couple who'd survived the unthinkable. And here was this loving woman who'd taken in a boy who'd needed a family, only to lose her own daughter. And somehow she still kept it all together.

"Can I ask you something, Melissa?"

"Of course."

Not sure how to ask my question or why I even wanted to ask it, I hesitated a moment. "How'd you do it? How'd you continue after . . . something like that?"

"You know, I've asked myself that many times. But you're the first person who's ever asked me that."

"I'm so sorry. It's personal. I shouldn't have—"

"No. It's okay. I don't talk about it much. The 'after,' I mean. I'm used to remembering Emily, used to talking about her with people who like to remember her too. But no one ever asks about what happens after. Maybe it feels too . . . messy or too invasive in some ways."

Melissa began walking down the steps, putting a hand on my back as she passed me. "You feel like another cup?" She glanced at my coffee. "I can use one myself."

I nodded and followed silently behind her toward the kitchen. Melissa filled my cup and set the creamer on the table before grabbing herself a cup and setting it down, along with some napkins and pastries from a box on the counter.

"Danishes from the best bakery around," she said. "The peach is the best." She slid one onto a napkin for me and then helped herself to one, slicing it in half delicately.

It looked amazing, but I wasn't in the mood to eat anything yet.

Melissa had one of those faces that let people know how loving she was. How welcoming. Or maybe I just felt that way because Ransom had spoken so highly of her and I knew she was both those things and more. I studied her features—the lines around her eyes and the soft curve of her lips, which were cracked a bit at the edges. Freckles dotted her cheekbones, giving a little color to her otherwise pale skin. Her face was soft. No sharp lines or striking features, but there was a quiet power in it.

I pulled a piece of my danish off because I didn't want to seem rude, but when I put it in my mouth, my taste buds told my stomach it was hungrier than it actually was. Melissa was right about the peach. Though to be fair, I hadn't tried any of the others.

"So," Melissa began after she swallowed a sip of coffee. "You wanna know about the after."

I nodded. "If you don't mind telling me."

She looked down at the liquid in her mug before speaking again. "Hard doesn't even begin to describe it. And if people tell you it gets easier with time, they're liars." I could tell she almost laughed but didn't quite get the sound out. Shaking her head, she said, "Nothing about losing a child gets easier. And for months after Emily passed, I would ask God *why me? Why us?* I've never considered myself religious, but I found myself angry with a God who could take something so perfect—so pure—away from this world."

Melissa sat quietly for a minute or so, but I could tell she had more to say, so I didn't fill the silence with my own words. I just sipped my coffee and waited until she was ready to continue.

After settling back into her chair with her cup in her hands, she said, "I'm not sure if Ransom ever told you this, but the reason we never had more children after Emily was born was because we couldn't. We'd always wanted a big family since Matt and I both come from them, but I guess the universe had other plans for us."

"I'm sorry," I whispered, needing to say something but not

wanting to sound like I was interrupting her.

"It's okay," she said almost as softly. "Life has a way of giving you only what you can handle."

Melissa sounded more religious than she claimed, but maybe spiritual more accurately described her.

"I had two miscarriages before Emily and one after. As soon as Em was a year old or so, our family and friends would ask when we were going to have our second. When we didn't have one by the time Emily was three, people went from asking us about it to telling us just to be patient and it would happen when we least expected it."

Her chest rose with the breath she'd taken, and once she released it, she rolled her eyes good-naturedly. "People mean well, but sometimes they say the wrong thing because they feel like they need to say *some*thing, you know?" I did, but now wasn't the time to vocalize that. "And usually they end up being wrong. We gave it a few more years, but staring at a single pink line every time I was a few days late became so emotionally draining. I eventually realized we were missing out on moments with the child we *did* have because we were putting so much energy into one we didn't."

Melissa shrugged. "So we decided we couldn't do that to ourselves any longer. We had this beautiful, smart, sassy-as-hell little girl. What did *we* have to be upset about? It didn't happen overnight, but eventually we accepted that our imaginary family of four or five or six would be three."

I thought I could see where this was going, but I waited for Melissa to take it there. It wasn't my story to tell.

She talked for longer than I'd expected about the birthdays and the family camping trips and about the three-hour drive to pick up Buddy from a breeder near her sister's house. The way she told the stories made me think it had been a long time since she'd spoken about them. I was glad she got to share all of it because the light in her eyes told me that talking about Emily brought her memory to life in a way Melissa didn't often get to experience. And I was even more happy it'd been *me* she'd shared them with.

"It was Emily's freshman year of high school when Ransom came to live with us. The second child we didn't think we'd ever have," she said. "The one who we realized somehow needed *us* less than we needed *him*."

I thought that was a beautiful way to look at it, like Ransom brought more happiness to the Holts than they thought they brought to him. Though I didn't think Ransom would agree.

"That picture of them in the snow was taken a few months after Ransom joined our family. It was his first Christmas with us, and of all the years I've lived in Georgia, I've maybe seen it snow a handful of times." Her eyes looked lost in the memory, like she was daydreaming in a way that felt real to her. I couldn't help but feel like my presence intruded on a private moment that I couldn't begin to understand. "Guess there were two miracles that year," she said with a smile.

I had no idea how Melissa wasn't crying, because I felt like if I blinked too hard, the dam might burst and I'd let enough tears out for the both of us. "You're so strong," I said, not realizing right away that I'd said it aloud.

Pushing back her chair, she let out a sound that resembled a laugh, like she thought my comment was a ridiculous one. "I'm not." She poured us both some more coffee before returning the pot to its place to stay warm. "I don't mean to minimize what we've gone through. I just mean that there are so many people with worse situations.

"I've met them," she continued. "After Emily passed, Matt and I joined a support group—my idea, not his, and he let me know it. There I met a woman whose ten-year-old daughter had gone missing. When I met the woman—Abby—her daughter would've been almost Emily's age. It'd been about eight years since she'd seen Grace, and they still had no idea if she was alive."

"That's …" I wasn't sure how to finish my sentence because there was no word in the English language that accurately seemed to describe how terribly sad that must've been. "I don't know what to say."

"I know," Melissa said. "Neither did I. We went for coffee one day after the group, and she told me that for months after her daughter disappeared, she and her husband felt guilty doing everyday things, like eating or sleeping, because they wondered if Grace had gotten to eat that day or if she was curled up on a cold concrete floor somewhere. They wondered if she was dead. And if she were, did she suffer at the end?"

Melissa swallowed hard, somehow still able to hold back tears. I couldn't remain as composed. Once the first tear fell, others followed, and I wiped them with a napkin, hoping Melissa didn't think less of me.

"There I'd been feeling sorry for myself all that time, and I know I had every right to … but I'd never even stopped to consider that there were people in the world who were suffering more than we were. And if Abby could wake up and get out of bed every day, I certainly could too."

I could see how that realization might help someone deal with whatever they were currently facing, but I wondered if comparing her own life and problems to someone else's was a healthy way to heal. There was always someone worse off.

Someone who *had* less and was *suffering* more. And if people constantly compared their lives to those in a more difficult situation, it would invalidate their grief or anxiety or whatever negative emotion they experienced because of it. And as Melissa said, she had a right to feel how she felt.

But as quickly as I'd been to consider Melissa's path a questionable one, I realized I had absolutely no room to judge someone else's coping mechanisms. I was a hot mess, and I hoped Melissa couldn't tell.

"I'd never thought of burying a child as a privilege until I met two people who didn't have the chance to say goodbye to theirs. And to be honest, that helped me deal with Emily's death more than any of the sessions with the group helped me." She looked up at me, and when she did, I watched a tear fall from her eye as well.

If I had to guess, I was pretty certain it was for Grace and her family, not for herself.

"I'm not strong," she said. "I'm just lucky. I know how Emily died. I know she suffered at the end but that it was over once she passed. I know—I *hope*—she's in a better place now." Melissa's voice cracked as she finished her sentence. "I got to say goodbye to her, to lay her body to rest. Becoming friends with Abby helped me view my situation in a very different light."

Melissa's story of Abby and her daughter Grace seemed to resonate in every cell in my body. My stomach tensed so much it felt like the organ was twisting on itself, and my blood felt like it'd been spiked with adrenaline so potent that my skin vibrated as it tried to hold the rest of me together.

"And Matt?" I asked, needing to know the effect all of this had had on them both.

"And Matt...doesn't say much," she answered with a quick smile that only touched the corners of her mouth briefly. "He never did. But he said even less after Emily's death. I said enough for the both of us, though. I screamed and I cursed and I got mad at the world and everyone in it. While I felt better talking about it, or *yelling*, Matt seemed to retreat further inside himself than he ever had. And when he couldn't stand being with even himself, he turned to alcohol for comfort. I'm sure Ransom's told you that, though," she said like it was a foregone conclusion.

I shook my head. "He hasn't."

She laughed harshly. "Well, that's kind of him, but we don't deserve it."

"I'm sure Ransom would say you deserve that and more."

"Yeah. Well, he usually does try to see the best in people." She smiled more broadly this time, and though it still held the seriousness of the moment, I thought her face seemed to lose some of the sadness that had been there only seconds ago.

"Yeah," I said with a chuckle. I wondered if she were referring to Kari or someone in particular or if the comment had just been a hyperbolic compliment, but I realized I might not ever know. Because even if Melissa had any less than flattering thoughts about Kari, to my knowledge she'd never shared them. At least not to Ransom.

She'd been a hundred percent supportive of his decision to reconnect with his mother after all these years. She'd even encouraged it. I guessed that had something to do with never getting the opportunity to see her own child again, but I'd probably never know the true reason. And who knew if Melissa even did.

It wasn't long before Melissa's eyes grew teary again.

"Emily always saw the best in people too," she said. "They were similar that way."

I searched my mind for an appropriate response that didn't seem cliché or manufactured to seem like I cared about someone I'd never even met. I'd already said all that I could, and I guessed her silence meant Melissa was done sharing as well. At least for now.

With a sigh, she pushed back in her chair and rose slowly, her posture never slackening as she headed to the sink. "I'll cook breakfast for everyone," she said without turning around. "Why don't you go get ready and see if you can't try an' wake the bear in a little while? Tell him I've got some candy bacon in the oven for him, extra crispy. He can sleep on the plane ride home," she said. "Matt and I wanna make sure we get to spend as much time as possible with him while he's here."

I didn't know whether her comment was more connected to losing Emily or the fact that Ransom didn't visit often, but the truth was, it probably didn't matter.

Chapter Eighteen

RANSOM

"Mmm," I groaned as I felt Taylor's arms slip around me and her body press against my back. She was warm and familiar, and I'd gotten so used to having her sleep beside me that the bed was beginning to feel too empty without her. Even this one at Matt and Melissa's that barely fit both of us. "Where'd you go?" I asked, my voice deep and groggy as I worked the sleepiness out of it.

"Just to get some coffee."

"Any left for me?"

I felt her nod against my shoulder before she kissed it. "And Melissa said to tell you she's making candy bacon. I'm not sure what it is, but it sounds delicious."

I let out a low laugh and turned over onto my back so I could see Taylor. She was still in what she'd worn to bed— one of my T-shirts, which was way too big for her, and a pair of sweatpants with the name of her college on the thigh. She looked sexy as hell with no makeup and her hair pulled up into a messy bun. She felt even hotter against me.

"I don't know what candy bacon is either or how she makes it, but it's amazing, and it'll ruin you for regular bacon."

She kissed my neck lightly as she spoke. "I'm torn between wanting to taste it and not wanting to feel different about plain bacon."

"That *is* a tough decision, but you're only gonna get it in one place, and that's the Holt household. It was Matt's mom's recipe, but only the women are allowed to know it for some reason. It's kinda sweet in a way, but it's also incredibly sexist."

Taylor laughed. "I think you're reading too much into it. It's just bacon."

"See if you stand by the phrase 'It's just bacon' once you taste it."

She slid her nails lightly over my stomach, and my breath quickened at the touch. "I think I'd rather taste you," she said. And when her face disappeared under the covers, all coherent thoughts of mine disappeared with it.

I tried to be quiet, and I tried to last. Unfortunately, I accomplished neither of those things. I was already hard after waking up, and her mouth was so hot, her tongue so wet. I never stood a chance.

And when I tried to warn her I was close—tried to grab her hair and pull on it a little—that only seemed to encourage her to keep going. After I was done, she kissed her way up my abdomen until her lips were close enough to my ear that she could whisper into it.

"Told you I wanted to taste you."

"I'm glad you keep your promises," I said, stroking her hair and staring into her eyes. Her words and her weight on me had me ready for round two. "Now it's your turn." I held her lower back as I flipped her over. The cotton sheets were soft against my skin, and I slid my hand underneath her shirt so I could feel the smoothness of her skin as well.

"It's okay," she said. "We should probably head down, or Melissa will wonder what we're doing up here."

"I think she'll have a pretty good idea what we're doing up here."

Taylor's hand connected with my bare ass. I liked it more than she'd probably meant for me to. "Well, if you're hoping that'll get me to *not* wanna stay up here with you, you should probably think of another form of punishment."

Her eyes grew more serious, and it made me wonder if I'd touched a nerve I didn't know existed. But before I could ask what was wrong, let alone apologize for it, she said, "Melissa said she wants to spend as much time with you as possible before we leave."

She pressed her lips together into a tight smile, like she was thinking about something and didn't know whether she should vocalize it. But I knew if something were on her mind that she wanted to share, she would.

"I guess this means I should get off you, then," I joked.

"It does," she answered, her demeanor a bit lighter. "Why don't you go have breakfast with Matt and Melissa while I take a shower, and I'll meet you downstairs in a little while?"

I knew she'd probably suggested that so I could spend time with them on my own, and I appreciated it, even though I didn't tell her. I'd spent most of the day yesterday with my biological family, but Matt and Melissa were family too, and being here with them—seeing them again in this house—filled me with regret for distancing myself from them, even if it hadn't been an intentional separation.

"'Kay," I said. "I'll see you downstairs when you're done."

Slowly, I climbed off her and put on sweatpants and a T-shirt before heading to the bathroom. After splashing some water on my face and brushing my teeth, I jogged downstairs. The scent of candy bacon and coffee drifted up the stairs and woke me up instantly.

"Morning," I called before my feet even touched the landing.

I hadn't realized Matt was up, but when I'd turned the corner toward the kitchen, he was cracking eggs for French toast. "Morning," he said. "Y'all sleep okay last night?"

"Yeah. Great. I'm thinking the accommodations here are better than what we would've encountered in the hotel. It didn't come with a complimentary breakfast like Hotel Holt."

Melissa smiled at me as she handed me a mug so I could get some coffee. "Thanks." I poured some coffee and then turned to Matt. "You're up early."

"I'm old."

He said it so dryly I couldn't help but laugh, even though he didn't. "You were old when I lived here too, but we usually had to drag your ass outta bed."

"All right, smartass, make yourself useful. Grab a spatula or some plates or something." He dipped the thick slices of bread into the batter and then placed them on the griddle. They sizzled immediately.

"I guess getting cranky is part of getting old too?" I joked, earning me a playful elbow to the stomach as I stood beside him.

I coughed dramatically.

"I see some things haven't changed," Melissa said.

Growing up, Matt had been an athlete too, and from time to time we'd spar in the living room until eventually one of us got injured by something other than each other. One time Matt backed into the coffee table, knocking over a glass and cutting himself when it broke.

Matt chuckled. "I'm tryin' to go easy on him."

"Right," I said with an eye roll.

Matt flipped the French toast over, revealing a perfectly golden-brown crisp of cinnamon and egg. "So what are your plans today?"

Taylor and I hadn't even talked about what we were doing, if anything. "I don't know. We don't really have any. I guess just relax before we need to fly back tomorrow."

"You think she'd be interested in seeing the town?"

I raised an eyebrow at him. "What part? There isn't really a whole lot to show off."

"Sure there is," Melissa said. "We thought it'd be fun to take Taylor on a little tour of the neighborhood and then maybe grab a bite to eat at Sully's."

The tour of the town would probably take about ten minutes since it had about six traffic lights, two parks, and only a handful of restaurants—including Sully's.

"Okay, yeah. If she's good with that, that's fine. Though I plan to eat until I feel sick this morning, so I'm not sure how hungry I'll be."

"Save room," Matt said. "You can't go to Sully's and pass up their brisket. Marilyn'll think you're sick or something."

Marilyn Sullivan was the wife of the owner, who'd been known only as Sully for as long as anyone in the town had known him. I wasn't even sure Marilyn knew his first name.

Taylor came down a few minutes later, just as we were finishing up preparing for breakfast. Matt stacked the French toast on a plate in the middle of the table, alongside syrup, butter, and powdered sugar. And Melissa pulled the pan out of the oven when we were ready to sit, so the bacon was still hot when we grabbed some.

"Oh my God," Taylor said with a moan that could've made my pants feel a little tighter if we weren't eating breakfast with my family. "This is . . ." She never found the word she was looking for so instead finished with "Ransom was right. This ruined me for plain bacon. What do you put on this?"

Melissa smiled, pleased with Taylor's reaction to her cooking. "All bad things, which is why it tastes so good. Some brown sugar, some butter, fresh maple syrup. A few other secret ingredients that only Holt women can know."

"Ransom told me about that," Taylor said.

"Maybe one day you'll get the recipe yourself." She winked at me, not so subtly, and I could've killed her if I didn't love her so damn much.

I'd absolutely thought about my future with Taylor, and I knew she'd thought about a future with me. We'd talked about it on more than one occasion, and though we'd never specifically discussed the M-word, it was clear we both saw the other when we closed our eyes and imagined our lives years from now.

But now that might all change with all this shit with Brad. Brody had texted twice yesterday to say that Xander was working on hacking into the autopsy results.

Of course he hadn't been so explicit. It had all been in Brode Code, a language I'd learned to decipher even before it'd become a legal necessity. Luckily, I was fairly sure no one else could crack it except maybe Sophia and Aamee.

Unsure of what a proper reaction to Melissa's comment would be, I tried to smile enough to make her feel like there was a chance her prediction might become a reality but not enough to freak out Taylor, who looked just as uncertain about the situation as I did. I was thankful we seemed to be on the same page.

"Tour starts at exactly eleven," Matt said, breaking the awkward moment. "Make sure you have your tickets in hand and meet me out front."

It was already ten thirty, which meant I'd have to get ready soon, so I finished up breakfast quickly and headed upstairs to take a shower. At some point, I realized that Taylor hadn't questioned what the tour was that Matt had mentioned, which meant that one of them—or both—had already discussed the plan with her and she'd agreed to it, but no one had told me. *Assholes*, I thought with a soft laugh.

It took me about twenty minutes to get showered and dressed, and I was back downstairs and ready to go. I could see through the kitchen window that they were already outside, so I headed out there as well. As I approached them, I noticed Matt had something in hand that he was showing Taylor.

I jogged up to them. "Whatcha lookin' at?"

"Taylor found Buddy's tag in the yard," Matt said. "I didn't even realize he was missing it. I'll have to get another ring for it, though, because I don't know where that is."

"Did you check to see if it's on his collar?" I asked.

"Actually no," Matt said. Then he disappeared inside. A minute or so later, he emerged from the house with Buddy on a leash. "You were right. It was on there the whole time."

"Why do you have him with you?" Melissa asked. "We're about to leave."

"Yeah, Buddy's coming with us. He wants to tour the town too."

Melissa rolled her eyes but looked like she couldn't

help but smile. "Hasn't he toured it enough all the times he's escaped?"

I could remember at least five times that Buddy had gotten out in the short time I'd lived with the Holts. One time he slipped through a rail in the fence that we hadn't even realized was broken, and a few other times he'd run out the front door when we came home. It was why everyone had started parking in the back, off the gravel alley that ran behind our block of houses. If we went in the back, we'd have the enclosed porch as a buffer to stop him from getting out.

"I don't think Taylor wants Buddy's breath all over her during the drive," Melissa said.

"It's really okay," Taylor told her, but I couldn't be sure if she'd said that to be polite or if she really didn't care.

It didn't seem to matter, though, because Matt already had the trunk open and was putting Buddy's ramp up so he could walk into the SUV. "See? It's fine."

I was pretty sure it wouldn't be the most relaxing ride we'd ever had, but since nothing about this trip had been easy, it seemed like a fitting decision to take Buddy.

TAYLOR

I'd spent the better part of the past hour in the car next to Ransom, with Matt and Melissa in the front stopping at various locations to give me an explanation about why that particular place was important. They'd shown me the diner where Ransom had bussed tables his junior year of high school when he'd first moved in with the Holts, and they'd driven the route that Ransom used to jog every morning during the football off-season to stay in shape.

Buddy seemed more excited to be on the tour than anyone else in the car, his tongue dangling out of his hot mouth behind me. Occasionally he tried to climb over the seat to sit in the back with us, but Ransom was able to keep him in place. For an old dog, he clearly had more than a spark of ambition left in him.

When we arrived at the high school Ransom had graduated from, I saw the nostalgia settle on his face. Matt pulled into the back lot so we could look at the football field.

"It hasn't changed," Ransom said, surprised. "I thought they were gonna redo it. Wasn't there talk of putting in lights and a snack bar and all that?"

"There was *talk*," Melissa said, "but not much more than that. The people in this town weren't about to let their taxes go up just so some kids could have a nicer place to play a game."

I'd imagined that football in this town, like a lot of southern towns, was more than a big deal, but that sentiment must've skipped their town, which seemed to care more about paying raised taxes than making sure the local high school had what it needed to be competitive.

Ransom stared out the window, his face within an inch or so of the glass like he couldn't quite get close enough.

"Do you wanna get out and walk around?" I asked him.

Ransom turned toward me, and I knew his answer before he said it. I doubted he realized the effect that being in his old town—at his old high school—would have on him, but it was clear from his eyes that the place pulled at his emotions.

"Yeah. Okay. You wanna come?"

Of course I wanted to come, but only if he didn't want the time to himself. "If it's okay with you."

He'd already unbuckled his seat belt and grabbed the door handle. A few seconds later, he was out of the car, motioning for me to follow him, so I did.

"Can we meet you guys at Sully's in forty-five minutes or so?" he asked Matt and Melissa. "It'll be nice to walk over."

Matt gave him a firm smile, but Melissa's looked more sentimental. My guess was they were both glad Ransom was taking the time to appreciate the place he'd been gone from for so long.

"See ya in a bit," Matt said.

Ransom closed the door and watched the SUV drive away before turning to face the football field. "It's weird," he said, "being back here like this. So much has changed for me, but looking at this . . . it's like the place is frozen in time."

I thought a lot of small towns were probably like that. Other than some minor changes—maybe some trees that had been cut down or planted or a house that had been painted— places like this weren't known for their transformations.

Other than acknowledging his comment with a "Really?" I didn't say anything else. And he didn't respond to my question, probably because it was a rhetorical one.

He looked toward the football field and then to the worn metal bleachers before grabbing my hand and walking toward them. Though I didn't need it, he helped me up the few steps to the first level and then up to the top so we had a full view of the field and the surrounding area.

We sat quietly, both of us taking in the scenery around us. Ransom's gaze locked on two boys who'd just arrived at the field and began tossing a football to each other. I watched them for a little while too, until my interest in their game of catch waned and my attention was drawn to the neighborhood beyond the field.

The school was nestled among rows of small homes with yards enclosed by mismatched fences. Driveways were in desperate need of repaving or consisted of only gravel. A group of kids playing hockey in a side street moved their nets when cars approached, and the drivers waved to them as they passed. Neighbors chatted from across the street, their rakes resting under their arms during their break from the yardwork.

It looked like a comfortable place to grow up, so drastically different from my childhood, where people focused so intently on their own lives and careers that they often came and went without so much as a wave. Not because they were rude but because they didn't notice what was happening beyond their immediate line of sight.

Everything seemed to move slower here. People walked leisurely, played hard, and worked to live instead of the other way around. Or at least that's how it seemed.

"You okay?" I asked when I noticed Ransom looking lost in thought. His eyes seemed fixed on an imaginary point somewhere ahead of him.

"Yeah." He took a moment to break from his trance or whatever had been pulling his attention elsewhere. "Yeah. I'm good."

"That was like . . . not at all convincing." I knew it had been an emotional few days—an emotional few weeks, if I were being honest—and asking Ransom if he was okay was probably one of the most naïve questions I'd ever had for him. But still, I wanted to know how I could help, because even though there was probably nothing I could do, it was important to me that he knew the offer was there. "Is there anything I can do?"

"I guess I'm just taking all of it in, ya know?"

I nodded. I understood as much as someone who'd never

been in Ransom's position could.

"It's weird being back. But it's a good weird." Breaking eye contact, he let his head fall toward the metal below his feet. He rubbed at a piece of dirt with the toe of his boot as he spoke. "I'm not sure when I'll be back, so I guess I just wanna commit all of it to memory. The feel of the bleachers under me." He rubbed his hands over the edge, massaging his palms on the metal like the motion relaxed him. Maybe it did. "The smell of burning leaves and Melissa's apple pie candles she always burns this time of year."

"You can come back."

Drawing in a quick breath, he snapped his head up to look out at the field again. I saw his exhale more than heard it, a heavy breath that came out in a visible cloud as it moved through the cool air.

"I hope so."

"Well, you can control that," I told him. "I'm sure Matt and Melissa are gonna miss the hell out of you when you leave."

The silence that followed didn't quite match the noise I knew was in his head. Knowing he would speak again when he was ready, I remained quiet, allowing him to take whatever time he needed to compose his thoughts.

I looked out over the field again, watching the two boys toss the ball to each other and then try to run past the one who'd just thrown it without getting tackled.

"I'm gonna come clean," Ransom said. "When we get back. I have to. I can't continue living my life like I didn't take someone else's."

I'd known Ransom would end up here. I just thought the path to that destination would've taken a little longer.

"I know," I said quietly.

I saw him turn toward me suddenly. "You're not gonna try to stop me?"

"Should I?"

"What kind of question is that?" He almost sounded annoyed by my response, and part of me wondered if he'd worked himself up in preparation for a battle he'd never have to fight—like a gladiator emerging from the tunnel, sword raised, only to realize his opponent was completely unarmed. "I've thought a lot about this."

"I know that too."

"How do you know that?" he asked, sounding more curious this time.

"Because I know you, Ransom. You're too good a man to run from something you know you should face."

He laughed sharply, sounding almost disgusted. "Don't do that. Don't act like I'm this good guy who's taking the high road."

"You are."

"Good guys don't kill people."

It had to be the loudest we'd ever spoken about what had happened with Brad, and it almost felt good to put it out into the air and see what the universe would do with it.

"It was an accident. You were *protecting* me. I'll make sure everyone knows that. This is my fault too."

"I had other options than beating him so badly he couldn't survive it."

"You didn't know that would happen. Neither of us did, or we wouldn't have left."

Shaking his head at me slowly, he looked almost disappointed. "That doesn't change the fact that it happened."

"No," I agreed. "It doesn't. But it changes whether you

deserve whatever will happen to you because of it."

"I don't get it. You aren't gonna stop me from turning myself in, but you're telling me I'm still a good person and I don't deserve to be punished?"

"Yeah," I said. "I guess that's exactly what I'm saying. I'll support whatever you want to do because I support *you*." Ransom didn't say anything to that, at least not before I added, "Brad's family's having a vigil for him in his hometown."

"How do you know that?"

"Sophia told me this morning."

"So . . . why are you telling me about it? I might feel like I need to take responsibility for what I did, but I sure as hell don't want to talk to Brad's family about it or hear them say what a great guy he was. Because he wasn't," Ransom said firmly. "He was stalking you, threatening you, *hurting* you. I'd never deliberately take someone's life, but I can't pretend the world isn't better without him in it."

"Whose world?"

"What?"

"Whose world is better without him in it?"

"Yours," he said. "Ours. Everyone's. Jesus, this isn't helping, Taylor."

"I'm sorry. I just . . . I talked to Melissa this morning. Or she talked to me, I guess. She told me about Emily and how it was difficult to lose a child, but she had a friend she'd met in her bereavement group whose daughter went missing—"

"I know this story," he said. "It's horrible, but Grace was an innocent child. *Emily* was innocent. They were good people. Brad wasn't, so if you're about to compare that piece of shit to Emily or Grace—"

"I'm not," I cut in. "There's no comparison obviously. Not

between Emily and Brad. I would never. But their families—their *parents*. All I'm saying is someone loved Brad. People cared about him. He was someone's son, someone's brother, someone's friend. And those people are grieving just like Melissa and Matt grieved. Just like you did. Grace's family never got the closure your family did, and it made it that much harder."

"Brad's family knows what happened to him, and when I turn myself in, they'll know who did it. That's all the closure they need, and that's all I'm prepared to give."

"What about closure for me?" I'd said it so softly, I wondered if my words had gotten swept away with the breeze. I couldn't look Ransom in the eye as I said it, so I retreated inside myself like a turtle pulling itself into its shell. I didn't exactly know why I didn't want to face Ransom. And the more I thought about it, the clearer it became to me that maybe it was more that I didn't want *him* to see *me*.

I felt his eyes on me even though I couldn't see them, and it made me want to crawl further inside.

"I never thought of that," he told me.

At his words, I managed to lift my head up to face him. His sunglasses shielded him from revealing any emotion I would've likely seen in his eyes, so I noticed his other features instead. He had more than a five o'clock shadow from yesterday, which I typically loved. It made him look less refined and a bit older than his twenty-four years. But today, his facial hair, which was darker than the light strands on his head, seemed to make him appear more worn out.

I had no doubts he'd been considering this decision for longer than he'd ever admit, and I was sure it had taken its toll on him. He'd probably been anxious about discussing it with me, and I couldn't blame him. I didn't want him to go to jail, but I'd also realized that living with that guilt would be more crippling to him than spending time in prison. At least mentally.

He didn't say anything afterward, and neither did I. I gave him time for his thoughts to marinate, both of us sitting on metal that stung our skin through our jeans.

Eventually he added, "So…what? We just show up to an event memorializing the person I killed so we can give our condolences?"

I hesitated, hoping that as time passed, Ransom's description of the situation would sound less ridiculous.

When it didn't, I finally said, "I think so."

We sat a while longer, and I couldn't be sure if Ransom felt relieved he'd been honest with me about wanting to confess. Hell, I couldn't be sure I'd done the right thing myself, because the more I convinced myself that the reason I wanted to attend Brad's service was because Brad's family deserved to hear the truth from us, the less convinced I actually became.

Like Ransom, I wanted to do the right thing because doing the right thing made *me* feel good in a situation that otherwise felt awful for everyone involved.

"We'd be taking the high road," I said. "The one less traveled. Robert Frost would've been proud." I only vaguely remembered the poem, but I had vivid memories of Mrs. Luvwell getting irritated when most of us misinterpreted the meaning.

Ransom laughed—one of those sounds that's released more out of frustration than humor.

"So you *do* know who Robert Frost is."

Then I laughed. "I'd forgotten all about that poem. But

then I helped my boyfriend escape manslaughter charges by fleeing the state, and it all came flooding back. Maybe I have more of an appreciation for poetry than I ever gave myself credit for. I wonder if it's too late to change my major," I joked.

"No way!" Ransom slung his arm over my shoulder and pulled me against him. "I can't think of anyone I'd rather have in my corner right now than a future lawyer."

Chapter Nineteen

RANSOM

"Don't panic," Taylor said from beside me.

I'd been leaning back in the uncomfortable airport chair, waiting to board our flight—which was still about an hour away—but at her words, I sat upright. "I honestly can't think of a *worse* sentence starter right now."

She smiled. "Sorry. It just occurred to me that we don't have anything to wear to Brad's viewing."

"We're going there to confess to"—I cast a surreptitious look around—"you know. I don't think our clothing is going to matter much."

She pulled a skeptical face. "I don't want to stand out more than we already will."

"More than when we're being escorted out, handcuffed by police, you mean?"

She sat back with a huff. "I know you think you're funny, but you're really missing the mark."

I actually didn't think I was being funny. A police raid on the church during Brad's service like we were some kind of notorious outlaws was exactly how I envisioned tomorrow going. But getting Taylor more stressed than she already was wouldn't help either of us, so I decided to tone it down.

"I think we passed a clothing store on the way to our gate."

"It's fine," she said. "We'll just wear jeans and sweatshirts."

I had to suppress a grin at her snarky tone. Bumping her shoulder with mine, I waited until she looked over at me before I started speaking. She flicked her eyes toward me in annoyance, which I figured was the best I was going to get.

"Come on. I'll buy you the best airport black dress we can find."

Normally I'd be worried about making such a promise, but this was a small airport, so I wasn't worried there'd be a lot of high-end shops. I hadn't noticed any as we'd walked to our gate.

She snorted. "You really know how to spoil a girl."

"Oh, baby, just you wait. I have years of spoiling in me. Convenience store coffee, street vendor hot dogs, vending machine jewelry. The sky's the limit."

She rolled her eyes, but the laughter in them was clear. "How could I ever say no to all of that?"

"You can't. I'm quite a catch."

"Totally," she said without much enthusiasm behind it, but the warmth in her eyes told me how she truly felt.

I stood and gathered my bag before extending my hand to hers. "Your couture appointment awaits."

"I'm impressed you know that word," she said as she stood and twined her fingers with mine.

"Awaits? Yeah, it is a tough one."

She huffed out a small laugh. "You're such a dork."

We wandered down the terminal toward where I'd seen

the store. When we arrived, I was relieved to see they sold men's and women's clothes, and most of it seemed to be business casual. A quick look at a price tag on a sweater made me almost break out in hives, but it was doable.

Taylor and I split up in hopes of making this venture end quicker. It didn't take me long to scoop up a pair of black slacks and a forest-green sweater, since the one I'd brought was looking a little rough after I'd worn it to the reunion. I had a fresh white button-down that I thought would work underneath to make me look appropriately dressed, since buying a suit from an overpriced boutique in an airport wasn't something I was willing to do.

Content with my selection, I looked around for Taylor. I furrowed my brow when I saw her sandwiched between two elderly women who seemed to be talking a mile a minute.

"Hi," I said when I reached them. "Find what you needed?" I asked her after giving a polite smile to the other two women.

Taylor looked relieved to see me. "Yes," she practically shouted. "Thank you so much for your help, ladies. We have a plane to catch, so . . ." Taylor didn't finish her sentence, instead just gesturing toward the cashier.

"Oh, that's okay. We're all done in here too. We'll come with you to pay," one of the women, a tiny thing with white hair puffed up high on her head, said.

I shot Taylor a look. What the hell was going on? I'd left her alone for five minutes, and she'd somehow attracted a fan club?

Taylor looked crestfallen at their pronouncement.

I was in the process of having a conversation with Taylor using only our eyes when I felt a thin arm snake through mine, causing me to startle. When I looked down, I saw the other woman, a little more filled out than her friend and with bright-red hair that had to be dyed.

"And what's your name?" she said in a raspy voice that I was worried was meant to be seductive.

"Oh, uh, Ransom, ma'am."

She fanned herself. "So polite. And Ransom. Such a . . . virile name. It's so nice that you came shopping with your sister."

My sister? Had Taylor told them that for some reason? I didn't want to blow her cover, which made me flustered in trying to respond.

Taylor, sounding vaguely annoyed, saved me. "He's my boyfriend, actually."

"Oh, really?" the woman said with such a fake tone of surprise it was clear she'd known that all along. "I'm sorry, he just looks so . . . mature and dominant. But that's okay. Some girls are into that I hear. Daddies, I think they call them."

Oh God.

Taylor's face took on a mischievous gleam, which worried me about what she would say next. "He's actually only three years older than me," she said. "So I'm not sure he qualifies as a Daddy quite yet."

"Oh, age has nothing to do with it. Being a Daddy is a mind-set," the white-haired woman said. "At least that's what my romance novels say." As she finished speaking, she reached into her bag and pulled out a paperback with a shirtless man on the front.

I nodded along dumbly because what was a guy supposed to say when a septuagenarian talked about the Daddy fetish she'd picked up from reading an X-rated novel she was waving around? Nothing in my previous twenty-five years of life had prepared me for a conversation like this.

"Doris, Fay, who do we have here?"

My eyes flew toward the voice. *Oh fuck. There are more of them.* Three more elderly women walked toward us, one of them eyeing me from top to bottom in a way that could only be described as lecherous.

"This is Ransom and . . . I'm sorry, dear. I don't think we got your name."

"Taylor," she grumbled.

"Ha, Taylor. Like a tailor. Which is funny because we're in a store that sells suits. Maybe you should work here," Doris or Fay said, making all their friends cackle.

"Ha-ha, yeah, funny. Anyway, we're going to . . . go . . . over there. Have a great flight, ladies," Taylor said, trying to steer me away from the granny gang that had surrounded us.

"We'll wait for you. We just love getting to know young people," the woman who still had her arm linked with mine said, shooting me an adoring smile. "Helps us keep a pulse on what's hip these days. Maybe we can all get a snack and chat."

Taylor shot me a look that let me know it was my turn to attempt an extraction.

"Oh, uh . . ." I was floundering again. "We don't, um, eat snacks."

This earned a confused look from the women, but I soldiered on. "It's . . . against our religion. Yeah, we're devout . . . antisnackers."

Taylor's eyes widened like she'd expected me to take the explanation in any direction but the one I'd chosen.

The women looked to be split between intrigue and outrage. "I've never heard of such a thing," one of them said. "What religion is that?"

"The name? Oh, yeah, right. The name. It's called the Believers of Divine . . . Macros."

"Huh, never heard of that," one of them said.

"Yeah, it's pretty new."

"Sounds like a cult," another one groused.

"Leave them be," Doris or Fay defended. "We all believed in stupid stuff when we were young."

Okay, so maybe less of a defense than I'd initially thought.

"Well, it's almost lunchtime. Are you allowed to have *meals*?" one asked.

"Yes, but we're still full from breakfast," Taylor said. "But thanks so much for the offer. We really must be going so we don't miss our flight."

The women looked sad to let us go but didn't follow us as Taylor dragged me away.

"Believers in Divine Macros?" she whispered.

"I panicked."

"Clearly."

"You're the one who attracted them in the first place," I accused. "They're probably part of some ancient coven that feeds on the souls of the young. We could've been killed because of you."

"I wish all people who accuse women of being the more dramatic gender could hear this conversation."

"It's probably easy to make jokes when you weren't the one being felt up by someone's great-grandmother."

Taylor rolled her eyes as we moved up to the register and put our clothes down so the woman could scan them. When the woman read the obscene total, Taylor looked at me expectantly.

"You said you'd buy me a black dress."

"I know. But you got black pants and a shirt, nullifying our deal. You also almost got us lured to some old lady's gingerbread house."

She stared flatly at me until I pulled out my wallet.

I returned her stare as I pulled out my credit card and handed it over. "Just so you know, making me pay makes me feel like maybe you *do* want a Daddy."

"Maybe I do. Any idea where I could find one?"

"You're a pain in the ass," I muttered, causing her to burst out laughing.

She huddled closer to me, wrapping herself around my arm like a vine. "Yeah, but I'm *your* pain in the ass."

As much as I wanted to on principle, there was no way I was ever going to argue with that.

TAYLOR

We'd wandered around for a bit after buying the clothes, so when we'd gotten back to our gate, they'd already begun boarding. We stood in line to show the attendant our boarding passes and then made our way onto the plane.

Since we'd made the reservations last minute, we hadn't been able to get seats next to one another, but we were close. My seat was across the aisle and one row up from where Ransom was seated. We'd decided that if the people next to us seemed friendly, we'd ask if any of them would mind switching.

As we scuttled down the aisle toward our seats, I felt my phone vibrate in my pocket. Suddenly, Ransom stopped short, causing me to bang into him from behind.

"What's wrong?" I asked.

"It can't be," I heard him mutter.

I looked around him to see what the issue was. I couldn't help the snort that escaped when I saw that the older women from the clothing store were sitting in Ransom's row of seats and in the row across the aisle. Thankfully they weren't in my row.

"Switch with me," he said.

"I love you desperately," I replied. "But there is no way in hell I'm doing that."

"Ransom?" one of the women I'd initially been speaking to said, her eyes lighting up as the circumstances dawned on her. "Are you sitting with us?" She gestured toward the open window seat.

Ransom whimpered, but it was low enough that only I heard him.

"Get in there, big guy," I said, giving him a nudge.

"Doris, move over," the woman across the aisle said. "That way Ransom can sit in the middle of all of us and we can find out more about him on the flight."

"Don't go to any trouble. I like the window," he tried to argue.

"Don't be silly. You're much too . . . big for that." As the woman said the words, her eyes dipped to his crotch, and I almost wavered in my resolve to not switch seats. Almost. A martyr I was not.

The women shuffled around, allowing Ransom to sit miserably in the aisle seat. My seat was the middle one, but thankfully it was between a middle-aged man who was already asleep and a woman who looked a few years older than me, typing away on her laptop. My seatmates were definitely preferable to Ransom's, who were already asking about his hobbies and favorite foods. I chuckled as I heard one ask for his address so she could mail him baked goods.

I'd gotten so wrapped up in eavesdropping, it took me a while to fish out my phone and check the missed call. It was from Xander.

But the flight attendant had come on to go over her spiel, and her volume was deafening, so I waited until she was done before checking voicemail. As I put the phone to my ear, I heard Xander's voice saying, "Seriously? Your phone is practically surgically attached to your hand and the one time I call, the only time I'll probably *ever* call anyone, because who even does that anymore? Everything can be a text message. Anyway, the one time I call, you don't pick up. For fuck's sake."

As I listened to his diatribe, I felt a hand tap me on the shoulder. I lowered the phone so I could look back at who'd touched me. It was part of the old lady brigade hovering over my seat.

"Yes?"

"You're not supposed to be on your phone."

"Oh, I have it on airplane mode. I'm just listening to a voicemail."

Her gaze was unwavering. "You're not supposed to be on your phone."

My eyes narrowed. "I can, actually. I just can't be on the internet."

"I had a dream last night."

I furrowed my brow at the strange non sequitur.

"We all died a fiery death due to our plane crashing. Because some young girl wouldn't get off her phone. Is that what you want? To kill us all?" Her voice had grown louder as she spoke, attracting the attention of those seated around us.

At their worried and annoyed stares, I decided my best recourse was to capitulate to her demands.

"No problem," I said, smiling the fakest smile I'd ever allowed to cross my face. "I'll listen later."

She nodded sharply before sitting back in her chair.

Sighing loudly, I let my phone drop into my lap. I was sure whatever Xander had to say could wait.

Chapter Twenty

RANSOM

"This was a bad idea," Taylor muttered.

Like mine, Taylor's attention was focused on the line that wrapped so far around the church we couldn't see its end.

"This was *your* idea."

"I know it was my idea, but unfortunately it might not have been one of my best."

The black heels Taylor wore clicked on the pavement as we approached the building. It wasn't too late to leave, but now that we were here and I'd accepted that we'd come to a funeral to tell the deceased's parents that I'd accidentally killed their son, it felt like a pussy move to back out.

"It'll be okay," I told her. "We're giving them closure, remember?" And Taylor was right. No matter how big of a shithead Brad was, no one deserved to mourn their child's death without knowing the circumstances surrounding it.

I wondered if my generic assurance had been at all convincing. Taylor was still walking, so maybe it had been. Or maybe she just didn't want to feel like a pussy either.

By the time we got to the back of the line, Taylor was practically shaking. I'd told her to wear a warmer coat, but she'd insisted she didn't have one with her that would look okay with her outfit, so she'd worn a thin sweater that was open in the front, and I could tell she regretted it. I pulled my own jacket off and put it around her shoulders, knowing that it would probably only help so much because at least some of her shaking was probably from the situation more than the cold.

"Thanks," she said.

Then both of us were quiet as we waited. Taylor barely looked up, and I wondered if she was worried about seeing someone she knew from school. We hadn't exactly talked about the specifics of how we'd reveal our role in Brad's death to his parents, and now that we were here, it became clearer that we should've taken some time to discuss it. We couldn't exactly plan our confession strategy while surrounded by mourners.

Were we just going to casually mention to Brad's parents on the way to the casket that "Oh, hey, you don't know me, but your son was stalking my girlfriend, so I had to kill him"? No parent would allow someone to leave after revealing something like that. The outlaws-in-handcuffs scenario was manifesting itself into a probable reality quicker than I cared to accept. Though that was preferable to Brad's family becoming an angry mob set on avenging their loved one's death.

Taylor was right. This was a bad idea. And the closer we got to the entrance, the clearer that fact became. Taylor already looked emotional, but I couldn't actually put my finger on what emotion had taken hold of her. Fear? Sadness? Embarrassment? A toxic mix of all of them?

I was sure she could hear, as I could, the quiet conversations of those around us discussing how young Brad was. How bright and full of life he was. Then there were the more intimate memories—the stories that only close friends and family would know.

I heard Taylor draw a shaky breath from deep inside her. I knew her well enough to recognize when she was about to lose it, and as we got closer to the casket, I worried about what her reaction would be when she actually had to look in it.

"I'm guessing those are Brad's parents?" I said, nodding toward the sharply dressed man and woman in their late forties in the receiving line. They cried softly and spoke to everyone, even if it was just to say a few polite words to friends of Brad's who they probably didn't know.

Taylor had mentioned that his parents were divorced, but Brad's dad was kind enough to hold his ex-wife as she cried softly. Somehow she managed to wipe her tears in a way that prevented her eye makeup from smearing.

"I'd assume so. I never met them, but that's gotta be."

In the receiving line were some other relatives, who I guessed were Brad's siblings or cousins and grandparents.

The people at the casket now had been up there for some time, providing a lull in the procession of people making their way to his family and then to the exit. "Maybe we should ask if we could talk to them afterward. Like just give them a heads-up so we don't bombard them with all of it unexpectedly."

Taylor hesitated. "You don't think they'll want to talk to us now once we mention it?"

I hadn't exactly meant that I'd reveal any details to them now, but Taylor's concern was still a valid one. "I guess they'll probably wonder," I said. "But they can't stop what they're doing to speak to us. It might be better this way because it'll give them some time to process what information could be coming their way."

"I doubt it'll cross their minds that we might be …" She seemed to remember that others were in earshot, so she left her sentence unfinished. I knew what she was going to say anyway without her having to voice it.

I sighed. "No. Probably not." I watched Brad's parents, both of them standing tall in the face of what had to be crippling. They should've been more fragile, I thought, like birds who'd been knocked from flight by a glass door. But they were holding it together better than the two of us—especially Brad's dad, who looked almost stoic. Maybe he was someone who broke down privately after the buildup of the day caused so much pressure inside him that the second he was alone, he exploded like a two-liter of Diet Coke that had been shaken.

And here we were about to throw a pack of Mentos into the bottle.

"I'll talk," I said. "It might be easier if I'm the one who mentions it to them. Then we can talk to them together afterward."

"So … what, I just stand there next to you like your manslaughter wingman," she whispered, "and let you do all the talking?"

"When you put it like that, it sounds ridiculous."

"It *is* ridiculous. This felt like a good idea when I thought of it, but now I feel like I'm looking out the door of an airplane trying to convince myself to jump."

"Why do all your metaphors have to do with aviation?" I asked her. "First the wingman and now this."

"Stop changing the subject."

"Fine," I said, placating her. "But why would we *want* to jump out of a plane?"

"Because we're skydiving in my hypothetical scenario,"

she replied, as if my question were the only stupid part of the conversation we were having. I watched her glance in the direction of Brad's parents before focusing back on me. "Though this feels more like jumping without a parachute."

"Well, if you ever have plans to make your hypothetical sky jump a reality, count me out."

"More terrifying than what we're doing now?" She stared at me as she let the question sink in. I didn't have to reply for her to know my answer. "Exactly."

"Well, we're almost to Brad's family, so you better get ready to jump." As the line moved again, we took a few more steps toward them.

"I can't jump," she said, sounding noticeably more panicked than she had only moments before. And she'd sounded pretty fucking panicked then too.

"Then I'll just have to pull you out with me."

I didn't wait for Taylor to respond because I didn't want to lose my nerve. I just took a deep breath, tried to quiet the voice inside my head that said this was a gigantic fucking mistake, and faced Brad's parents.

No doubt there had been countless students who'd come through here to pay their respects to Brad and express their condolences to his family. And I was sure they probably thought Taylor and I were more of the same: two innocent college kids who were mourning the loss of one of their own.

I wasn't quite sure how to begin, other than to say I was sorry for their loss and to introduce myself as someone who knew their son, though not well, of course. "And my girlfriend, Taylor"—I put my arm on her back but couldn't bring myself to look at her—"went to school with your son. Dated him, actually," I said, though I don't know why.

Brad's mother looked almost pleased. "He had a girlfriend?" She shook her head slowly. "We didn't even realize."

"We weren't together when he passed" was all Taylor said as a way of explaining the situation as simply as possible.

"I see," his mother said.

I wondered if Brad's own parents even realized what a creepy fuck their son was, because his mom, at least, seemed surprised to hear he'd been able to convince someone to date him.

"I know this probably isn't the best time," I said, hoping to get to the point sooner rather than later. It would be our turn at the casket soon, and I'd finally have to face—literally—the person I'd killed. The strangest shit was that somehow this conversation seemed more painful than staring at Brad's dead body. "But we're only in town tonight," I continued, "and I was wondering if we might be able to talk to you for a few minutes after the viewing. We'd like to talk to you about… what happened to your son. I know the circumstances of his passing weren't exactly clear—"

"I'm sorry, who did you say you were?" Brad's father asked me.

"My name is Ransom. I'm sure that doesn't mean much to you right now, but I knew your son a little—"

"You have information about my son's death?" Brad's mom cut in, sounding about as excited as someone could possibly seem at their child's funeral. Though I was sure her emotion more closely resembled desperation. "Please. Tell me. We just don't even know what he was doing there that night," the woman said. "To be found in an alley like some sort of drug dealer or thug or something… It doesn't make any sense to us. He was such a good kid. So smart. Brilliant, really. And he'd made so many friends at college. I can't think of anyone who would want to hurt him." Her eyes had been cast down as she spoke, but she brought her gaze up to me when she said the last part. "Can you? What is it that you know?"

I wasn't expecting her to take hold of my wrist like she did, and the action startled me. My instinct was to break away, but her grip was nowhere near strong enough to cause me to feel physically threatened. It felt more frantic than anything else, like a silent plea for me to tell her more.

Brad's father placed his hand gently on her back and leaned down to her. "Not here," he said, staring at the line behind us before glancing up toward the casket.

Relieved that his dad's social etiquette overruled any desire for more information—at least for the moment—I pulled my hand away slowly. I watched Brad's mother's eyes close for a second, and I could tell she thought if I walked away from her, anything I knew about Brad's death might leave with me.

"We'll talk when you have a few minutes," I said to them quietly.

His mom nodded but didn't say anything else.

"I'm freaking out," Taylor said after we moved up a few feet closer to the front of the line. "Now it's real. We're about to see Brad. And we just told his parents we have to talk to them after the service." I could hear the panic in her voice, and I wished I could've convinced her not to do this here. Who knew if we'd even get to leave after we revealed our part in their son's death.

We moved again, and this time I realized there were only two people ahead of us, and I thought they were together.

"Can you do this?" I asked, giving a nod toward the coffin. "You sure you'll be okay?"

Taylor nodded quickly and muttered a soft "yes," like if she didn't answer immediately, she was scared she might change her mind. "It's just…a lot. Being here, seeing him, talking to his parents. I don't know why I thought this would be easier, but I clearly overestimated myself."

As the area in front of the casket cleared, I grabbed a hold of her hand and gave it a firm squeeze that I hoped would be comforting. I didn't know how she'd react once she saw the actual body. Maybe she'd burst into tears or hyperventilate, or maybe she'd let out an audible gasp at the sight of him lying lifeless in a box that I'd essentially put him in. Whatever her reaction was, I'd be ready for it. Ready for *her*. We'd come this far together. We'd see it through together too.

She closed her eyes as she took the two steps toward him, and though I looked at the body for a quick second, most of my attention went to Taylor.

She took a deep breath before opening her eyes and looking down at Brad's body. Her lips parted slightly as her eyes took in his body. Like his parents, he was well-dressed too. A dark-gray suit covered his body that would've been much paler without the makeup. And his dark hair had been styled to the side neatly.

When I heard Taylor let out a small sound similar to a whimper, I looked over to see her covering her mouth with the hand that wasn't holding mine. She pulled in a sharp breath through her nose before allowing her fingers to move enough that she could speak.

"Oh my God," she whispered. "Oh my God."

"I know," I whispered back.

"No, you really don't," she said, her voice suddenly holding a sense of panic I hadn't seen until now. "We gotta get out of here."

"What? Why? What's wrong?"

"Nothing," she answered quickly. She glanced back at Brad's parents, causing me to do the same. Despite their speaking to other people at the moment, both of them had their eyes trained on us. "Or everything. Jesus. Fuck."

"Taylor, tell me what's going on," I said, holding her steady to face me.

Closing her eyes, she drew in a few deep breaths, and I could tell she was trying to breathe more slowly with each one. When she finally opened them to look at me again, her lips opened for a few seconds before she moved them to speak. And when she did, she uttered the best, and most confusing, set of words I'd ever heard.

"That's not Brad."

TAYLOR

"What?" Ransom asked, his jaw dropping open so far I could practically see down his throat.

"That's not Brad," I whispered through gritted teeth. It felt like the best news ever and the worst news ever all at the same time. "We gotta get the hell out of here."

"That's not Brad? What do you mean that's not Brad?"

"I mean it's not him. I don't know *how* it isn't him. I just know that it isn't."

When I'd laid eyes on the person inside the casket, I'd needed to make sure my eyes were telling a truth I wanted so badly to be true. Because although the person in the casket looked familiar and with his dark hair and similar age and body type could've easily been Brad, it wasn't.

I don't think I've ever opened and shut my eyes that many times or that quickly in my life, almost as if I believed every blink might possibly reveal a new sight before me, like pulling a handle on a slot machine.

I'd been glancing around looking for the closest exit as I grabbed Ransom's hand and led him off to the side of the casket.

"Maybe he just looks different because he's dead," Ransom offered, because, really, how could we have thought we killed someone we didn't?

"Do you know how many times I pictured what Brad would look like dead?" I pulled Ransom toward the side of the church and headed toward an exit. "I know that sounds . . . totally fucked up, but it's true. He's haunted me almost as much dead as he did when he was alive. Or I guess he's maybe *still* alive." Grabbing Ransom's hand suddenly, I said, "Oh, my God! Do you think Brad's still alive?" Even though I knew the answer, I asked anyway.

"Um . . ." He hesitated, probably more because he didn't *want* to tell me than because he didn't know *what* to tell me. "I think he probably is, right? He has to be." His voice sounded filled with the same heaviness I felt. The implications of all of this were too much to ponder right now.

"We gotta get out of here," I said again.

"Shouldn't we at least tell Brad's . . . or whoever that was in the casket's parents that we made a mistake? I mean, we just told the parents of whoever *that* guy is that we know something about their son's death."

"Well, we can't exactly go back there and tell them we accidentally killed someone who *wasn't* their son."

"Isn't that better than saying we killed someone who was?" Ransom asked. "We can't just leave. We came to help give a grieving family closure about the passing of their son. We just made it worse for them."

"I'll write them a letter to explain," I said. "They'll understand."

"A letter? How?"

Jesus, my boyfriend asked a shit ton of questions that shouldn't matter at the moment. We were standing at the double doors on the side of the church that led to the parking lot, but neither of us had opened them yet. At least at this angle, the family of the deceased could no longer see us.

"Because," I said. "I know *him* too."

"You know him? The dead guy? *That* dead guy? How? What do you mean you know him?"

"Maybe *know* isn't the correct word, but I've seen him before." I could swear I did, though I couldn't place him. "I'm not even sure of his name, though. I can't . . . I don't know how this is even happening."

Ransom lifted both hands to his head and massaged them through his hair anxiously. "What the fuck are we gonna do?" He groaned loudly before letting his hands fall to his sides with an "Ugh, this is so fucked up."

"I don't know," I said slowly. Then I let him have the moment to himself and simply be in his own mind until whatever thoughts were running through it finished their jog. Both of us were silent as we leaned against the church wall next to the exit. "But you're right," I conceded. "We can't just let these poor people think we know something about . . ." I gestured toward the casket.

"I'll get us a prayer card before we go talk to them so we at least have his name," Ransom promised. "You figure out what the hell we're gonna say to them."

He was gone, heading toward the entrance of the church before I had time to try to bargain with him to switch tasks.

I waited by the door for him, trying to make sense of what we'd discovered. Here was a kid who looked familiar, and apparently he'd died exactly as we thought Brad had died. But we'd had nothing to do with it. At least not directly.

But when Ransom returned, I still hadn't come up with a clear idea of what we'd say to the grieving parents that would be both a comfort and the truth. The scent of incense, flowers, and unexplained death clouded my mind too much for me to think clearly. My only hope was that seeing the name on the card would help me connect the dots I wasn't even sure I wanted to connect.

Ransom put the card in my hand. "His name's Peter."

It didn't immediately ring a bell, but when I saw his last name was Faulkner, I knew exactly where I'd seen him. We'd had some English lit class together as freshmen. The professor had commented during the first class about how Petey, as he'd introduced himself, shared his last name with a famous author.

I'd hated the class, mostly because I was horrible at it. As if fishing wasn't boring enough to experience, who wanted to read a *book* about some fisherman searching all over the ocean for a whale to kill? But Petey, an avid part of the class discussions, always seemed to enjoy it.

I knew that I couldn't leave without speaking to his parents. I just hoped I didn't make an already horrible situation worse for them.

Ransom and I made our way toward Mr. and Mrs. Faulkner cautiously, not wanting to disrupt the line or interrupt a conversation with family if Petey's parents couldn't talk. But as soon as they spotted us, it was clear they weren't going to let us out of their sight again without talking to us. His father locked eyes with me and then immediately said something to the people he'd been speaking with before leading his wife toward where we stood between the pews.

"I'm sorry," I said, "about before. We shouldn't have told you something like that during such a difficult time. I just—"

"Don't be sorry," Petey's mom said, her eyes filled with a hope that I was scared I would crush. "I'm glad you're here. If you have information about our son's death—"

"We don't," I told her. "I'm sorry if it came across like that. I went to school with Petey. We had a freshman English class together, and he was . . . so smart."

"Jesus," his father said, the low volume of his voice doing nothing to disguise his anger. "Everyone here knew my son. You implied you had something important to tell us. My wife and I thought that you knew something that would help explain the circumstances of his death."

Ransom's eyes were wide as he watched me.

"I live in the town where your son passed away," I said, "and I just wanted to let you know that if I hear anything or if I can be of any help to you, I'll reach out."

His mom's expression seemed to deflate, but neither of his parents looked angry now. They seemed to be processing the information, their eyebrows furrowing in the same way Ransom's were.

Apparently all of us, myself included, were trying to figure out the implications of Petey's whereabouts that night. It was a big city and a college town. Petey could've easily known someone there who he was visiting. Still, it seemed unlikely, given the distance from his own school.

"Thank you," his mother said. "We appreciate that. If you could maybe even ask around . . ."

"I will," I said, thinking that might not be a lie. Now that we weren't involved in a murder investigation, maybe we could do a little investigation of our own. "I'm not sure I know anyone who knew Petey."

"So you don't know this Lacey girl either?" his mom asked, looking disappointed.

"No. I'm sorry. I don't know any girls with that name."

Their shoulders slumped with the news. "We've been trying to figure out who this girl is, but we've gotten nowhere. All Petey told us was that he was planning to hang out with Lacey all weekend, and then he's found dead in an alley hundreds of miles away. We don't have a last name for this girl, and the police don't seem to be much help locating a student by that name. Or anyone there who Petey would've been in contact with."

"I wish we could be more helpful," I told them. "It seems . . . strange to me too, to say the least."

"We should probably get going," Ransom said, more to Petey's family than to me. "We have to get back home."

"We appreciate you coming out to pay your respects," his mom said. "I know this isn't necessarily the appropriate time, but would you mind if I got your number? Or at least your email? Just in case we hear anything else, I mean. With you living in the city where he was . . ." She cast her gaze to the floor. "Well, just in case," she said again.

"Um, yeah, of course," I told her, already pulling out

my phone while simultaneously regretting agreeing to share my contact information with her but knowing I had no good reason not to.

After I sent her a text so she'd have my number, Ransom and I excused ourselves and headed for the exit. Once we were outside, I felt like I could breathe for the first time in weeks, and the look on Ransom's face told me he felt the same way. I didn't want to ruin it, but I knew the feeling would be temporary.

The two of us leaned against the side of the building for a minute before Ransom looked over at me. "It's okay," he said. "We're gonna be okay. I mean, it's a crazy fucking coincidence that this Pete guy went to your school, but still. It means I didn't kill anyone." He almost smiled.

"No, you didn't."

"Then why do you look so worried?" he asked.

Unsure of whether I really wanted to tell him now, as Ransom seemed freer than I'd seen him look in weeks, I remained quiet as he studied my expression.

"What? What is it?"

Fuck it. Whatever all this turned out to be, we were in it together. "Because Brad's last name is Lacey."

Chapter Twenty-One

RANSOM

Returning to normal life after thinking we'd murdered someone was not as easy as one might expect. We'd carried a belief—albeit false—that we'd irrevocably changed the course of a family's life, so it was difficult to adapt to mundane things like laundry and catching up on schoolwork.

Thinking like that probably made me an asshole, as if killing someone somehow made me special, but I couldn't deny it felt . . . unsettling to suddenly be thrust back into pre-alley life.

Thankfully, my professors were understanding of my absences. Even though it had felt like a lifetime, I'd only really missed a few classes, and since I'd never missed any before, they were all accommodating.

Since Taylor's classes were online and self-directed, she had more leeway in catching up, but with the semester quickly drawing to a close, she also had some added stress of making sure all her requirements were completed so she could graduate.

I was so fucking proud of her. She was on track to graduate Magna Cum Laude, *and* she'd done well on her LSATs. Who'd have ever thought I'd land a girl who could accomplish all of that? Definitely not my aunt Renee, that's for damn sure.

Speaking of family, things had been quiet on that front. Kari texted a couple of times, but she didn't push to rehash what had happened after the reunion. She seemed content, at least for now, to let the chips of our relationship fall where they may.

What surprised me was how I hadn't heard from Hudson. Not even a text, which I thought was weird. I'd thought I'd made it known that I wanted her in my life, but maybe I hadn't been clear. I needed to call her to set things right, but it had been a busy week. I guessed I couldn't fault her for not calling when I hadn't done so either. I'd call her soon and be a more involved brother from here on out.

Taylor and I continued to spend almost all our free time together, her at my place or me at hers. It just felt normal now for the two of us to be together, sharing meals and the details of our day. It felt normal to share our *life*.

And while we hadn't discussed next steps, I felt like we could weather anything that came at us. I wasn't sure where Taylor planned to apply to law school, where I'd find a job after graduation, or even if Brad was still lurking in the shadows. But we'd figure it out. Together.

When we'd gotten home from Pete's funeral, the Scooby Gang had descended on us like rabid mother hens, but we'd held them off for the most part—other than Xander, who thoroughly berated us for not listening to his voicemails. He'd called to warn us the viewing wasn't for Brad after all—a fact that would've been helpful to know before walking in there.

I blamed the old ladies.

We had so much to process, and we felt we deserved to give ourselves time to digest at least some of it. But time was up.

Sophia was on her way over for breakfast to get the scoop, and she'd mobilized the troops to join her. Thankfully, they were all bringing something, and Carter and Toby offered to cook up some waffles. Taylor and I were not gifted enough in a culinary sense to feed all these people, nor were we volunteering since the gathering hadn't been our idea.

Taylor came into the room, tying her hair back in a loose ponytail. She'd just showered, and while the impulse had been there to join her, I'd needed to straighten up a bit before the crew arrived. Who knew friends would be such an epic cockblock?

"How much time do we have?" she asked, her gaze drifting toward the clock on the TV.

I opened my mouth to reply, but a knock on the door answered for me. "I guess none." I walked over and swung open the door to reveal Toby and Carter.

"Sorry, we're early. We wanted to get things prepped for breakfast," Toby explained, a blush blooming across his cheeks.

I wasn't sure he was embarrassed they'd potentially interrupted us or if it was something else, but I simply smiled and held the door open for them. "No worries. Come on in."

"What's up, man?" Carter said by way of greeting as he gave me a bro-shake.

"Hi, guys," Taylor said as she settled in next to me. "Can I take your coat?" she asked Toby.

"Oh, uh, yeah," he replied as he looked down at his arms that were full of groceries.

"Maybe after you put everything down," she suggested.

He smiled. "That's probably a good idea."

Carter dropped a quick peck on Taylor's cheek as a greeting before we all made our way to my kitchen.

"Do you have a casserole dish?" Toby asked.

"A what now?" I asked.

Toby's shoulders slumped as he turned to Carter. "I told you we should've brought ours."

Ours? They were sharing cookware now?

"He's got one," Carter assured him. "He just doesn't know it." He shot me a wink before ransacking my cabinets. "Ah-ha!" he declared as he pulled out a rectangular glass dish from my cupboard.

I'd gotten it as part of a set at a garage sale a few years back because it looked like something I might need. I hadn't. While the things had clearly seen some use from its previous owners, I'd made no contributions to the few burn marks that scarred it.

Taylor took Toby's coat when he slid it off and disappeared with it, likely putting it in the bedroom.

"You guys need any help?" I asked.

"Nope," Carter replied. "And Toby doesn't really like an audience, so if you don't mind . . ."

Toby's cheeks flamed red, making me think his mind had gone somewhere other than me leaving the kitchen.

"You got it," I said. I returned to the living room just as another knock came.

"Everyone else can't be early too," I heard Toby whine.

"Relax. We're not preparing a meal for Gordon Ramsay. These are college kids. They'll eat anything."

I laughed at Carter and Toby's conversation as I made my way to the door.

Little by little, our friends trickled in. Even Aamee had shown up. Xander and Aniyah argued about...whatever those two argued about. Brody regaled Drew and Sophia with some story about how someone had thought he was Chris Hemsworth at a bar, to which Sophia questioned the health of the person's vision. Aamee pecked at her phone as she rolled her eyes behind Brody, finally breaking in with "For the last time, he said you looked like a kid he grew up with named Chris Hemingway."

"Hemingway, Hemsworth, I know what he meant."

"I'll tell you what he *didn't* mean," she mumbled.

Drew's brother Cody burst into the room a few minutes later, completing the group. "Why aren't we eating? I'm starving," he said immediately upon entering.

"It's nice to see you too, little brother," Drew teased.

"Yeah, yeah, hi and whatever. You all know food comes before family for me."

"I'll go see how things are coming with the chefs," I said. I went into the kitchen and saw Carter and Toby moving around one another with a practiced ease.

They were probably more fluid with one another than Taylor and me.

"Hey, guys. Just checking if you needed anything," I said, since bursting in and demanding to know when we were eating seemed tactless.

"Nah, we got it. Should only be about five more minutes," Carter said.

"Awesome. Thanks." I turned to leave, but Carter stopped me.

"How was giving Owen a ride home?"

"Pretty good. He's...interesting. But it all worked out

for the best because my truck ended up dying and his dad's a mechanic."

Owen had shown up with my truck the day after we got back. His dad had done incredible work, and it was running as good as new. The inside was a little worse for wear since Owen had brought Gimli back with him, but I figured I couldn't bitch about that when his dad had only charged me for parts and Owen had helped him do the work.

Owen hadn't stayed long. He needed to figure out a way to sneak Gimli past his elderly landlord. He hoped she spent enough time high that he could convince her she was hallucinating if she ever heard barking. I'd told him to keep me posted, and he seemed pleased by the fact I'd given him an opening to contact me again. It seemed like I was collecting friends all over the place recently.

"He is a bit of a loose cannon," Carter said with a laugh. "But he's a good dude."

"He is," I agreed. Just as I was about to say more, my phone began to ring in my pocket. Withdrawing it, I saw Hudson's name flash on the screen. A wide smile spread across my face—I was happy she must've been thinking about me too. "Hey, Blink. How's it going?"

There was silence on the other end of the line for long enough to make my lips drop into a frown. I pulled the phone away to see that the call was still connected. "Hudson?"

A sniffle came over the line. "Ransom. Hi, um …" And then her sigh came down the line.

I moved out of the kitchen and into a corner of the living room so I could hear her better. Her voice sounded tinny and low, like she was whispering in a place with bad reception.

"What's wrong?" I asked. My voice must've conveyed

the alarm I felt, because the room went quiet around me, and I felt a hand settle on my back before Taylor entered my periphery.

Who is it? she mouthed.

"Hudson," I murmured back.

My sister was crying on the other end—that much I could make out—but she was also rambling off words that I couldn't put together, especially since it seemed every third one cut out. I put the phone on speaker, hoping Taylor could help me make sense of what Hudson was saying.

"Hudson, you gotta slow down and speak louder. I can't understand what you—"

"Everyone's going to be so disappointed in me."

"Why would anyone be disappointed in you?" I asked.

"I should've known better. God, this is the kind of stuff you hear stories about, but you never think it'll happen to you. I'm such a cliché."

"Hudson, please. You gotta tell me what's going on." I felt my anxiety rising, a pain in my chest starting to radiate outward, headed straight toward panic.

"There was this guy. He was . . . nice. At least I thought he was. But he . . . he wasn't. He got me . . . I can't even believe I fell for his shit. I don't know what to do. I can't tell Mom or Aunt Renee. Or Grandma. Oh God, what's Grandma going to think when she finds out?"

Considering none of the women she named were saints, I didn't think they had much room to say anything. Sharing that sentiment probably wouldn't have helped the situation, though. My brain started to put the pieces together, and my eyes widened as I realized what she was telling me. "Hudson, are you—"

"I'm in trouble, Ransom. A lot of trouble. I can't... I can't stay here. It isn't safe. This guy, he wants... but I can't give him... I don't know what to do."

"Where are you right now?"

"I'm in South Carolina, but my car isn't going to make it much farther. God, I can't even afford a decent car. How am I ever going to afford—"

"It's okay. We'll figure it out. Can you do a quick search and figure out which airport you're closest to? I'm going to buy you a ticket up here. You can stay with me until we figure this all out." I wasn't exactly rolling in money after our trip, but I'd make it work.

"I... really?" she said, her voice grateful, even though it was still heavy with tears.

"Yes. Just do a quick search and then text me the info. I'll take care of it and call you back."

"Ransom, I... I don't know what to say. Thank you. I'm so sorry that I'm—"

"Stop. I'm your brother, and I love you. I *want* to help. Okay?"

She sniffled again and cleared her throat. "Yes," she replied, sounding more herself. "Okay." She hesitated a second before adding, "I love you too, Ransom."

I couldn't help but smile a bit at that. "We'll talk soon."

"Okay."

She disconnected the call, but I couldn't stop staring at the phone in my hand. Was this really happening? When I looked up, I was gazing into Taylor's concerned face.

"Did my sister just tell me she's pregnant?"

Taylor looked almost pained when she replied. "Yes. I think she did."

And with her words, my heart felt like it fell from my body. What the hell were we going to do now?

CONTINUE READING IN

Tag, We're It

THE LOVE GAME: BOOK SIX

Keep reading for an excerpt!

Chapter One

RANSOM

"What time is Hudson's flight getting in?" Taylor asked, her voice breathy.

"She said she'd call when she landed." Her flight had been delayed, so it had been over twenty-four hours since her frantic call, but I was relieved she was on her way.

"With our luck, she'll call as soon as you start something."

I started kissing down her jaw. "Maybe you should start it, then."

"Mmm, think you beat me to it."

"I can stop," I said as I pulled away from her a little.

She reached up and pulled my head down to hers until our lips touched. "Don't you dare," she mumbled against me before drawing me into a heated kiss.

I began moving us toward the couch so we could stretch out, preferably with less clothes on. As soon as Taylor's back made contact with the fabric and I settled on top of her, we began grinding desperately. This was how I always hoped things were for Taylor and me: incendiary. I wasn't sure anyone could go from zero to sixty like we could.

I reached a hand down between us to pop the button on her jeans and then began gliding the zipper down. I'd just gotten my hand inside to tease along her underwear when there was a knock at my door.

Groaning, I buried my face in her neck. "If that's one of our friends, I'm disowning them."

"Well, they tend to travel in packs, so it's probably more than one. They're also impossible to get rid of. Kind of like the herpes of humanity."

I laughed as another knock came. "Yeah, yeah, I'm coming," I yelled, hoisting myself off Taylor.

She snorted. "Not now, you're not."

Jerk. When I reached the door, I gave a quick look over my shoulder to make sure Taylor was decent. Seeing that she'd refastened her pants and was sitting up on the couch made a wave of longing rush through me. Was it so much to ask to have spontaneous sex with my girlfriend one last time before my sister moved in?

I was going to kill whoever was on the other side of the door. Though not literally. I'd already avoided one murder rap. No need to tempt fate.

Taking one more deep breath to make sure my body was back under control, I opened the door, ready to give hell to whoever was on the other side.

But as my eyes settled on who was there, my head jerked back in surprise. "Hudson?"

A frown marred her face. "Yeah. Were you...not expecting me?"

I snapped out of my shock and moved to envelop her in a hug. "I thought you were going to call from the airport."

Feeling her shrug against me, she said, "I didn't want to make you come all the way down there to get me. It was just as easy to Uber."

"I would've been happy to come get you." In fact, I was a little irritated she hadn't called. She didn't need to be traipsing all over the place in her condition. She'd been through enough already. But coming down on her for it wouldn't help anything. What was done was done. "How did you know my address?" I asked as I pulled away and gestured for her to come in.

"You texted it to me when you moved in, and I saved it in my phone."

That made me smile. *I'm important to her.*

"How'd you get in the building?"

"Someone opened the door for me because I was holding my bags, so it would've been tough for me to get to my keys."

"Because you don't have any."

"Minor detail," she said with a smile.

"Well, I'm glad to know my apartment's got top-notch security." It was one of the more high-end complexes in the area, which was one of the reasons Taylor had stayed here so many nights when Brad had been lurking around town. Though clearly that hadn't done much to protect her from him.

"Well, in case you haven't noticed, I'm not the most threatening human being. Most people aren't very scared of teenage girls."

"Tell that to my high school self," I said with a laugh before grabbing Hudson's bags from her shoulders and bringing them inside.

I held the door so she could enter, and after closing the door, I spun and saw Taylor hugging Hudson.

"We're so glad you're here," Taylor said.

Hudson chuckled, the sound a little awkward. "I'm sure you have better things to do without being inconvenienced by me. But I appreciate you letting me come anyway." Hudson turned to look at me. "I promise, I'll get my shit sorted and get out of your hair as quickly as I can."

"Don't be silly," I said. "You're not inconveniencing anyone, and you're welcome to stay as long as you need."

She smiled at me, but I could see hesitation in her eyes. I'd just have to work on convincing her that I wanted her here.

"I'll take your stuff into the bedroom. Do you need anything? I ran to the grocery store and got a bunch of things, but if there's anything you like that's not in there, I could run back out."

Settle the hell down, Ransom.

The words had poured out of me almost frantically. I just wanted her to know I was happy to have her here, but I didn't want to oversell it either. She'd probably interpret it as disingenuous if I was too effusive.

"I'm sure it'll be fine," she said, giving me a sweet smile. "I'm not picky."

Maybe she wasn't yet, but I'd heard cravings were a thing when a woman was pregnant. And hormones. *Should I ask about her hormones?* Damn it, I probably should've spent more time on Google instead of with my hand down Taylor's pants.

"Let me take your coat," I said as I started to pass her.

She pulled it off and handed it to me, and I made a mental note to take her shopping sometime soon. Her coat was sufficient for Georgia, but she'd freeze in a winter here. She'd probably also need some maternity clothes eventually. Not that I really knew what made something maternity, but I assumed it was . . . stretchier.

"We should go clothes shopping," I blurted.

Hudson looked at the jacket in my arms and then down at herself before focusing back on my face. "Why? Is something wrong with what I'm wearing?"

I tried to ignore the *what the fuck is wrong with you* look Taylor was shooting at me as I stammered out a reply that wouldn't put her on the spot to discuss something she maybe wasn't ready to.

"Oh, uh, no, I just...thought...um, new place, new clothes, ya know?"

Hudson looked confused, her reply cautious. "I'm good. For now, at least."

Right. For now her clothes still fit, so she was fine. Maybe shopping for pregnant lady stuff was too much change all at once.

"Ransom." Taylor's voice shook me from my internal musings.

"Huh?"

"Weren't you putting Hudson's things in the bedroom?" she asked.

Oh. Yeah. Shit. I'd been standing here like a doofus. "Right. Yeah, I'm just gonna...do that."

As I walked away, I heard Hudson whisper, "Is he okay?"

"Sure. He's always super weird and awkward. Don't worry about it."

That wasn't exactly how I'd always dreamed of being described by the love of my life, but at the moment it was stunningly accurate, so I decided to go with it rather than argue.

I had a feeling that would be my approach to a lot of things in the coming months.

Ransom needed to slow his roll way down. He'd been hovering over Hudson since she'd arrived an hour ago, and I could tell she was beginning to question if coming up here had been a good idea.

Watching him was cute, honestly. He was fluffing pillows, fetching drinks, messing with the thermostat, offering blankets, whatever he could think of to make Hudson comfortable. When—a long, long, long time from now—I was pregnant, he was going to be amazing. Until I got tired of it and killed him. But it would be a really enjoyable few hours before he made me homicidal.

I was watching some reality show with Hudson when Ransom burst out of the kitchen, clutching his phone. "I read something about feet. Do yours hurt?" The look on his face was so earnest I almost laughed.

"Uh, no," Hudson replied carefully. She looked like she'd just realized he may be a pod person she'd need to escape from.

"Ransom, can you help me with something in the bedroom?" I asked as I stood.

His brow scrunched up, and his lip curled in disgust. "My sister is here."

My eyes narrowed in disbelief. "Are you serious right now?" Did he really think I was suggesting we disappear into the bedroom to have sex while his sister channel surfed on the couch?

"I . . . don't know how to answer that," he replied.

Pointing toward the bedroom, I gritted out. "Go."

Sighing, he made his way across the room toward the

hallway that led to the bedroom. As he passed the couch, he hesitated. "Do you like tea?" he asked Hudson.

"Oh my God," I yelled.

"What? It can settle the stomach."

I simply pointed again, though more emphatically this time.

"Okay, okay. I'm going."

When he'd disappeared, I turned to Hudson. "He's just really excited you're here, so he's trying too hard."

A small smile played over her lips. "That's . . . really sweet. Totally unnecessary. But definitely sweet."

I gave her a smile in return before following Ransom into the bedroom. When I arrived, I saw him sitting on the edge of the bed with his head in his hands.

"I'm being annoying, aren't I?"

After closing the door, I leaned back against it. "Like next-level annoying."

He groaned. "I just want her to be comfortable and feel welcome."

I truly felt for him. He'd never gotten to have a real relationship with his sister. And now that opportunity was in front of him, and he wanted to make sure he did everything right. But it was turning him into some kind of leech on speed. He hadn't left Hudson alone for more than three minutes since she'd arrived.

I sat down on the bed and put an arm around him. "I know you do."

"She hasn't mentioned the baby or anything."

"She's had a rough few days. She's probably embarrassed by the way everything went down."

He looked over at me, brow furrowed. "She doesn't have

anything to be embarrassed about."

"We know that. But us knowing it and her feeling it are two different things. She'll get there. Just give her time to adjust to the shock of it all."

"That makes sense."

"And please stop treating her like some kind of IED. She's not fragile. You don't have to . . . hover."

"I'm not hovering."

"Baby, you're practically a helicopter."

He snorted a laugh and rocked his body into me gently. "Don't call me baby when my baby sister is having a baby."

I laughed. "Now say it five times fast."

After a few seconds, he sat up straighter. "Okay. I'm ready to stop being a basket case."

"That's what I like to hear."

Leaning in, he pressed a quick kiss to my lips. "Thanks for being here with me."

I smiled. "Nowhere else I'd rather be."

Continue reading in *Tag, We're It*

Also by
ELIZABETH HAYLEY

The Love Game:
Never Have You Ever
Truth or Dare You
Two Truths & a Lime
Ready or Not
Let's Not and Say We Did
Tag, We're It

Love Lessons:
Pieces of Perfect
Picking Up the Pieces
Perfectly Ever After

❤

Sex Snob
(A Love Lessons Novel)

Misadventures:
Misadventures with My Roommate
Misadventures with a Country Boy
Misadventures in a Threesome
Misadventures with a Twin
Misadventures with a Sexpert

Other Titles:
The One-Night Stand

Acknowledgments

First and foremost, we have to thank Meredith Wild for allowing us to achieve our dream of writing a rom-com series. This has been a cathartic experience for us, and we'll always be grateful to you for this opportunity.

To our swolemate, Scott, these books wouldn't be what they are without you. Thanks for giving us room to push boundaries while reeling us in when it's necessary.

To Robyn, thank you for managing our writing lives—haha. We're honestly not sure how we made it this far without you.

To the rest of the Waterhouse Press team, you simply kick ass. Thank you for everything you do to help us be as successful as we can. You're an amazing group of people, and we're lucky to have the honor of working with you.

To our Padded Roomers, we don't even know where to begin to express how amazing you all are. You're funny and crazy and supportive and crazy and fierce and crazy, and... have we mentioned crazy? You make this process all the more enjoyable because we get to share every success and setback with you. Thank you for everything you've done for us, such as posting teasers, sharing links, reading ARCs, writing reviews, and making us laugh. We don't deserve you, but we're damn glad to have you.

To our readers, there's no way to accurately thank you for taking a chance on us and for your support. Thank you for letting us share our stories with you.

To Stephanie Lee, thank you for coming up with the name Ransom. It's perfect for him.

To Google, thank you for providing the means for us to research things including, but not limited to, fraternities, sororities, marketing degrees, alcoholic drinks, dean responsibilities, business class topics, college codes of conduct, Gen Z lingo, and popular clothing trends.

To our sons for inspiring the last names of our main characters. Our lack of originality strikes again.

To Elizabeth's daughter for being a spitfire and inspiring the way she writes female characters.

To our husbands, we know it's not easy. Thanks for hanging in there. We honestly don't deserve you.

To each other for pushing one another forward when we stall. The ride hasn't been easy, but it's sure as hell been a lot of fun. On to the next.

About

ELIZABETH HAYLEY

Elizabeth Hayley is actually "Elizabeth" and "Hayley," two friends who love reading romance novels to obsessive levels. This mutual love prompted them to put their English degrees to good use by penning their own. The product is *Pieces of Perfect*, their debut novel. They learned a ton about one another through the process, like how they clearly share a brain and have a persistent need to text each other constantly (much to their husbands' chagrin).

They live with their husbands and kids in a Philadelphia suburb. Thankfully, their children are still too young to read their books.

Visit them at AuthorElizabethHayley.com